Other Books by Judas Jung:

Dirty Deeds Done Dirt Cheap: A Collection of Stories
A Silver Moon Over Sunset: An Eleanor 'Ellie' Vance Mystery

A HUNGER GROWS IN HOLLYWOOD

An Eleanor 'Ellie' Vance Mystery

JUDAS JUNG

NONGE PUBLISHING

Copyright © 2025 by Judas Jung

ALL RIGHTS RESERVED

PRINTED IN THE UNITED STATES OF AMERICA

ISBN: 979-8-9934898-1-0

No part of this publication may be reproduced, distributed, or transmitted in any form or by any means, including photocopying, recording, or other electronic or mechanical methods, without the prior written permission of the publisher, except as permitted by U.S. copyright law. For permission requests, contact JJUNGINQUIRY@gmail.com

This story, all names, characters, and incidents portrayed in this production are fictitious. No identification with actual persons (living or deceased), places, buildings, and products is intended or should be inferred.

Book Cover by Judas Jung

1st edition 2025

For

The Eleanor Vances of the world: the ones who not only don't look away when things get ugly, they don't walk away from it, either. They face the ugliness head on and get to the truth.

and

'Dawn'

Without whom Ellie would never have made it out to the world.
Thank you.

Contents

PART ONE – THE VELVET COFFIN

1. The Critic in the Corner — 3
2. A Mother's Fear — 11
3. The Immortal Artist — 23
4. The Girl with the Glass Ambition — 35
5. Party for the Damned — 45
6. The Serpent's Kiss — 53
7. One Last Pitch — 62
8. The Tragedy of Zelda Kettleton — 72

PART TWO – THE BLOOD KISS

9. In the Archives — 87
10. The Stakeout at the Velvet Vesper — 97
11. The Artist's Message — 109
12. The Ghost on the Wire — 118
13. A Warning in Silver — 129
14. The House on the Hill — 142
15. The Critic — 154
16. An Invitation to the Premiere — 167

PART THREE - A BLADE IN THE DARK

17.	Gearing Up	183
18.	The Deathtrap	192
19.	The Sleeping Guardians	203
20.	The Artist's Legacy	213
21.	Sanctum	222
22.	The Beautiful Lie	234
23.	A Blade in the Dark	244
24.	Epilogue	253

PART ONE
THE VELVET COFFIN

The Critic in the Corner

April in Los Angeles. Six months since the night the monsters showed their teeth and I'd learned what really hunted in this city after dark. The spring air held the kind of warmth that used to make me think about second chances, about maybe finding a life that didn't revolve around other people's secrets and lies.

That was before I'd discovered some secrets had claws.

I stood at my third-floor office window on Spring Street, watching the morning commuters hurry along the sidewalk below. Same building my father had rented back in '32, same peeling paint on the door that read "Vance Investigations." Pop had started this business with fifty dollars, a used desk, and the stubborn conviction that Los Angeles needed at least one honest detective. When I'd enlisted right after Pearl Harbor in '41, he'd been proud but worried. When I'd mustered out in '44, he'd been waiting with a job offer and three years' worth of detective lessons.

I'd planned to put my Army Medical Corps training to work in some nice, quiet hospital. Figured I'd seen enough blood and guts to last several lifetimes. But Pop needed help with the business, and the Army had taught me that duty was duty, whether you liked it or not. Those three years learning the trade from him had been good ones—right up until his heart attack in '47 left me running Vance Investigations alone.

Course, I'd never imagined I'd end up seeing more blood and guts as a private investigator than I had patching up wounded soldiers in field hospitals.

The shoulder holster under my light spring jacket held a Colt .38 Super semi-automatic now instead of the .38 revolver I'd carried before October. I'd started calling it Pops—seemed fitting, since Pop would have approved of the upgrade and, as a plus, it meant he was still at my side, in a way. The bullets weren't standard issue either—each one blessed by Father Martinez down at St. Vibiana's, then loaded with silver powder I'd gotten from a jewelry supplier who thought I was making religious medals.

Let him think that. The truth would've had him reaching for the nearest psychiatry ward's phone number.

The silver-plated stiletto in my boot was new, too. Six inches of blessed steel that had cost me two weeks' grocery money but might mean the difference between walking home and being carried out. After what happened in October, I'd learned that some things only stayed dead if you killed them with the right materials.

My desk drawer held a rosary that had belonged to Detective Frank Miller—God rest his soul—along with three spare clips for Pops and a hip flask filled with holy water. Frank had died saving this city from a pack of werewolves that had been treating Los Angeles like their personal hunting ground for sixty years.

Most people would call that story insane.

I'd call those people lucky.

The phone rang, cutting through my morning inventory of the weapons that had become as essential to my routine as coffee and cigarettes. Dating Irene Stout for six months had changed a few things. These days I checked my watch before walking into dark alleys, wondered if I'd make it home for dinner. Funny how having someone to come home to made staying alive seem more important.

"Vance Investigations."

"Morning, Ellie." Irene's voice still sent a warm flutter through my chest, even after all this time. "Sleep well?"

"Like a baby. A very paranoid baby who checked the locks twice and kept a loaded gun on the nightstand."

She laughed, and the sound pushed back some of the morning's shadows. "Still having those dreams?"

Fangs and claws. Gunfire echoing down basement corridors where good men died fighting monsters. I'd been having them since October, and they showed no signs of stopping. Dr. Carlisle at the Veterans Hospital called it "combat fatigue," but he'd never seen the kind of combat I'd seen.

"Some," I admitted. "Nothing I can't handle."

"Liar. But I'll let you get away with it this time." Her voice held warmth that hadn't been there when we'd first met. Back when she'd asked me to dinner, pretending it was about a newspaper interview. We'd both known better.

"Breakfast at Philippe's?"

Philippe's French Dip had become our regular morning spot. Close enough to both our offices, public enough that nothing supernatural would risk showing itself there. Safe, which mattered more these days than I cared to admit.

Irene Stout had been covering crime for the L.A. Times for eight years before the werewolves grabbed her last October. She'd been investigating the same missing persons cases that had led me to the Crescent Club, and she'd paid for that curiosity with three weeks in a cage, waiting to be served up as dinner for monsters that most people didn't believe existed.

But she'd survived, and more than that, she'd understood. When I'd pulled her out of that hellish ceremony chamber, covered in dirt and blood but still fighting, she'd looked at me with eyes that held no illusions about what kind of world we really lived in.

"It's been a long time since I had dinner with someone who understands that monsters are real," I'd told her that first night. She'd smiled and said she was buying.

Six months later, she was still buying breakfast, and I was still grateful to wake up next to someone who didn't think I was crazy when I checked the shadows twice before going to sleep.

"Twenty minutes," I said. "I want to finish balancing the books."

"How bad is it this month?"

"Let's just say Pop's fifty-dollar startup fund is looking pretty ambitious right about now."

"Maybe I should write that article about you after all. 'LA's Only Supernatural Private Eye.' It would bring in business."

"And get us both killed by things that prefer to stay in the shadows."

"Point taken." The warmth in her voice carried clearly through the phone line. "See you at Philippe's. Try not to shoot any monsters before breakfast."

She hung up, and I was left holding the receiver with something that might have been a smile trying to work its way across my face. Irene had that effect on me—she made me remember what it felt like to have something worth protecting besides my own stubborn hide.

The books, when I finally looked at them, weren't as bad as I'd feared but weren't good enough to make me stop worrying about next month's rent. April had been slow, mostly divorce cases and missing persons work that didn't involve anything more supernatural than human selfishness. After six months, the honest cases were starting to feel strange.

I locked Pops in my desk drawer—Philippe's frowned on customers who came armed, even customers who'd learned the hard way that Los Angeles was full of things that went bump in the night—and headed downstairs.

Spring Street was busy with the kind of morning energy that made this city feel almost innocent. Office workers hurried past with newspapers tucked under their arms, shop owners swept their storefronts, and somewhere a radio played Dinah Shore singing about buttons and bows. Normal people living normal lives, blissfully unaware that their city had been under supernatural control for sixty years until a stubborn ex-Army medic and a handful of allies had burned it all down.

I walked the six blocks to Philippe's, enjoying the feel of sunshine on my face and the weight of the silver stiletto in my boot. Strange how both had become equally comforting.

The restaurant was busy with the usual crowd of downtown workers grabbing coffee and conversation before heading to offices that wouldn't see monsters no matter how many real ones walked past their windows. I chose a table near the front window where I could watch the street—old habits from the war, reinforced by newer habits from the aftermath.

Irene arrived exactly on time, looking professional in a navy dress that brought out her eyes and a hat that sat at just the right angle to frame her face. She'd always been pretty, but six months of shared secrets had given her beauty an edge of strength that made my pulse quicken in ways that had nothing to do with danger.

"You look tense," she said, settling into the chair across from me.

"Just the usual morning paranoia. Nothing a cup of coffee and some normal conversation won't cure."

"Define normal."

"Conversation that doesn't involve fangs, claws, or things that should be dead but aren't."

The waitress brought coffee and took our orders. I watched Irene add cream to hers, noting the steady hands and calm expression that had made her one of the Times' best crime reporters long before she'd learned what real crime looked like.

"Speaking of normal," she said, "I've been thinking about what you said last week. About maybe taking some time off. Going somewhere that doesn't have a supernatural underground."

"Like where?"

"San Francisco. Seattle. Hell, Kansas City. Anywhere that doesn't have a sixty-year history of monster infestation."

I'd been thinking the same thing myself, though I hadn't said so. The idea of walking down a street without checking the shadows, of sleeping through the night without keeping one ear open for sounds that shouldn't exist—it held an appeal I wasn't entirely comfortable with.

"And do what? Go back to being a nice, normal detective agency that only handles simple cases like cheating spouses and insurance fraud?"

"Would that be so bad?"

Before October, I'd have said yes without hesitation. I'd thrived on the danger, the challenge, solving cases the police couldn't touch. Now, with Frank Miller's rosary in my desk drawer and Irene holding my heart like it was made of spun glass, the idea of a quiet life didn't feel like giving up anymore.

"Maybe not," I admitted. "But who'd watch over Los Angeles if we left?"

"Bill Kowalski's still here. The federal boys have their eyes open now. Maybe this city doesn't need Eleanor Vance anymore."

Maybe it didn't. The werewolf pack was broken, their human collaborators dead or fled, and Agent Reynolds had left me a phone number that connected directly to a federal task force that specialized in supernatural threats. Los Angeles had other protectors now, official ones with government backing and resources I could never match.

But every morning when I read the papers, I found myself checking the crime reports for patterns that didn't belong, for deaths that couldn't be explained by human motives. Old habits, Frank Miller would have called them. The kind that kept you alive in a city where the real predators wore human faces right up until they didn't.

"Earth to Ellie." Irene was smiling at me across the table. "You were somewhere else entirely."

"Just thinking about what you said. About leaving."

"And?"

"And maybe you're right. Maybe it's time for Eleanor Vance to try being normal for a while."

The food arrived before she could answer, which was probably just as well. Normal was a nice idea, but I'd learned not to make plans too far in advance. In my experience, Los Angeles had a way of reminding you that some responsibilities couldn't be walked away from, no matter how much you might want to.

We ate in the comfortable silence that had developed between us over months of learning each other's rhythms. When I checked my watch, it was already past nine.

"I should go," I said, reaching for my wallet.

"Breakfast is on me. But I want something in return."

"What's that?"

"Dinner tonight. Somewhere nice. Somewhere we can talk about San Francisco or wherever without looking over our shoulders for things that might be listening."

I looked at her across the table, this woman who'd somehow become essential to my life without either of us quite planning it. She was offering me something I'd thought was lost forever—a future that might include more than just surviving from one case to the next.

"I'd like that," I said.

"Good." She stood and kissed me, quick and warm. "Seven o'clock. I'll pick the place."

I walked back to my office with her taste on my lips and her words echoing in my head. San Francisco. A new start. A chance to be the kind of detective my father had been—someone who solved human problems with human methods, who never had to worry about whether his bullets were blessed or his blade was silver.

By the time I reached my building, some of the morning's optimism had started to fade. The shadows between buildings seemed deeper, more active. A man in an expensive suit walked past and turned to look back at me with eyes that held too much intelligence, too much interest. A woman at the bus stop watched me with the kind of predatory patience I'd learned to recognize.

Or maybe I was seeing things that weren't there. Maybe six months of hunting monsters had finally pushed me over the edge, and I was starting to see them everywhere I looked.

But as I climbed the stairs to my office, I could feel the weight of the silver stiletto in my boot, and I knew that whether I was sane or paranoid didn't matter nearly as much as being prepared.

Los Angeles was beautiful in the spring sunshine. It was also patient, and hungry, and full of secrets that wore human faces right up until they decided they didn't need to anymore.

Most days, that knowledge felt like a burden I'd give anything to put down.

Today, with Irene's kiss still warm on my lips and the promise of dinner somewhere safe hanging in the air between us, it almost felt like just another part of a life that might be worth living.

Almost.

I unlocked my office door and stepped inside, breathing in the familiar mixture of coffee, cigarette smoke, and the particular kind of loneliness that came with being one of the few people who knew what really prowled this city after dark.

Pop's old desk sat exactly where he'd left it, still bearing the coffee stains and cigarette burns of thirty years' worth of cases that probably never involved anything more supernatural than human greed and stupidity. His picture hung on the wall behind it—a serious-faced man in a cheap suit who'd believed that right and wrong were as clear as black and white, and that a good detective's job was to make sure the right side won.

I'd inherited his business, his desk, and his stubborn sense of justice. I'd also inherited a world where the line between right and wrong had been redrawn in blood and silver, where monsters wore movie stars' faces and the only thing standing between ordinary people and the things that wanted to eat them was someone foolish enough to fight back.

Some inheritance.

But tonight, I was going to have dinner with a beautiful reporter and talk about San Francisco and the possibility of a life where monsters were just things in fairy tales. Tonight, for maybe the first time in a long while, I was going to pretend that normal was something I could still choose.

I settled into Pop's chair and pulled out the morning paper, scanning the headlines for anything that might need a private investigator's attention. Nothing jumped out at me—the usual mix of political scandals, traffic accidents, and society gossip that kept Los Angeles running.

Maybe that was a good sign. Maybe the city was finally settling into a rhythm that didn't include supernatural predators hunting in the shadows.

The spring sunshine streaming through my office window felt warm and innocent and full of promise.

For now.

A Mother's Fear

I'd left Irene still warm and sleepy in my bed, her blonde hair tangled across the pillow. She didn't have to be at the Times until ten, lucky girl, and I'd hated leaving her there. Six months ago, I couldn't wait to get to the office each morning. These days, I found better reasons to stay in bed as long as possible.

But bills didn't pay themselves, and Vance Investigations wasn't going to run itself.

The phone started ringing before I'd even hung up my jacket and hat. I stood there in my office doorway, keys still in one hand, listening to the insistent bell that probably meant my peaceful morning was about to become a memory.

I crossed to the desk and lifted the receiver on the fourth ring.

"Vance Investigations."

The voice on the other end belonged to a woman who sounded like she'd been crying for hours.

"Miss Vance? This is Dorothy Walker. I got your name from the police department. I called looking for Detective Miller about a case, and they told me he'd been killed in the line of duty last October." Her voice caught. "The sergeant I spoke with said Frank worked with you on a case right before he died, and that maybe I should give you a call for the kind of help I need."

Frank Miller's name hit me like a punch to the gut, even six months later. He'd handed out my card to people who needed help that didn't come with official badges and departmental oversight. People who'd found themselves face to face with the kind of evil that most cops weren't equipped to handle.

"What can I do for you, Mrs. Walker?"

"It's about my daughter. Margaret. She's in trouble, and I don't know where else to turn."

I grabbed a pencil and pulled a legal pad closer. "Tell me about Margaret."

"She's twenty-one. An actress, or trying to be one. Beautiful girl, talented, but this city..." Mrs. Walker's voice turned hard. "This city chews up girls like her and spits out the bones."

I'd heard this story before. Hell, half the waitresses in Hollywood had the same one—bus ticket from some small town, fifty bucks, and a head full of dreams.

"When did you last see Margaret?"

"Three weeks ago. She was supposed to come to dinner on a Sunday, like she always did. But she didn't show up, didn't call. When I went to her apartment in West Hollywood, the landlady said she'd moved out in the middle of the night. Packed everything and left with some European gentleman."

European gentleman. That phrase started setting off alarms in my head.

"Did the landlady describe this gentleman?"

"Tall, she said. Well-dressed, expensive clothes. Dark hair with some silver at the temples, like a movie star. Very handsome, very charming. He had this accent, she said. French, maybe, or German. And his eyes..." Mrs. Walker paused. "She said his eyes were the most beautiful thing she'd ever seen."

I wrote down 'beautiful eyes' and underlined it twice. That phrase came up when people were describing someone they probably shouldn't have trusted.

"Mrs. Walker, have you heard from Margaret at all since she left?"

"That's just it—I have. She calls me every few days, but always at night. Very late, sometimes past midnight. And she sounds different."

"Different how?"

"Tired, like she never sleeps. But also excited, like she's discovered some wonderful secret. She keeps talking about this man she's with, this Julian Croix. Says he's going to make her a star, that he's showing her a new way of living. But when I ask to see her, she always has excuses."

Julian Croix. I wrote the name down, though something about it was familiar in a way I couldn't place.

"What kind of excuses?"

"She's busy during the day—says the sunlight gives her terrible headaches now, that she has to avoid it. All her important meetings are at night. She's working on a special film project, she says, something that will change everything for her."

The Colt .38 Super was cold against my ribs. I had a feeling I might need it before the day was through.

"Mrs. Walker, I'd like to meet with you in person. Can you come to my office this afternoon?"

"Yes, of course. But Miss Vance, there's something else. Something that really frightens me."

I waited.

"Last time Margaret called, she sounded hungry. That's the only way I can describe it. Like she hadn't eaten in days, but not hungry for food. Hungry for something else. And when I asked her about it, she just laughed and said Julian was teaching her about different kinds of appetite."

My pencil snapped between my fingers.

"Mrs. Walker, what's your address? I'm coming to see you right now."

"But I thought you said this afternoon—"

"Change of plans. This can't wait."

I hung up and stared at my notes. Julian Croix, European, beautiful eyes, nocturnal habits, talks about different kinds of appetite. It could be drugs—Hollywood was full of pushers who specialized in starlets. It could be some kind of cult, the type that promised enlightenment through unconventional means.

Or it could be something much worse.

I unlocked my desk drawer and clipped the holster for Pops to my belt. The silver stiletto was already in my boot, and I added a small cross to my jacket pocket—the one Father Martinez blessed after I'd told him a carefully edited version of what happened in October.

Mrs. Walker lived in a modest house in Glendale, the kind of place that was a good investment twenty years ago and was still holding its value. The neighborhood was quiet, full of middle-class families whose biggest worries should have been mortgage payments and whether their kids would make it through school without getting into trouble.

She answered the door on the first knock, a woman in her early fifties with graying brown hair and the kind of worry lines that came from too many sleepless nights. She wore a simple blue dress and clutched a handkerchief like a lifeline.

"Miss Vance? Thank you for coming so quickly."

The house was neat and clean, filled with furniture that spoke of financial comfort without showing off. Family photographs lined the mantelpiece—Margaret at various ages, school pictures and graduation photos showing a pretty blonde girl with bright eyes and an infectious smile.

"Tell me about Margaret's acting career," I said, settling into a chair that probably cost more than my office rent.

"She'd been in Los Angeles for three years, ever since high school. A few small parts in pictures, mostly background work. She was persistent, though. Went to auditions, took acting classes, worked part-time at a dress shop to pay for it all." Mrs. Walker twisted the handkerchief in her hands. "She was getting discouraged, though. Said the competition was getting fiercer, that the studios only wanted a certain type of girl."

"What type?"

"Blonde, busty, not too smart. Margaret was blonde enough, but she wanted to be taken seriously as an actress, not just cast as decoration. She'd been talking about giving up, maybe going back to school. Then this Julian Croix came along, and suddenly everything changed."

"How did they meet?"

"At some party, I think. One of those industry things where young actors go hoping to be discovered. Margaret came home excited, said she'd met a European director who saw unusual potential in her. She showed me his card—very expensive-looking, with just his name and a phone number."

"Do you still have the card?"

"No, she took it with her when she left. But I remember the name—Julian Croix. Said he was making art films, the kind that wouldn't be shown in regular theaters but would establish her reputation among serious artists."

The story was depressingly familiar. Struggling actress meets mysterious man who promises to make her dreams come true, if only she'll trust him completely and cut ties with everyone who cares about her.

"Mrs. Walker, did Margaret mention anything else about Croix? Where he lived, what kind of films he made?"

"She said he had an estate somewhere in the hills. Very private, very exclusive. The films he made were about transcending human limitations, about discovering what we're truly capable of when we stop being afraid." Mrs. Walker's hands were shaking. "Miss Vance, my daughter is a smart girl. But this man has done something to her, made her believe things that don't make any sense."

"Did she describe this estate?"

"Something about it being perfect for night shooting, she said. Lots of Gothic architecture, like something out of a Dracula picture." Mrs. Walker paused. "When she told me that, she laughed, like it was funny. But I didn't hear any humor in it."

I kept my expression neutral, but inside, every alarm bell I'd developed was going off. European director, Gothic estate, night shooting, themes about transcending humanity—it was like someone had taken every vampire story ever written and decided to make them real.

"Has Margaret mentioned any other people involved with these films?"

"A few names, but she was always secretive about them. Said Julian insisted on discretion—that the work was too important to risk having it misunderstood by small minds." Mrs. Walker's voice cracked. "She used to tell me everything. Every audition, every callback, every disappointment. Now she acts like her old life was something to be ashamed of."

"What about friends? People who might have seen her recently?"

"That's another thing that worries me. Margaret had a circle of friends in the acting community—other girls trying to make it, young men from her drama classes. But in the last month, she stopped seeing all of them. Said they wouldn't understand the important work she was doing."

Classic isolation tactics. Whether it was a cult, an abusive relationship, or something supernatural, the pattern was always the same—cut the victim off from their support system, make them dependent on the predator for validation and connection.

"Mrs. Walker, I'm going to take your daughter's case. My fee is twenty-five dollars a day plus expenses."

"Money is no object. I just want Margaret back."

"I need you to understand something. If Julian Croix is what I think he might be, getting Margaret away from him could be dangerous. For both of us."

"What do you mean?"

I chose my words carefully. "Some men who prey on young women in this city have connections to very dangerous people. People who don't like interference in their business. If I take this case, I need to know you're prepared for the possibility that things might get complicated."

Mrs. Walker's jaw set in a way that reminded me of mothers I'd known during the war—women who'd sent their boys off to fight and were prepared to fight themselves if necessary.

"Miss Vance, Margaret is my only child. Her father died in the Pacific, and she's all I have left in this world. If someone is hurting her, I don't care how dangerous they are. I want them stopped."

I respected that kind of determination, even if it came from someone who probably had no idea what she might be up against.

"All right. I'll need a recent photograph of Margaret, the address of her old apartment, and a list of any friends or colleagues she mentioned. I'll also need the name of the dress shop where she worked."

Mrs. Walker nodded and began gathering the requested items. As she moved around the room, I noticed she'd installed new locks on the doors—heavy deadbolts that looked out of place in the genteel neighborhood.

"Mrs. Walker, are you concerned about your own safety?"

She glanced at the locks, then back at me. "Three nights ago, I had a visitor around eleven-thirty. A man claiming to be from Margaret's talent agency, said he needed to discuss an urgent contract matter. When I looked through the peephole, he seemed normal enough—well-dressed, professional. But something made me keep the chain on."

"What kind of something?"

"He was too still. People fidget, shift their weight, you know? This man just stood there like a statue. And when I told him through the door that Margaret didn't live here anymore, he didn't ask where she'd gone. He just said, 'We know where she is. We wanted to make sure you understood that she's being well cared for.'" Mrs. Walker's voice dropped. "Then he smiled at the peephole, like he knew I was watching, and walked away."

My hand instinctively moved toward Pops under my jacket. "Did you call the police?"

"They said it was probably just a strange agent, that entertainment people can be eccentric. But Miss Vance, the way he moved when he left—it wasn't normal. Too smooth, too quiet. And the next morning, I found footprints on my porch. Someone had been standing at my door for a long time."

This was getting worse by the minute. If Julian Croix had people watching Mrs. Walker, it meant he knew she was looking for her daughter. And that made this whole situation significantly more dangerous.

"Keep your doors locked and your curtains drawn at night. If you see anyone suspicious, call the police immediately. And Mrs. Walker—" I wrote down my office number on a card. "—if anything feels wrong, call me. Day or night."

An hour later, I was driving through West Hollywood with Margaret Walker's photograph on the passenger seat beside me. She was a pretty girl, blonde and fresh-faced with the kind of wholesome looks that could go either innocent or sultry depending on the lighting. The kind of face that would stand out in a crowd, but not so much that people would remember specific details about her.

Perfect prey for someone who specialized in making people disappear.

Margaret's former apartment was in a building that had seen better decades, the kind of place where aspiring actors lived while they waited for their big break. The landlady was a sharp-eyed woman in her sixties who looked like she'd heard every sob story in the book.

"You're not the first person asking about Margaret Walker," she said, leading me up a narrow staircase that smelled of cigarettes and unfulfilled dreams.

"Oh? Who else has been interested?"

"Couple of men came by last week. Said they were from some talent agency, wanted to know if she'd left a forwarding address. But they didn't look like talent agents to me."

"What did they look like?"

"Professional types, expensive suits, but something was off. They moved wrong—too smooth, like dancers or something. And they kept asking the same questions over and over, even after I'd answered them. Gave me the creeps."

The apartment was small and mostly empty, but a few personal items remained—a jewelry box, some costume pieces, a stack of acting headshots. I flipped through the photographs, noting the progression from fresh-faced newcomer to someone who was trying harder to project sophistication and worldliness.

"She was a quiet tenant," the landlady said. "Paid her rent on time, didn't throw parties. But in the last month, she started keeping strange hours. I'd hear her coming in at dawn, leaving at sunset. And the visitors..."

"What about the visitors?"

"Always men, always well-dressed, always after dark. They didn't look like the usual Hollywood types—agents, producers, casting directors. These guys looked like they'd stepped out of some old European movie."

I found what I was looking for in the bedroom closet—a small appointment book that Margaret apparently forgot in her hurry to leave. I flipped through the pages, noting auditions, acting classes, and social engagements. Then, about a month ago, the entries changed.

Instead of specific appointments, there were just cryptic notations: "J.C. - estate" and "night shoot" and "artistic consultation." The final entry, dated three weeks ago, simply read: "transformation begins."

Transformation begins. I'd seen enough horror movies to know that wasn't the kind of phrase that usually led to happy endings.

The dress shop where Margaret worked was called "Celestial Fashions," a boutique in Beverly Hills that catered to women who could afford to pay too much for clothes that looked like they belonged in a museum. The owner was a thin, nervous man named Felix Crane who spoke with the kind of affected accent that suggested he'd grown up somewhere far less glamorous than he wanted people to believe.

"Margaret was one of our best girls," he said, adjusting and readjusting the arrangement of scarves in a display case. "Beautiful, charming with the customers, never late. Until the end."

"What happened at the end?"

"She started missing shifts, showing up pale and distracted. Said she was working on an important film project that required her full attention. Then one day, she just stopped coming in. Sent a message saying she wouldn't be needing the job anymore."

"Did she mention this film project?"

"Some art film with a European director. Very hush-hush, very exclusive. She was quite excited about it, said it was going to change her life." Felix's expression darkened. "I've been in this business long enough to know what usually happens to girls who get involved with mysterious European directors and their 'exclusive' projects."

"What do you think happened?"

"Best case scenario? She's someone's kept woman, living in luxury until he gets bored and trades her in for a younger model. Worst case..." He shook his head. "Let's just say I've known too many girls who got involved with the wrong crowd and were never seen again."

I was starting to get a clearer picture of Margaret Walker's last weeks in Los Angeles. A struggling actress, growing desperate as her career stalled, suddenly presented with an opportunity that was too good to be true. A mysterious director who promised her stardom, who saw "unusual potential" in her, who introduced her to ideas about transcending human limitations.

It was a predator's playbook, whether the predator was human or something else entirely.

By the time I returned to my office, the sun was starting to set over Los Angeles, painting the sky in shades of orange and red that reminded me of dried blood. I sat at Pop's old desk and spread out everything I'd learned about Margaret Walker and Julian Croix.

The pattern was clear enough—find vulnerable young women with show business aspirations, isolate them from their support systems, gradually introduce them to increasingly strange ideas and activities. Make them dependent on you for validation and connection, then... what?

That was the question I needed to answer. Whether Julian Croix was running some kind of sophisticated prostitution ring, a religious cult, or something supernatural, his end game involved making young women disappear from their old lives completely.

The phone rang, interrupting my thoughts.

"Vance Investigations."

"Miss Vance? It's Dorothy Walker. Margaret just called me."

I grabbed a pencil. "What did she say?"

"She sounded different than before. Excited, but in a frightening way. She said she wanted to see me, that she had wonderful news to share. But when I suggested she come here, she insisted I meet her instead."

"Where?"

"Some nightclub in Hollywood. A place called 'The Crimson Room.' She said Julian would be there, that she wanted me to meet him." Mrs. Walker's voice was tight with worry. "Miss Vance, she sounded so strange. Like she was reading from a script, or like someone was telling her what to say."

The Crimson Room. I'd heard of it—an after-hours club that catered to Hollywood's more adventurous crowd. The kind of place where starlets went to be seen with men who could advance their careers, where deals were made that never appeared in any official contracts.

"Mrs. Walker, I don't want you meeting her alone."

"But she's my daughter—"

"And someone has spent the last month isolating her from everyone she cared about and filling her head with dangerous ideas. This could be a trap."

"What do you suggest?"

I looked out my window at the deepening twilight. Somewhere out there, Margaret Walker was either in terrible danger or had become dangerous herself. Either way, tonight was going to provide answers to questions I wasn't sure I wanted to ask.

"I suggest we go to The Crimson Room together. But Mrs. Walker, you need to understand something. If Julian Croix is what I think he might be, seeing your daughter again might not be the reunion you're hoping for."

"What do you mean?"

"I mean sometimes the people we love change in ways that can't be changed back. And sometimes, trying to save them puts everyone in danger."

There was a long pause on the other end of the line.

"Miss Vance, I've already lost my husband to the war. I'm not losing my daughter to whatever's happening in this city. If she's in danger, I'm going to help her. If she's become dangerous..." Mrs. Walker's voice hardened. "Well, then I suppose we'll cross that bridge when we come to it."

I looked at the silver stiletto lying on my desk next to the blessed bullets for Pops. Los Angeles was full of things that looked human until they didn't feel like pretending anymore. I'd learned that the hard way.

"Mrs. Walker, I'll pick you up at nine o'clock. Wear something dark, and bring identification. Just in case."

"Just in case what?"

"Just in case we don't come home."

I hung up and started checking my weapons. The Crimson Room was the kind of place where predators went to hunt, and if Julian Croix was holding court there, I was going to make sure I was ready for whatever kind of predator he turned out to be.

Outside my window, Los Angeles settled into its nightly rhythm of dreams and nightmares, and somewhere in the darkness, a young actress named Margaret Walker was about to learn whether the promise of stardom was worth the price her mysterious benefactor was asking her to pay.

    I had a feeling we were all about to find out.

The Immortal Artist

The Los Angeles Public Library smelled like dust, old paper, and the dreams of people who'd come looking for answers they couldn't afford to buy. I'd been there since nine in the morning, working my way through every film industry publication I could get my hands on, searching for any mention of Julian Croix.

So far, I'd found nothing.

That should have been impossible. Directors didn't just appear out of thin air in Hollywood, especially ones making the kind of money it took to rent Gothic estates in the Hills and throw lavish parties for the city's hungriest social climbers. There should have been trade publications announcing his arrival, gossip columns speculating about his projects, industry directories listing his credentials.

Instead, Julian Croix might as well have been a ghost.

I pushed back from the reading table and rubbed my eyes, trying to focus on what I'd learned instead of what I hadn't. Three hours of research had turned up exactly one reference—a brief mention in Variety from six weeks ago about a European art film director exploring "themes of immortality and transcendence" at a private screening for Hollywood types.

The article gave no details about his background, previous work, or how long he'd been in Los Angeles. It read like a planted story, the kind of publicity piece someone paid good money to get printed without asking too many questions.

I made a note of the date and tucked it into my jacket pocket next to the blessed cross. If Julian Croix was trying to erase his past, he'd done a professional job of it. But in my experience, people who worked that hard to hide their history usually had good reason.

The question was what he was hiding, and whether Margaret Walker was still alive to be saved from it.

My next stop was RKO Studios, where Margaret had auditioned for small parts over the past three years. The casting director was a harried-looking woman named Ruth Steinberg who remembered Margaret but seemed more interested in getting back to her appointment book than helping a private investigator.

"Pretty girl, decent actress, nothing special," she said, lighting a cigarette with fingers that shook slightly. "Comes in here twice a month like clockwork, always prepared, always professional. Then about five weeks ago, she just stops showing up."

"Did she say why?"

"Got herself a benefactor, from what I heard. Some European director who promised her the moon and stars. Happens all the time in this business—girls think they've found their big break, disappear for a few months, then come crawling back when reality sets in."

I showed her Margaret's photograph. "When was the last time you saw her?"

Ruth squinted at the picture through cigarette smoke. "Beginning of March, maybe? She seemed different that last time. Excited, but also nervous. Kept checking her watch, said she had an important meeting that evening."

"Did she mention Julian Croix?"

"That name doesn't ring a bell, but like I said, girls are always talking about some mysterious producer who's going to make them famous. Half the time the guy doesn't even exist."

But Julian Croix existed, all right. The question was what kind of existence he was offering Margaret Walker in return for her cooperation.

I spent the rest of the morning making the rounds of other studios and talent agencies, following the same pattern Margaret had walked for three years. The story was always the same—a young woman growing increasingly desperate as her opportunities dried up, then suddenly full of hope about a mysterious benefactor who'd promised to change her life.

Nobody had actually met this benefactor. Nobody could verify his credentials or describe his previous work. He was like smoke, substantial enough to lure vulnerable young women into his orbit but too insubstantial to pin down.

By noon, I was starting to think I'd need a different approach.

I found it at a small art house theater on Melrose that specialized in experimental films and foreign imports. The owner was a thin, intellectual-looking man named David Roth who wore wire-rimmed glasses and spoke with the careful precision of someone who'd learned English as a second language.

"You're asking about Julian Croix," he said when I mentioned the name. "Yes, I know of him. Brilliant filmmaker, though his work is... challenging."

Finally, someone who'd actually encountered my mysterious director.

"Challenging how?"

Roth gestured toward a poster on the wall advertising something called "The Eternal Moment." The image showed a woman's face in close-up, her eyes wide and staring, her lips parted as if in ecstasy or terror. In the corner, elegant script credited Julian Croix as writer and director.

"His films explore themes that most Hollywood productions wouldn't touch. The nature of immortality, the relationship between art and eternity, whether true creativity requires transcending human limitations." Roth removed his glasses and polished them carefully. "Very avant-garde, very European in sensibility."

"Have you shown his work here?"

"Just once, about a month ago. A private screening for a select audience. The film was... provocative."

I studied the poster more carefully. The woman's face seemed familiar, though I couldn't place where I might have seen her before. "What was it about?"

"A young actress who discovers that the key to creating truly immortal art lies in embracing a different kind of existence. She undergoes a transformation that allows her to transcend the limitations of mortal creativity." Roth replaced his glasses. "The imagery was quite striking, though some viewers found it disturbing."

"Disturbing how?"

"The transformation sequences were very realistic. Almost documentary in style. Some people left during the screening."

I felt the familiar chill that came with recognizing a pattern I'd hoped never to see again. "Mr. Roth, do you know where I could see this film?"

"I'm afraid that would be impossible. Mr. Croix was very specific about the screening being a one-time event. He collected all the prints afterward, said the work was too important to risk having it misunderstood by inappropriate audiences."

"Did he say what made an audience appropriate?"

Roth hesitated, as if choosing his words carefully. "He seemed most interested in people who were artists themselves. Actors, writers, directors. People who understood what it took to create something worth remembering."

"What kind of sacrifices?"

"The willingness to give up everything that holds you back from achieving your full potential. Conventional morality, social expectations, even basic human limitations." Roth's expression grew troubled. "He spoke very passionately about the idea that only immortals could create truly eternal art. That mortal artists were fundamentally limited by their brief lifespans, their biological needs, their attachment to temporal concerns."

I thought about Margaret Walker's appointment book, the final entry that had read "transformation begins."

"Mr. Roth, was Julian Croix recruiting people at that screening?"

"Not recruiting, exactly. But several young artists approached him afterward, very interested in his ideas about transcending human limitations. He was quite selective about who he chose to speak with privately."

"Do you remember any names?"

"I'm afraid not. But I got the impression he was looking for a particular type—young, talented, perhaps a bit desperate for recognition. People who felt their current circumstances were holding them back from achieving greatness."

Margaret Walker fit that description perfectly.

I thanked Roth and left the theater with more questions than answers, but at least now I had a clearer picture of Julian Croix's methods. He wasn't just a predator hunting vulnerable young women—he was something more sophisticated, more dangerous. A collector who used philosophy and art to justify whatever he was doing to his victims.

What bothered me most was how he was operating completely outside the system. In 1949, you didn't just show up in Hollywood and start making movies. The studios controlled everything—who got cast, who got financing, who got distribution. MGM, Paramount, Warner Brothers, they had the town sewn up tight. Even the independents like David Selznick had to work within the system.

But Julian Croix seemed to exist in his own world, with his own money and his own private estate and his own collection of artists. Like Howard Hughes, but more secretive, more selective. The studios tolerated Hughes because he had oil money and airplane factories. What did Croix have that let him operate in the shadows?

My next stop was the Los Angeles County Recorder's Office, where I hoped to find some trace of Croix's business activities. Real estate transactions, business licenses, anything that might give me a lead on where he was operating from.

The clerk was an elderly man named Morris Katz who looked like he'd been filing paperwork since the city was founded. He listened to my request with the patient expression of someone who'd heard every possible variation of "I need to find information about someone who might not want to be found."

"Julian Croix, you said? European fellow?"

"That's right. Probably renting or buying property in the Hills, maybe under a business name."

Morris disappeared into the filing system for twenty minutes, returning with a thin folder and a puzzled expression.

"Found something interesting," he said, opening the folder. "Property lease for an estate on Mulholland Drive, signed six weeks ago. But here's the curious part—the lease is paid for a full year in advance, in cash."

I studied the paperwork. The address was 1847 Mulholland Drive, and the lease was indeed signed by Julian Croix. But the signature looked old-fashioned, like something from a different era entirely.

"Who's the property owner?"

"That's where it gets strange. The owner is listed as J. Croix Enterprises, incorporated in Nevada last year. But when I checked with Nevada, they show the incorporation papers filed by someone named Julian Croix."

I felt that familiar chill again. "So he leased the property from himself?"

"Looks that way. It's not illegal, just unusual. Most people don't go to that much trouble to obscure a simple rental agreement."

Unless they had something to hide that went beyond simple business privacy.

I copied down the address and headed back to my car, thinking about what I'd learned. Julian Croix was operating out of a Gothic estate on Mulholland Drive, making avant-garde films about immortality and transcendence, and recruiting young artists who felt held back by human limitations. He'd gone to considerable trouble to erase any trace of his past, and his business dealings were structured to avoid scrutiny.

It was starting to sound less like a cult and more like something much worse.

The drive up Mulholland took twenty minutes, winding through the Hills past estates that belonged to studio executives and established stars. 1864 was at the end of a private road, hidden behind wrought-iron gates and mature trees that blocked most of the view from the street.

I parked where I could watch the gates and settled in to wait. If Croix was following the pattern Margaret's mother had described, he'd be sleeping during the day and active after sunset. But I might learn something from watching who came and went during daylight hours.

For two hours, nothing moved except the occasional delivery truck and a gardening crew that worked on the landscaping visible through the gates. The estate looked expensive but not ostentatious—the kind of place where someone could conduct business without attracting unwanted attention from neighbors or authorities.

Then, around three o'clock, I saw something that made me reach for my notebook.

A black Cadillac pulled up to the gates, which opened automatically. Behind the wheel was a woman who looked to be in her thirties, pale and thin with dark hair pulled back severely. She wore sunglasses despite the overcast afternoon, and she moved with the careful precision of someone who wasn't entirely comfortable with daylight.

I'd seen that type of careful movement before, in October, from people who'd been changed into something that preferred darkness to light.

The gates closed behind her, and I made a note of the license plate and time. If Croix was building a collection of transformed artists, this might be one of them. Someone who'd undergone the same process he was promising Margaret Walker.

At four-thirty, the pattern repeated. Another car, another pale, careful driver wearing sunglasses on a cloudy day. This time it was a young man who looked like he might have been an actor before whatever had happened to him happened.

By five o'clock, I'd counted four visitors, all showing the same characteristics—pale skin, careful movements, unnecessary sunglasses, and an overall appearance that suggested they were more comfortable after dark.

I was looking at Croix's "immortal cast and crew," the people he'd recruited with promises of transcending human limitations. The question was whether they were still human enough to be saved, or if whatever transformation Croix offered was permanent.

As the sun started setting behind the Hollywood Hills, I made a decision that would probably qualify as the stupidest thing I'd done since October, but seemed like the only way to get the answers I needed.

I was going to get a closer look at Julian Croix's operation.

The estate was surrounded by a high wall topped with decorative iron spikes that would discourage casual trespassers but weren't impossible to overcome for someone with Army training and adequate motivation. I waited until full darkness, then made my approach from the back of the property where the landscaping would provide cover.

Getting over the wall was easier than I'd expected. Getting to the main house without being seen was harder.

The estate was much larger than it had appeared from the street, with the main house set well back from the gates and surrounded by gardens that had been designed for nighttime entertaining. Subtle lighting illuminated paths and architectural features, and I could hear the sound of music and conversation coming from somewhere behind the house.

A party was in progress.

I worked my way through the gardens, staying in the shadows and moving carefully toward the source of the sounds. What I saw when I finally got close enough made me understand exactly what kind of artist Julian Croix really was.

The party was being held on a large terrace behind the main house, lit by torches and decorated in a style that seemed to blend classical European architecture with Hollywood glamour. There were perhaps thirty people in attendance, all of them young, attractive, and dressed in expensive clothing that managed to look both fashionable and somehow timeless.

And every single one of them had the same pale skin, careful movements, and aversion to direct light that I'd observed in the afternoon visitors.

At the center of it all stood Julian Croix himself.

He was exactly what you'd expect from a European film director who'd convinced dozens of young artists to transform themselves for the sake of their art—tall, distinguished, with silver-touched dark hair and features that belonged in a Renaissance painting. He wore an expensive suit that fit like it had been tailored specifically for his frame, and when he moved, he did so with the kind of unconscious grace that suggested he was very, very old and very, very dangerous.

But it was his commanding presence that held my attention. Even at thirty yards, there was something about the way he moved and spoke that reminded me of someone who'd been in complete control for far longer than any normal person should be.

He was speaking to the gathered crowd, his voice carrying clearly in the still night air.

"True art," he was saying, "requires more than talent. It demands immortality. The greatest artists in history were limited by their brief mortal spans, their biological needs, their attachment to temporal concerns. They created beauty, yes, but it was always haunted by the knowledge of its creator's mortality."

The crowd listened with the rapt attention of converts, hanging on every word.

"But imagine art created by immortal minds. Imagine creativity freed from the constraints of human limitation. Imagine beauty that could be refined and perfected over centuries, not mere decades." Croix gestured elegantly toward the estate around them. "This is what we are creating here. Not just films, but a new form of artistic expression. A cinema of eternity."

I thought about Margaret Walker, somewhere in this crowd of transformed artists, and felt my hand move instinctively toward the silver stiletto in my boot.

"Each of you has made the choice to transcend your mortal limitations," Croix continued. "Each of you has discovered that true creativity requires abandoning the petty concerns that bind ordinary humans. You are no longer merely actors or directors or writers. You are eternal artists, freed from death to create works that will outlast civilizations."

A young woman near the front of the crowd raised her hand. Even in the torchlight, I could see she was beautiful in the way that Margaret Walker was beautiful—fresh, wholesome, with the kind of face that could have belonged to the girl next door if the girl next door had been transformed into something that fed on human blood.

"Master Croix," she said, and I realized with a chill that this might be Margaret herself, "when will we begin work on the new project?"

Croix smiled, and even at a distance, I could see his canine teeth were longer and sharper than they had any right to be.

"Soon, my dear. Very soon. We have one more artist to add to our company, and then we can begin creating the masterpiece that will announce our presence to the world." His gaze swept over the crowd. "A film that will show ordinary mortals what true immortal art looks like. A work of such beauty and power that it will inspire others to seek the same transcendence we have achieved."

I'd heard enough. Julian Croix wasn't just running a cult—he was something worse. The pale skin, the nocturnal activities, the talk of immortality and transcending human limitations, the way his followers moved like they were uncomfortable in their own bodies. It was starting to add up to a pattern I recognized from the supernatural research I'd done after October.

Whether he was exactly what I suspected or just something similar, he was definitely using whatever he'd become to recruit victims. He'd turned filmmaking into bait, using promises of eternal creativity to lure vulnerable young people into his web.

And Margaret Walker was either his latest victim or about to become one.

I started backing away from the terrace, planning to return to my car and figure out how to get Mrs. Walker to safety before confronting Croix directly. But I'd only made it twenty yards when I heard footsteps behind me.

"You're not one of our usual guests," a woman's voice said.

I turned to find myself facing the pale, dark-haired woman I'd seen arriving in the black Cadillac. Up close, she was even more obviously not entirely human—her skin had the waxy quality of someone who hadn't seen sunlight in months, her movements had that same careful precision I'd observed earlier, and when she smiled, there was something predatory about the expression that made every instinct I'd developed scream danger.

"Just enjoying the evening air," I said, keeping my voice casual while my hand moved slowly toward my boot.

"I don't think so." Her smile widened. "Who are you? What are you doing here?"

"Just out for a walk," I said, keeping my voice steady. "Heard there was a party. Thought I'd take a look."

"A walk." She tilted her head, studying me with the kind of attention a cat gives a mouse. "At midnight. In the hills. Behind a private estate."

"I get restless at night."

"How interesting." She took a step closer. "Most people sleep at night. But then, most people aren't carrying weapons specifically designed to hurt my kind, are they?"

My hand froze halfway to my boot. She'd noticed the silver.

"I don't know what you're talking about."

"Oh, I think you do." Her voice dropped to almost a whisper. "Silver blade, blessed no doubt. You know exactly what we are, don't you? The question is, what are you planning to do about it?"

The silver stiletto was halfway out of my boot when she moved. She was fast—faster than anything human had a right to be—but I'd been fighting supernatural predators for six months, and I'd learned a few things about staying alive when the odds were against me.

I rolled sideways as her claws raked the air where my throat had been, came up with the stiletto ready, and drove six inches of blessed silver between her ribs before she could recover her balance.

She screamed—a sound that was part human agony and part animal rage—and staggered backward. The silver had done its work, burning her from the inside, but she was still standing, still dangerous. Blood that looked too dark in the torchlight seeped through her expensive dress.

"Silver," she hissed, looking at me with eyes that held too much anger for someone who should have been dying. "Clever little girl."

I could hear voices calling out from the terrace, movement in the gardens, and the distinctive sound of predators organizing a hunt. Whatever she was, her scream had attracted the attention of her friends.

Time to go.

I ran for the wall, using every bit of Army training I possessed to stay ahead of whatever was coming after me. Behind me, I could hear Julian Croix's cultured voice calling out instructions, organizing his immortal artists into a search pattern that would have impressed a military commander.

"Find her," he said, his voice carrying clearly through the night air. "But don't harm her. I want to meet this detective who's been so interested in our work. She may prove useful to our next project."

I cleared the wall with nothing to spare and dropped into the darkness beyond, running for my car and thinking about everything I'd learned.

Julian Croix was a vampire who'd turned art filmmaking into a sophisticated recruitment operation. He'd collected dozens of transformed artists who believed they were creating immortal art when they were actually serving as his personal army of predators. And he had plans for a masterpiece that would reveal their existence to the world and attract new victims.

Margaret Walker was either already lost or about to be, and her mother was walking into a trap that could get them both killed.

But at least now I knew what I was up against.

As I drove back down Mulholland toward the city lights of Los Angeles, I started planning how to stop a vampire who thought he was Orson Welles and save a young actress who might already be beyond saving.

It was going to be a long night.

The Girl with the Glass Ambition

I got back to my apartment at two in the morning, still wound tight from the night's work. Irene was asleep in my bed, blonde hair spread across the pillow, one arm reaching toward the space where I should have been. She stirred when I sat down on the edge of the mattress to pull off my boots.

"How'd it go?" she mumbled, not opening her eyes.

"About as well as breaking into a vampire's estate usually goes."

That got her attention. She rolled over and switched on the bedside lamp, squinting at me in the sudden brightness. "Jesus, Ellie. Look at you."

I glanced down at myself—torn jacket, grass stains on my skirt, scratches on my hands from climbing walls and running through gardens. I looked like exactly what I was: someone who'd spent the evening playing hide-and-seek with supernatural predators and barely made it out alive.

"It's not as bad as it looks," I lied.

"Uh-huh." Irene sat up, fully awake now. "And what did you learn from tonight's adventure?"

I told her everything while she cleaned the scratches on my hands with iodine that stung worse than the vampire's claws had. Julian Croix's estate full of pale, careful people who moved like they weren't comfortable in daylight. The party where he preached about immortal art to a crowd of transformed followers. The woman who'd tried to kill me and taken a silver blade between the ribs without going down.

"So he's building an army," Irene said when I finished.

"Looks that way. Question is, what's he planning to use them for?"

"You said he mentioned a masterpiece. Something that would announce their presence to the world."

I nodded. "Which probably means more people are going to disappear before this is over. Starting with Margaret Walker."

Irene was quiet for a long moment, thinking. Finally she said, "You know, this might be exactly the kind of story Zelda's been looking for."

"Zelda?"

"Zelda Kettleton. She works research at the paper—brilliant woman, knows everything about everyone in this city. She's been asking me about your cases lately, particularly anything involving the entertainment industry."

I'd heard the name before, but I couldn't place where. "Why would she be interested?"

"Because she used to be a playwright. A damned good one, from what I hear. Had a play almost make it to Broadway back in '44, but the funding fell through at the last minute. Since then, she's been stuck doing research work and watching other people's dreams come true."

The kind of person Julian Croix would love to get his hands on. A talented artist whose ambitions had been crushed, who might be desperate enough to believe promises about transcending human limitations and creating eternal art.

"Irene, I don't think it's a good idea to involve your colleague in this."

"I'm not talking about involving her. I'm talking about picking her brain. Zelda knows more about the people behind the scenes in Hollywood than anyone else at the Times. If Julian Croix has connections to the industry, she'll know about them."

That made sense, but something about it still bothered me. Maybe it was the memory of all those pale, transformed faces at Croix's party. People who'd probably started out as researchers and struggling artists, convinced they were going to create something immortal.

"Just be careful," I said. "People who get too interested in Julian Croix have a tendency to disappear."

"I'll be careful. But Ellie, if this bastard is collecting artists, we need to know how he's choosing them. Zelda might be able to help us figure out his pattern."

She had a point. And if Zelda Kettleton really did know everyone's business in Hollywood, she might be able to give me leads that would take weeks to develop on my own.

"All right," I said. "But we meet her somewhere public, and we don't tell her everything."

"Agreed." Irene smiled and kissed my forehead. "Now get some sleep. You look like you've been hit by a truck."

I did feel like I'd been hit by a truck, but sleep was a long time coming. Every time I closed my eyes, I saw Julian Croix's commanding presence and heard his cultured voice talking about eternal art. I thought about Margaret Walker, somewhere in his collection of transformed artists, and wondered if she was still human enough to be saved.

Most of all, I thought about the woman who'd tried to kill me in Croix's garden. The way she'd moved, the way she'd looked at me after I'd put six inches of silver between her ribs. The casual way she'd called me "clever little detective," like she'd been expecting me.

They'd been waiting for me. Which meant Julian Croix knew exactly who I was and what I'd been doing. The question was whether he saw me as a threat to be eliminated or a potential addition to his collection.

I had a feeling I'd find out soon enough.

The next morning brought rain and a phone call from Dorothy Walker that I'd been dreading.

"Miss Vance, I haven't heard from you since yesterday. Did you learn anything about Margaret?"

I'd learned that her daughter was probably beyond saving, but I wasn't ready to tell a desperate mother that her child had been turned into something that fed on human blood.

"I'm making progress, Mrs. Walker. But I need you to promise me something. If Margaret calls you again, don't agree to meet her anywhere. And if anyone else comes to your house claiming to be connected to her, don't let them in."

"You sound frightened."

"I am frightened. The people Margaret's gotten involved with are more dangerous than I initially thought. I'm going to need a few more days to figure out how to approach this safely."

There was a long pause. "Miss Vance, you don't think she's coming back, do you?"

The honest answer was no, I didn't think Margaret Walker was coming back as anything her mother would recognize. But sometimes the truth was too cruel to speak aloud.

"I think the people who have her are very good at making promises they can't keep," I said instead. "Just give me some time to work on this, and please be careful."

After I hung up, I sat at my desk and stared at the notes I'd made about Julian Croix. A vampire who collected artists, promising them eternal life and eternal creativity. It was sophisticated, targeted, and probably more effective than anything the werewolves had ever tried.

The werewolves had been predators, pure and simple. They'd killed for food and entertainment, and they'd done it clumsily enough that Detective Miller and I had been able to track them down. But Julian Croix was something different. He was a predator who understood psychology, who knew exactly what desperate people wanted to hear.

He was also smart enough to operate completely outside the established systems that might have caught him. No studio connections, no official film permits, no paper trail that would lead back to anything concrete. Just a carefully constructed mythology about art and immortality, and an estate full of people who'd bought into it completely.

I was still thinking about how to approach the problem when Irene called around noon.

"I talked to Zelda," she said. "She's very interested in your case. Wants to meet this afternoon at Musso & Frank's."

Musso & Frank Grill on Hollywood Boulevard was about as public as you could get—a restaurant that had been serving writers, actors, and industry types since 1919. If we were going to talk to someone about Julian Croix, it was exactly the kind of place to do it.

"What did you tell her?"

"Just that you were investigating a missing actress and a mysterious European director. She got very excited when I mentioned the European part."

"Excited how?"

"Said she'd been hearing whispers about someone like that for weeks. Apparently there's been talk in certain circles about a new player in town, someone with money and connections but no visible means of support."

That sounded like our Julian Croix. "Did she mention anything about films?"

"Art films. Underground projects. The kind of thing that gets people talking at parties but never seems to result in anything you can actually see in theaters."

"All right. Set it up for three o'clock. And Irene?"

"Yeah?"

"Don't leave me alone with her. Something about this whole thing feels like a setup."

I spent the afternoon reading everything I could find about vampires in the occult books I'd collected since October. Most of it was folklore and superstition, but some patterns emerged that matched what I'd observed at Croix's estate.

They were master manipulators, capable of inspiring fanatical loyalty in their victims. They often posed as artists, philosophers, or religious leaders—anything that would give them authority over people's minds as well as their bodies. And they were notoriously difficult to kill, requiring specific methods and materials that most people wouldn't think to use.

The silver stiletto had hurt the woman in Croix's garden, but it hadn't killed her. According to the books, that would require either decapitation with a blessed blade, a wooden stake through the heart, or exposure to direct sunlight. None of which were particularly practical for someone trying to rescue kidnapping victims.

I was beginning to understand why most people who ran into vampires ended up dead.

Musso & Frank's was busy with the usual crowd of industry types conducting business over martinis and red meat. Irene had claimed a booth in the back, and she wasn't alone. The woman sitting across from her was in her early thirties, with dark hair pulled back in a severe bun and intelligent eyes behind wire-rimmed glasses. She wore a simple blue dress that looked expensive, and when she stood to shake my hand, she moved with the kind of nervous energy that suggested she had more ideas than she knew what to do with.

"Eleanor Vance," she said before I could introduce myself. "I've heard so much about you."

"Ms. Kettleton. Irene tells me you might be able to help with some research."

"Please, call me Zelda. And yes, I'm very interested in what you're working on." She gestured toward the booth. "Shall we sit? I have quite a lot to tell you."

I slid in next to Irene, noting that Zelda had positioned herself where she could watch the entire restaurant. Either she was naturally paranoid, or she'd learned to be careful about who might be listening to her conversations.

"Irene mentioned you were looking into a European film director," Zelda said, leaning forward with the intensity of someone who'd been waiting for this conversation for weeks. "Julian Croix, by any chance?"

The fact that she knew the name without me mentioning it put me on edge. "You've heard of him?"

"Heard of him? I've been trying to find him for over a month." Zelda's eyes lit up with the kind of excitement that made me think of Margaret Walker talking to her mother about unusual potential. "He's exactly the kind of director the industry needs right now. Someone who understands that cinema can be more than just entertainment."

"What do you mean?"

"Art, Miss Vance. True art. The kind that explores the deepest questions about human existence, that pushes boundaries, that refuses to be constrained by commercial considerations." Zelda pulled a notebook from her purse and flipped through pages covered with her handwriting. "From what I've been able to learn, he's creating films that deal with themes Hollywood wouldn't touch. Mortality, transcendence, the relationship between art and immortality."

I exchanged a glance with Irene, who looked as troubled as I felt. Zelda Kettleton wasn't just interested in Julian Croix—she was fascinated by him. And that fascination had the same quality I'd heard in the voices of Croix's transformed followers at the estate.

"How did you first hear about him?" I asked.

"Through my work at the paper. I research background stories for the entertainment writers, and I started noticing references to this mysterious European director. Nothing definite, just whispers and rumors. People talking about private screenings, experimental films, a new approach to cinema that was supposed to revolutionize the industry."

"Did you see any of these films?"

Zelda's expression grew frustrated. "No, and that's what's been driving me crazy. Every time I thought I'd found a way to contact him or attend one of his screenings, the lead would dry up. It's like he's deliberately staying hidden from anyone who might want to write about his work."

Or like he was being very careful about who he allowed into his circle. I was starting to understand Julian Croix's method. He'd let rumors about his work circulate in exactly the right circles, building interest among the kind of people he wanted to attract. Then he'd make himself difficult to find, so that when someone finally did make contact, they'd feel like they'd accomplished something special.

"Zelda," I said carefully, "what kind of themes are you interested in as a writer?"

"The same themes Croix is exploring. The limitations of what we're allowed to write about in this town, the possibility of creating something that transcends commercial demands." Her voice grew passionate. "I've been working on a novel, you know. 'The Eternal Hour.' I've sent it to every publisher in New York, every studio story department in Hollywood. Same response every time - too intellectual, too philosophical for general audiences."

"What was your novel about?"

"A group of writers who discover that true creativity requires them to abandon everything that connects them to ordinary commercial success. The studio system, audience expectations, conventional storytelling—all the things that hold real artists back from achieving their full potential." Zelda's eyes gleamed. "It ended with them choosing to embrace a kind of pure artistic existence that would allow them to create without compromise for eternity."

I felt like I was listening to Julian Croix's recruitment speech, performed by someone who'd never even met him. Zelda Kettleton had somehow independently arrived at exactly the philosophy he was using to lure victims into his circle.

She was perfect bait for his trap.

"Zelda," Irene said gently, "don't you think there's something to be said for art that comes from human experience? From the connections we have to other people?"

"Of course," Zelda said, but her tone suggested she was just being polite. "But imagine what we could create if we weren't limited by human lifespans, human needs, human emotions. Imagine art that could be refined and perfected over centuries."

She was quoting Croix almost word for word, and she'd never even heard him speak. It was like she'd been primed for his message her entire life, just waiting for someone to come along and validate her belief that ordinary human existence was inadequate for true artistic achievement.

"Have you tried to contact him directly?" I asked.

"I've been working on it. There are ways to get messages to him, if you know the right people to ask. I was actually planning to attend one of his gatherings this week."

Every instinct I'd developed was screaming danger. "Zelda, I don't think that's a good idea."

"Why not? You're investigating him yourself, aren't you? What's the difference?"

The difference was that I was armed with blessed silver and a healthy understanding of what Julian Croix really was. Zelda Kettleton was walking into his web with nothing but enthusiasm and a philosophy that perfectly matched his recruitment pitch.

"The difference is that I'm investigating a missing persons case. A young actress named Margaret Walker disappeared after getting involved with Julian Croix. Her mother hired me to find her."

Zelda's expression grew troubled. "You think something happened to her?"

"I think Julian Croix collects artists the way other people collect paintings. And I think once you become part of his collection, you don't get to leave."

"But surely—" Zelda began, then stopped. I could see the conflict in her face, the battle between her fascination with Croix's artistic philosophy and her journalist's instincts that something wasn't right.

"Zelda," Irene said, "promise me you won't try to contact him until Ellie's finished her investigation. If this Margaret Walker really is missing, then there's something dangerous going on."

For a moment, I thought Zelda was going to agree. She looked troubled, uncertain, like someone who'd just realized that her dream opportunity might be too good to be true.

Then her expression hardened. "I appreciate your concern, but I've been waiting years for a chance like this. If Julian Croix is really creating the kind of art I think he is, then I can't afford to wait. Opportunities like this don't come along twice."

"Zelda—" Irene started, but she was already standing up.

"I'm sorry, but I have to follow my instincts on this. If there's a chance that Julian Croix could help me create the kind of work I've always dreamed of, I have to take it." She picked up her purse and notebook. "Thank you for telling me about him, Miss Vance. You may have helped me change my life."

She walked away before either of us could stop her, moving with the determined pace of someone who'd finally found what she'd been looking for.

"Shit," Irene said quietly.

I watched Zelda Kettleton disappear into the crowd of Hollywood Boulevard, thinking about Margaret Walker and all the other young artists who'd probably walked away from similar conversations with the same expression of determined hope.

"We have to stop her," I said.

"How? She's an adult, she can make her own choices."

"Even when those choices are going to get her killed?"

Irene was quiet for a long moment. Finally she said, "What do you want to do?"

"I want to follow her. If she's really planning to contact Julian Croix, then maybe she can lead us to wherever he's keeping Margaret Walker."

"And if she gets herself turned into one of those things you saw at his estate?"

I thought about the woman who'd tried to kill me in Croix's garden, the way she'd looked at me with eyes that held too much anger for someone who should have been dying.

"Then we'll have to figure out how to save her too."

But as I watched the rain start to fall on Hollywood Boulevard, I had a feeling that Julian Croix had just been handed another perfect recruit. Someone brilliant, frustrated, and desperate enough to believe that the answer to her problems lay in abandoning her humanity for the promise of eternal art.

I was going to have to move fast if I wanted to save anyone from the mistake Zelda Kettleton was about to make.

The question was whether I was already too late.

Party for the Damned

I spent the next three days watching Julian Croix's estate. Three days of sitting in my car with binoculars and bad coffee, learning the rhythm of a vampire's daily routine.

Same pattern every day—dead quiet until sunset, then the place came to life. Cars started arriving around eight, passengers moving like they were made of glass. Pale as milk and wearing sunglasses when the sun was already down.

What I was waiting for was the kind of gathering Croix mentioned to his followers—a recruitment party where he'd hold court for potential new additions to his collection. The kind of event where someone like Zelda Kettleton might show up, convinced she was about to meet her artistic salvation.

I got my chance on Friday night.

The preparations started at sunset. Catering trucks, florists, musicians carrying instrument cases. By eight o'clock, the estate blazed with light—torches lining the driveway and subtle lighting turning the gardens into something from a movie set.

Expensive and elaborate, like everything else about Julian Croix. Or a very expensive trap.

I'd positioned myself on a hillside about two hundred yards from the estate, hidden behind scrub brush with a pair of binoculars I'd borrowed from Bill Kowalski. The view was perfect—I could see the main terrace where the party would be held, the gardens where guests would mingle, and most of the approaches to the house.

The guests started arriving around nine.

They came in expensive cars—Packards, Cadillacs, a few Rolls-Royces that probably belonged to studio executives or established stars. But this wasn't the usual Hollywood crowd. These people moved wrong—too careful, too pale, like they'd forgotten how to be human.

Croix's vampires, coming to help with the hunt. I counted fifteen of them as they arrived.

By ten o'clock, maybe fifty people on the terrace. Moving with that same careful grace, clustering around the bar, conversations that looked casual but were predatory underneath. They were hunting, but they were patient about it.

Then the real guests started arriving.

These were different. Normal movements, wide-eyed at all the sophistication. Expensive clothes that didn't quite fit, like somebody dressed them for the occasion. And that eager, desperate energy—people who thought they were about to get everything they'd ever wanted.

I counted twelve of them. Young, attractive, talented in that Hollywood way—actors stuck in background work, writers with scripts nobody would read, directors whose vision exceeded their prospects.

Fresh meat.

I watched through the binoculars as the two groups mingled. Croix's people were smooth, drawing the newcomers into conversations that looked casual but were clearly planned. Every new arrival getting surrounded, isolated, given individual attention that must have been intoxicating after years of rejection.

Watching predators work was always disturbing, but this was different. No claws, no teeth, just words and smiles and the promise of everything you'd ever wanted.

Then Julian Croix himself appeared.

He emerged from the main house at exactly ten-thirty, moving through the crowd like he owned it. Which he did. Elegant black suit, expensive as sin, and when he spoke to people, they listened like he was God himself.

With his transformed followers, he was casual. A touch on the shoulder, knowing smiles, the easy familiarity of someone who'd known these people forever.

With the newcomers, he was different. Focused. Intent. Gave each one individual attention, speaking with the kind of concentrated interest that made them stand straighter, smile brighter, lean in to catch every word.

He was shopping. Deciding which ones were worth keeping.

Around eleven, the formal part of the evening began.

The crowd gathered on the main terrace, with Croix at the center and his transformed followers arranged in a loose circle around him. The newcomers found themselves on the periphery, looking in with expressions that said they hoped they were about to be let into an exclusive club.

Croix began to speak, and even at two hundred yards, his voice carried clearly in the still night air.

"My friends," he said, his accent making every word sound important, "we gather tonight to celebrate something that Hollywood has forgotten—the true purpose of art."

The crowd listened like he was preaching gospel. Even the transformed followers, who must have heard this speech before, watched him like they'd never get tired of it.

"This city was built on dreams. Dreams of creating something beautiful, something lasting, something that would touch the human soul. But somewhere along the way, those dreams got corrupted. Commerce. Compromise. The limitations of being mortal."

I could see heads nodding among the newcomers. They were eating this up, probably thinking about every rejection, every door slammed in their faces, every time they'd been told they weren't good enough.

"You have all experienced this," Croix said, his voice growing passionate. "The frustration of being told your vision is too complex, too sophisticated. That audiences want simple entertainment, not challenging art."

The newcomers were completely hooked now. I could see it in how they leaned forward, the expressions on their faces. Julian Croix was telling them exactly what they wanted to hear—that their failures weren't their fault, that their lack of success proved they were better than everyone else.

"But what if I told you there was a way to create without these limitations? What if the greatest artists in history were held back not by lack of talent, but by lack of time? That mortality itself is the enemy of true creative achievement?"

This was where it got dangerous. The transformed followers grew more alert, watching the newcomers' reactions. Hunting for the ones who responded strongest to Croix's message, identifying the best candidates.

"Consider the masters. Leonardo, Michelangelo, Shakespeare. Imagine what they could have created if they had been freed from human limitation. Imagine the works of art that were never created because their creators died before they could finish."

He gestured toward his transformed followers. "The people you see around you tonight have made that choice. They have chosen to transcend mortal existence, to dedicate themselves entirely to eternal art. They have discovered that true creativity requires abandoning everything that binds ordinary humans."

Several newcomers exchanged glances, shifting from simple interest to genuine fascination. These were people who'd spent years being told they weren't good enough. Now they were being told their failures proved their superiority, that there was a way to achieve everything they'd ever dreamed of.

It was brilliant and horrifying. Recruitment by validation.

"The work we do here is unlike anything in Hollywood's studios. We explore themes commercial cinema dare not touch. We create beauty that will outlast civilizations. We are artists in the truest sense—freed from the compromises that constrain mortal creativity."

A young woman near the front raised her hand. She had the kind of wholesome beauty perfect for romantic comedies, but her eyes held the hungry intensity of someone who wanted more than bit parts.

"Mr. Croix, how does someone become part of your artistic community?"

Croix smiled, and even at a distance, I could see the predator in it. "The process is... transformative. It requires abandoning everything that has held you back. Your attachment to conventional success, to the approval of those who lack vision, to limiting beliefs about what art should be."

Another newcomer spoke up, a young man who looked like a writer. "What kind of commitment does it require?"

"Complete commitment. The kind that allows no room for doubt, no turning back. Once you begin, you become part of something larger than individual ambition. Part of a vision that will change not just your art, but the entire nature of creative expression."

I was sick listening to it. He was describing vampirism as artistic enlightenment. Getting them complicit in their own destruction by convincing them it was what they'd always wanted.

The worst part was how well it was working. I could see the excitement building, the way the newcomers looked at the transformed followers with new understanding and envy. These weren't just pale strangers—they were the chosen ones, the artists brave enough to transcend human limitation.

"The transformation takes place gradually, over weeks. You'll find your perspective changing, your creativity expanding, your understanding deepening beyond anything you've imagined. And when the process is complete, you'll have unlimited time to perfect your craft, unlimited energy to pursue your vision."

One of the newcomers, a woman who looked like a failed screenwriter, asked: "What happens to our old lives?"

Croix's expression grew sympathetic. "You leave them behind. Everything that connected you to your limited existence—family members who don't understand, friends who accept mediocrity, the entire network of relationships that kept you bound to conventional thinking. It's a sacrifice, yes, but one every great artist must eventually make."

The crowd was completely under his spell. I could see it in their faces, how they hung on every word. He was offering them everything they'd ever wanted—artistic validation, unlimited time to create, membership in an exclusive community of superior beings. All they had to do was give up their humanity.

"Those of you interested in learning more will have the opportunity to speak with me privately before the evening ends. But understand—this decision is not to be made lightly. Once you begin the transformation, there is no returning. You will become something more than human, but you will no longer be human."

The formal presentation ended, and the crowd began to disperse into smaller groups. But several newcomers lingered, clearly hoping for one of those private conversations. The transformed followers moved smoothly through the crowd, identifying the most interested candidates and guiding them toward separate areas of the terrace.

It was a sorting process, and it happened with military precision.

I watched for another hour as the evening played out. Some newcomers left early, probably deciding whatever Croix was offering was too strange. But six of them stayed until the end, and I saw each have brief private conversations with Croix himself.

By the time the party wound down around two in the morning, Julian Croix identified his next batch. Six more young artists who would disappear from their old lives over the next few weeks, becoming part of his growing collection of immortal predators.

The whole thing was conducted with the efficiency of a business meeting and the seductive power of a religious revival. Croix turned vampire recruitment into performance art, complete with philosophical justification and artistic validation.

As I packed up my binoculars and prepared to leave my hillside position, I thought about Margaret Walker, somewhere inside that estate, probably helping with recruitment now that she'd been transformed. Had she started out as eager as the newcomers I'd watched tonight? Had she listened to Croix's speech with the same hungry fascination?

The answer didn't matter now. What mattered was stopping this before Zelda Kettleton ended up on that terrace, listening to Julian Croix explain why giving up her humanity was the key to artistic fulfillment.

I made my way back to my car, thinking about everything I'd observed. Croix's operation was more sophisticated than anything the werewolves attempted, more psychologically complex than simple predation. He'd turned vampirism into a lifestyle choice, complete with philosophical framework and artistic justification.

That made him more dangerous than any monster I'd ever encountered, because he made his victims want to become monsters themselves.

But it also gave me an idea for how to stop him.

Julian Croix's strength lay in his ability to convince people that transformation was what they wanted. His recruitment parties worked because they made victims complicit in their own destruction, turned them into willing participants rather than unwilling prey.

But that same psychology might be his weakness. If I could find a way to expose the reality behind his artistic philosophy, to show his potential victims what transformation really meant, I might be able to break the spell he cast over people like Margaret Walker and Zelda Kettleton.

The question was how to do it without getting myself killed in the process.

As I drove back toward Los Angeles, the lights of Julian Croix's estate disappearing behind me, I started planning an approach that would probably qualify as the most dangerous thing I'd ever attempted.

The drive gave me time to think. The sophistication of Croix's operation was staggering. He'd turned vampire recruitment into performance art, complete with philosophical justification and psychological manipulation that would make a Madison Avenue executive weep with envy.

But more than that, he'd identified the perfect hunting ground. Hollywood in 1949 was full of desperate, talented people who'd been told repeatedly they weren't good enough. They were primed for someone who would tell them their failures were proof of their superiority, that there was a way to transcend the limitations that had held them back.

It was brilliant, in a horrifying way. Instead of hunting random victims, Croix created a system where victims came to him willingly, already half-convinced that whatever he was offering was exactly what they needed.

The six people I'd seen recruited tonight would probably spend the next few days thinking about their conversations with Croix, building up their excitement. By the time they showed up for whatever came next, they'd be completely committed to the idea that giving up their humanity was a small price to pay for artistic immortality.

But if I could show them the reality—if I could expose what Julian Croix really was and what transformation really meant—I might be able to save a lot of people from making the worst mistake of their lives.

If it worked, it might save a lot of people from making the worst mistake of their lives.

If it didn't work, I'd probably end up as another pale, careful predator in Julian Croix's collection, helping him recruit the next batch of victims.

Either way, I was going to find out just how committed I was to stopping monsters who made their prey grateful for the privilege of being destroyed.

The Serpent's Kiss

The call came at six-thirty Monday morning, dragging me out of the kind of sleep that comes after too many nights spent watching vampires recruit their next victims. The phone's harsh ring cut through the fog in my head like a silver blade through undead flesh.

"Vance," I muttered into the receiver, not bothering to hide the exhaustion in my voice.

"Miss Vance? This is Sergeant Ray Torres, LAPD. We've got a situation down in Griffith Park you might want to take a look at."

I sat up, suddenly awake. Torres was one of the few cops who'd actually worked with me on cases instead of trying to shut me out. If he was calling this early, it was important.

"What kind of situation?"

"Dead girl. Young, blonde, probably early twenties. Name's Margaret Walker. I know her mother hired a private investigator to look for her, and I heard your name come up as someone who was recommended. You working this case?"

"I am," I said, the words hitting me like a punch to the gut. I'd known this was coming, had seen it in Julian Croix's predatory smile and the way Margaret's mother described her daughter's transformation. But knowing something and hearing it confirmed were two different things entirely.

"Where in the park?"

"Near the old zoo site, down by the picnic area off Crystal Springs Drive. You know the spot?"

I knew it. A section of Griffith Park that was isolated enough for privacy but accessible enough that someone would eventually find what was left behind. Exactly where vampires might dump a body they wanted discovered.

"I'll be there in thirty minutes."

I hung up and stared at the phone for a moment, thinking about Dorothy Walker sleeping in her Glendale house, probably still hoping her daughter would come home safe. By tonight, she'd know the truth, and it was going to destroy her.

The bedroom door opened, and Irene appeared in her robe, hair tousled from sleep. She took one look at my face and knew something was wrong.

"What happened?"

"They found Margaret Walker."

Irene's expression went through the same progression mine had—understanding, then pain, then resigned anger at watching monsters win another round.

"Do you need me to come with you?"

I considered it. Having Irene there would mean having someone who understood what we were really dealing with, someone who wouldn't buy whatever story the police were already constructing to explain away the supernatural elements. But exposing her to another crime scene meant another reminder that the monsters we fought left real victims behind.

"No," I said, pulling on yesterday's clothes. "Stay here. I'll call you when I know more."

The drive to Griffith Park took twenty-five minutes through morning traffic that was just starting to build. Los Angeles was waking up to another sunny day, full of people heading to jobs and school and all the normal concerns of mortal life. None of them knew that vampires were recruiting artists in the Hills, that young women were being drained of blood and left in parks like discarded props from a horror picture.

I envied them their ignorance.

The crime scene was exactly where Torres had said it would be—a patch of scrubland near the abandoned Griffith Park Zoo that had closed three years earlier. Police cars, an ambulance, and the coroner's wagon were arranged in a loose perimeter around something I couldn't see from the road.

Torres met me at the perimeter tape, a stocky man in his forties with kind eyes and the weary expression of someone who'd seen too many crime scenes like this one. He handed me a cup of coffee from a thermos without being asked.

"How bad is it?" I asked.

"Bad enough. Come take a look, but fair warning—this one's gonna stick with you."

He led me past the cluster of uniforms and detectives to where the body lay at the base of an old oak tree. Margaret Walker was spread out on her back, arms at her sides, looking almost peaceful except for the unnatural pallor of her skin. She wore an expensive evening dress that I recognized from the photographs in her mother's house—midnight blue silk that probably cost more than most people made in a month.

But it was her neck that told the real story. Two small puncture wounds, barely visible unless you knew what to look for, marked where Julian Croix had fed on her. The skin around them was pale as paper, drained of the blood that had once brought color to her cheeks.

"Coroner says she's been dead maybe twelve hours," Torres said, lighting a cigarette with hands that shook slightly. "No obvious signs of struggle, no defensive wounds. Like she just lay down and died."

"What's the official theory?"

"Suicide. Girl was despondent over her career, came out here to end it all. Took some kind of poison that doesn't show obvious symptoms, then lay down to wait for it to work."

It was a neat theory that ignored everything that didn't fit. The location miles from where Margaret lived. The expensive dress she wouldn't have worn to kill herself. The fact that there was no suicide note, no poison bottle, no means of death that would explain her condition.

Most of all, it ignored the puncture wounds that every cop on the scene was pretending not to see.

"You buy that?" I asked.

Torres took a long drag on his cigarette and stared at Margaret's body. "Hell no. But it's what the department's going with, and arguing about it won't bring her back."

I understood the logic. A vampire murder was something the LAPD couldn't solve, couldn't prosecute, couldn't even acknowledge without sounding insane. A suicide was clean, simple, and wouldn't require them to admit that Los Angeles had monsters living in estates in the Hills.

But understanding the logic didn't make it any easier to swallow.

"Can I have a few minutes alone with the scene?"

Torres looked around at the other cops, most of whom were busy avoiding eye contact with Margaret's body. "Five minutes. Then we've got to clear out and let the coroner do his thing."

He walked away, giving me space to examine Margaret without an audience of uniforms who'd already decided what they weren't seeing. I knelt beside the body, looking for anything the official investigation would miss or ignore.

The puncture wounds were precise, professional. Croix had fed carefully, taking exactly what he needed without the savage fury that marked amateur vampire attacks. This wasn't about hunger—it was about sending a message.

Her hands were crossed over her chest, fingers interlaced in a pose that was too perfect to be natural. Someone had arranged her body after death, positioning her like a sleeping princess waiting for a kiss that would never come.

It was theater. Julian Croix staging his victim for maximum psychological impact.

I was about to stand up when something caught the morning light near Margaret's left shoulder. A small metal object, almost hidden by the dark fabric of her dress. I glanced around to make sure none of the cops were watching, then carefully worked it free from where it had been pinned to the inside of her collar.

A silver pin, no bigger than a dime, crafted in the shape of a serpent eating its own tail. The ouroboros—an ancient symbol of eternal life, death, and rebirth. The perfect calling card for an immortal predator to mark his work.

I palmed the pin and stood up, slipping it into my jacket pocket before anyone could see what I'd found. The police might be willing to pretend this was a suicide, but I wasn't going to let them ignore the one piece of evidence that might lead to Margaret's killer.

"Time's up," Torres called from the perimeter.

I took one last look at Margaret Walker, thinking about the bright young woman her mother had described, the aspiring actress who'd believed Julian Croix could help her transcend the limitations of ordinary existence. He'd kept his promise, in a way. She'd definitely transcended mortality.

The question was how many other young artists would end up the same way before I found a way to stop him.

"Learn anything useful?" Torres asked as I ducked under the crime scene tape.

"Maybe. You said no defensive wounds, no signs of struggle. But did anyone check for injection sites? Places where someone might have drugged her before bringing her out here?"

Torres frowned. "You think someone knocked her out, then dumped her?"

"I think a young actress doesn't drive herself to a deserted part of Griffith Park to commit suicide. Especially not dressed like she was going to a party."

"The coroner will do a full examination. If there's evidence of foul play, we'll follow up on it."

We both knew that was unlikely. The LAPD had already decided what Margaret Walker's death meant, and they weren't interested in evidence that might complicate their neat, simple explanation. A suicide was a closed case. A murder would mean work, investigation, and questions they couldn't answer.

I handed Torres my card. "If anything else turns up—anything at all—give me a call. Her mother hired me to find her daughter. I owe her a complete report."

Torres tucked the card into his shirt pocket. "I'll do what I can. But Vance? Be careful with this one. There's something about the whole thing that doesn't sit right. Girl like that doesn't just end up dead for no reason."

He was right, but not in the way he thought. Margaret Walker hadn't died for no reason. She'd died because she'd gotten involved with a vampire who collected artists like other people collected stamps. And unless I found a way to stop Julian Croix, she wouldn't be the last.

The drive back to my apartment gave me time to think about what I'd seen. The careful positioning of Margaret's body, the expensive dress, the silver pin hidden where only a thorough examination would find it. Julian Croix wasn't just killing his victims—he was making art out of their deaths.

It was sophisticated, psychological warfare. A message designed to let me know that he was aware of my investigation, that he could kill the people I was trying to protect whenever he chose, and that there was nothing the police could do to stop him.

But leaving the ouroboros pin was a mistake too. By marking his work, he'd given me evidence of his involvement. A link between Margaret's death and his artistic philosophy that wouldn't mean anything to the cops but might mean everything to the people who were still alive to be saved.

People like Zelda Kettleton.

I was still thinking about Croix's psychological games when I climbed the stairs to my apartment. The familiar weight of the silver pin in my pocket was a reminder that the conflict between us had just escalated. Margaret Walker was his opening move.

Now it was my turn.

Irene was waiting in the kitchen, dressed for work and nursing a cup of coffee that had probably gone cold while she worried. She looked up when I walked in, and I could see the questions in her eyes.

"It was her," I said, hanging my jacket on the back of a chair. "Margaret Walker. Found dead in Griffith Park this morning."

"How?"

I sat down across from her and pulled out the silver pin, setting it on the table between us. "Officially? Suicide. Unofficially? Julian Croix drained her blood and left her body staged like a work of art."

Irene picked up the pin, examining the intricate serpent design. "This is his signature?"

"Has to be. The ouroboros is a symbol of eternal life. Perfect for a vampire who thinks he's an artist."

She set the pin down carefully, like it might bite her. "What are you going to tell her mother?"

That was the question I'd been avoiding. Dorothy Walker had hired me to find her daughter, and I'd found her. But the truth—that Margaret had been murdered by a vampire who collected artists—wasn't something I could put in an official report. And the lie—that Margaret had killed herself—would destroy a mother who'd spent weeks hoping for her daughter's safe return.

"I don't know yet," I admitted. "But I know what I'm going to do about Julian Croix."

Irene's expression grew worried. "Ellie, whatever you're thinking—"

"I'm thinking that he just declared war. Margaret Walker was a message, a demonstration of what he can do to the people I'm trying to protect. Well, I've got a message for him too."

I picked up the ouroboros pin and closed my fingers around it. The silver was warm from Irene's touch, but it felt cold and sharp against my palm.

"He wants to play games? Fine. But he's going to learn that some games have consequences he didn't plan on."

Irene reached across the table and covered my hand with hers. "Just promise me you won't do anything reckless. Margaret Walker is dead, but you're still alive. I'd like to keep it that way."

I looked at her serious expression, thinking about how much I had to lose and how much that made me vulnerable to exactly the kind of psychological manipulation Julian Croix specialized in. He'd killed Margaret to send me a message, but he'd also killed her to show me what happened to people who got in his way.

The smart thing would be to back down, to tell Dorothy Walker that her daughter was dead and leave Julian Croix to the authorities. Let someone else figure out how to stop an immortal predator who turned vampire recruitment into performance art.

But I'd tried backing down from monsters before, and it never worked. They didn't stop because you left them alone. They just moved on to the next victim, and the next, until someone finally found the courage to fight back.

Margaret Walker had been transformed by Julian Croix, then murdered when she was no longer useful to him. Her mother would never know the truth about what had happened to her daughter. The police would close the case as a suicide and forget that Margaret Walker had ever existed.

But I would remember. And Julian Croix would learn that some private investigators didn't back down when monsters started playing games.

"I won't do anything reckless," I promised Irene. "But I won't let him get away with this either."

She squeezed my hand and nodded, understanding that this was bigger than just one case, bigger than just one dead girl. This was about whether monsters like Julian Croix could operate freely in Los Angeles, collecting artists and transforming them into predators without anyone willing to fight back.

I stood up and walked to the window, looking out at the city waking up under another perfect California morning. Somewhere out there, Zelda Kettleton was getting ready for another day at the Los Angeles Times, probably still thinking about Julian Croix and the artistic opportunities he might represent.

Somewhere else, Julian Croix was probably sleeping through the daylight hours, satisfied that his message had been delivered and that I understood the stakes of our conflict.

What he didn't understand was that killing Margaret Walker hadn't intimidated me—it had given me a target. The ouroboros pin was evidence, but it was also a promise. Julian Croix had signed his work, and now I knew exactly what I was hunting.

The only question was whether I could find him before he added Zelda Kettleton to his collection of dead artists.

I pulled out my notebook and started making a list of everything I knew about Julian Croix's operation. His estate on Mulholland Drive. His recruitment parties and artistic philosophy. The careful way he selected victims who wanted to transcend human limitations.

Most importantly, his need to turn killing into art, to make every death a statement about immortality and artistic vision. That psychological compulsion was his strength, but it was also his weakness.

Monsters who were content to hide in the shadows were almost impossible to catch. But monsters who needed to make statements, who turned their crimes into performances, left trails that could be followed.

Julian Croix had just left me a very clear trail, marked with a silver serpent eating its own tail.

Time to see where it led.

I picked up the phone and dialed Dorothy Walker's number. She deserved to know that her daughter was dead, even if I couldn't tell her the whole truth about how Margaret had died. It would be the hardest call I'd ever made, but it was also necessary.

After that, I was going to start hunting vampires.

The phone rang twice before Dorothy Walker answered, her voice thick with sleep and hope.

"Hello?"

"Mrs. Walker? This is Eleanor Vance. I'm afraid I have some bad news about Margaret."

One Last Pitch

The call to Dorothy Walker had gone about as badly as I'd expected. Three hours of tears, questions I couldn't answer honestly, and the kind of grief that comes from learning your daughter is dead without knowing why. I'd told her what I could—that Margaret had been found in Griffith Park, that the police were investigating, that I was sorry for her loss. I'd left out the puncture wounds, the staging, and the silver pin currently sitting in my desk drawer like a promise of violence.

By the time I hung up, I felt like I'd been worked over by a team of professional thugs.

Irene found me slumped at my kitchen table around noon, still in yesterday's clothes and nursing a cup of coffee that had gone cold hours ago. She took one look at my face and poured herself a drink from the bottle of rye I kept on the counter.

"That bad?" she asked.

"Her daughter's dead, and I can't tell her why. How do you think it went?"

She sat down across from me, and I could see the exhaustion in her eyes. The Los Angeles Times had been running stories about the "rash of young actress suicides" that had been plaguing Hollywood over the past few months—Margaret Walker wouldn't be the first talented girl to be found dead in a park with no clear explanation for why she'd wanted to die.

Of course, the papers didn't know that the girls weren't actually killing themselves. They were being murdered by a vampire who collected artists like other people collected butterflies. Margaret

Walker had been different though—from what her mother had described, she'd been partially transformed, then something had gone wrong. Maybe she'd fought back against the process, or her body had rejected the change. Either way, Croix had killed her and arranged the scene to avoid police scrutiny—though his artistic nature had turned even that disposal into a kind of performance.

"Any word from Zelda?" I asked.

Irene's expression grew worried. "That's actually why I came by. She didn't show up for work today, and she's not answering her phone. Her landlady says she left last night around eight, all dressed up like she was going to some fancy party."

The cold feeling that had been sitting in my stomach since Torres's phone call got worse. "Did she say where she was going?"

"Just that she had an important meeting about her writing career. Something that was going to change everything."

I closed my eyes and tried not to think about Margaret Walker's pale face and carefully arranged hands. "She went to him. After everything we told her, she went to Julian Croix anyway."

"We don't know that for sure."

"Don't we?" I stood up and walked to the window, looking out at another perfect Los Angeles afternoon. Somewhere in the Hills, Julian Croix was probably sleeping through the daylight hours, satisfied with his latest acquisition. "She's been obsessed with him since we mentioned his name. A European director who makes art films about transcending human limitations? It's exactly what she's been waiting to hear her entire life."

Irene joined me at the window, and I could feel the tension radiating from her. "So what do we do?"

"We go looking for her. Tonight, when the sun goes down and Croix's people start moving around. Maybe we can find her before..." I didn't finish the sentence. We both knew what happened to young artists who got too close to Julian Croix.

But even as I said it, I had a feeling we were already too late. Zelda Kettleton had walked into that estate with the same eager determination Margaret Walker had shown, convinced she was about to get everything she'd ever wanted.

Instead, she was about to lose everything she'd ever been.

The rest of the afternoon crawled by like a wounded animal. Irene went back to the Times to see if she could learn anything more about Zelda's disappearance, while I spent the time cleaning my weapons and trying to plan an approach to Croix's estate that wouldn't get us both killed.

Pops was loaded with regular ammunition—I'd use the silver bullets if things got bad enough, but I needed to save them for when they'd do the most good. The silver stiletto was sharp and blessed, tucked into my boot where I could reach it quickly. I added a wooden stake to my jacket pocket, carved from a chair leg I'd broken during the werewolf case last October. If the vampire lore was accurate, driving it through a monster's heart would put him down permanently.

All the preparation in the world wouldn't help if we couldn't find where Croix was keeping Zelda, assuming she was still alive to be found.

I was still working on that problem when Irene returned around six, looking like she'd aged ten years in the past few hours.

"I talked to everyone at the paper," she said, collapsing into a chair. "Zelda spent most of yesterday asking questions about exclusive Hollywood parties, particularly ones that might be attended by European directors or avant-garde filmmakers. She seemed especially interested in events that weren't covered by the regular society pages."

"Like recruitment parties for vampires."

"She didn't know they were recruitment parties. She thought she was researching networking opportunities for serious artists." Irene pulled out a notebook and flipped through several pages. "But here's the interesting part—she talked to Mickey Torrino in the entertainment section. He covers the industry parties that are too weird or too exclusive for the main society reporters."

Mickey Torrino was a gossip columnist who specialized in Hollywood's stranger corners—the occult societies, the underground art scenes, the kind of parties where studio executives went to indulge in interests that wouldn't look good in the trades. If anyone would know about Julian Croix's gatherings, it would be him.

"Did he tell her anything useful?"

"He told her about a party happening tonight at an estate in the Hills. Very exclusive, very artistic, hosted by some European director who's been making waves in certain circles. Invitation only, but Torrino thought he might be able to get her in if she was really interested."

My blood went cold. "He gave her an invitation?"

"He gave her press credentials and the address. Told her to say she was covering the event for a story about underground cinema in Los Angeles." Irene closed the notebook and looked at me with scared eyes. "She left the office yesterday evening with everything she needed to walk right into Julian Croix's estate."

I thought about the recruitment party I'd observed from the hillside—the careful way Croix had evaluated potential victims, the smooth efficiency with which his followers had identified the most promising candidates. Zelda Kettleton would have been perfect for his purposes: brilliant, frustrated, desperate for artistic validation, and convinced that her failures were proof of her superiority rather than evidence that she needed to try harder.

"We have to go get her," I said.

"Ellie, if she's really at one of Croix's parties, she might already be... you know. Changed."

I thought about that possibility. If Julian Croix had already begun Zelda's transformation, we might be walking into a trap designed to capture or kill anyone who came looking for her. But if there was a chance she was still human, still saveable, I had to try.

"Then we'll have to deal with that when we find her. But I'm not leaving her there to become another Margaret Walker."

Irene nodded, understanding that this was bigger than just rescuing one person. This was about stopping Julian Croix from adding another artist to his collection, another predator to his pack of transformed followers.

We spent the next hour planning our approach. The estate on Mulholland Drive was isolated, surrounded by walls and gates that would make a direct assault difficult. But I'd observed enough of Croix's parties to know that they followed a pattern—guests arrived around nine, the formal presentation began around eleven, and the selection process happened in the hours afterward.

If Zelda had attended last night's party, she might still be on the estate, either held prisoner while Croix decided whether to transform her, or already beginning the change that would turn her into one of his followers.

Either way, we were running out of time.

The drive up Mulholland Drive took forty minutes through evening traffic. Los Angeles was settling into another warm night, full of people heading home from work or out for dinner and entertainment. Normal people with normal problems, no idea that monsters were throwing cocktail parties in the hills above them.

I envied them their ignorance, but I also envied them their safety. Tonight, Irene and I were heading into territory controlled by an immortal predator who'd already demonstrated his willingness to kill anyone who got in his way.

The gates to 1864 Mulholland Drive were closed when we arrived, but there were lights visible through the trees and several expensive cars parked along the estate's private road. Another party was underway—Julian Croix's systematic recruitment of Hollywood's most desperate artists.

I parked where we could watch the gates without being seen from the estate, then settled in to wait for an opportunity. Getting inside would be tricky, but I'd done it before. The question was whether we could find Zelda and get out again without attracting the attention of Croix's transformed followers.

"There," Irene whispered, pointing toward the estate's perimeter.

A delivery truck was approaching the gates—catering for the evening's event, probably, or supplies for whatever theatrical presentation Croix had planned. The gates opened automatically, and the truck disappeared down the private road toward the main house.

"Can you drive?"

"Well enough. Why?"

"Because we're following that truck."

I checked my watch. Ten o'clock. The party would be hitting its stride, which meant Croix and his followers would be focused on their potential victims rather than watching for intruders.

Irene started the engine, and we followed the delivery truck through the gates before they could close again. The private road wound through mature trees and carefully maintained landscaping, designed to give the estate privacy while showcasing its wealth and sophistication.

We passed the main house—a Gothic revival mansion that looked like it belonged in a European horror film—and continued toward what appeared to be service buildings. The delivery truck was parked near a kitchen entrance, with uniformed staff unloading boxes and equipment.

I had Irene park behind a gardening shed where the car wouldn't be visible from the main house. From there, we could hear the sounds of the party—music, laughter, and the kind of animated conversation that suggested people were having the time of their lives.

People who didn't know they were attending a recruitment party for vampires.

"Stay close," I told Irene. "And if things go bad, run for the car and get out of here. Don't try to be a hero."

She nodded, but I could see in her expression that she had no intention of leaving without me. I hoped it wouldn't come to that, but I had a feeling this evening was going to end badly for someone.

We made our way through the estate's gardens toward the sounds of the party. The layout was similar to what I'd observed during my surveillance—a large terrace behind the main house, with smaller seating areas scattered throughout the landscaped grounds. Perfect for the kind of intimate conversations Julian Croix specialized in, where he could evaluate potential victims and begin the process of psychological manipulation that would make them willing participants in their own destruction.

The party was in full swing when we reached a position where we could observe without being seen. Maybe sixty people scattered around the terrace and gardens—the same mix of transformed followers and potential victims I'd seen before. The followers were easy to identify: pale, careful in their movements, wearing sunglasses despite the evening hour. The marks looked like kids on Christmas morning—nervous but excited, finally invited to the cool kids' table.

And there, near the main terrace, talking intently to a woman who was definitely one of Croix's transformed followers, was Zelda Kettleton.

She looked exactly as I'd expected—animated, engaged, hanging on every word of her conversation partner. She wore an expensive dress that probably represented a month's salary, and she moved with the kind of nervous energy that suggested she was having the most important conversation of her life.

She had no idea she was talking to a vampire who was evaluating her for transformation.

"There she is," I whispered to Irene.

"Is she...?"

"Still human, as far as I can tell. But not for long if we don't get her out of here."

The problem was that Zelda was surrounded by Croix's followers, positioned in the center of the party where any rescue attempt would be immediately noticed. We'd have to wait for an opportunity—a moment when she moved away from the crowd, or when the followers' attention was focused elsewhere.

That opportunity came around eleven o'clock, when Julian Croix himself appeared on the main terrace.

He commanded attention the moment he stepped into view—tall, elegant, moving with the kind of predatory grace that made everyone around him seem clumsy by comparison. The entire party began gravitating toward him, including Zelda, who pushed through the crowd to get closer to the man she believed could validate her artistic ambitions.

It was exactly the same pattern I'd observed during my surveillance, but watching it happen to someone I knew made it infinitely more horrifying.

Croix began his presentation—the same speech about transcending human limitations, about art that would outlast civilizations, about the necessity of abandoning everything that held true artists back from achieving their full potential. And just like before, his audience was completely captivated.

Especially Zelda, who stood near the front drinking in every word like it was the gospel.

"We have to get her away from there," Irene whispered.

But even as she said it, I could see that it was too late. Croix had noticed Zelda's intense attention, and he was directing part of his presentation toward her specifically. Making eye contact, speaking about themes that would resonate with a frustrated writer who'd spent years collecting rejection slips.

He had her hooked. Same technique he'd used on Margaret Walker and dozens of other young artists who'd believed his promises about eternal creativity and unlimited time to perfect their craft.

The formal presentation ended around midnight, and the crowd began to disperse into smaller groups. But Zelda didn't move away from the main terrace. Instead, she lingered, clearly hoping for a chance at one of the private conversations Croix held with his most promising candidates.

She got her wish. One of the transformed followers—a woman who might have been an actress or model before her transformation—approached Zelda and said something that made her face light up with excitement. Then the woman led her away from the main crowd, toward a secluded area of the gardens where several other small groups were engaged in what appeared to be intimate conversations.

"Now," I said. "While they're distracted."

We moved through the shadows at the edge of the gardens, using the landscaping and outdoor sculptures for cover. Getting close enough to intervene would be tricky—we'd have to time it perfectly, create enough of a distraction to get Zelda away from her conversation partner without alerting the entire party to our presence.

But when we reached a position where we could see the conversation clearly, it was obvious that we were too late.

Zelda was completely under the spell of whatever the transformed woman was telling her. Her eyes were bright with excitement, her whole body leaning forward with eagerness. She was nodding enthusiastically, asking questions, clearly agreeing to whatever was being proposed.

And then Julian Croix himself appeared, approaching their secluded conversation area with the satisfied expression of a hunter who'd successfully cornered his prey.

He spoke briefly to the transformed woman, who smiled and withdrew, leaving Zelda alone with the vampire who'd been orchestrating her seduction all evening. Croix said something that made Zelda laugh—a bright, musical sound that made my stomach clench. I'd heard that kind of laughter before, from Margaret Walker in her final days.

Then he offered her his arm, and she took it without hesitation.

They walked together toward the main house, Zelda's hand tucked into the crook of his arm like they'd known each other for years. Like she trusted him completely. Zelda looked back once at the party she was leaving behind, and in that glance I could see everything Julian Croix had promised her: artistic validation, unlimited time to create, membership in an exclusive community of superior beings.

Everything she'd ever wanted. All it would cost her was her soul.

The last I saw of Zelda Kettleton, she was disappearing into the Gothic mansion with Julian Croix, thinking she was finally getting her big break. Instead, she was about to become something that would hunt people like her.

"We have to go after them," Irene whispered.

But even as she said it, we could see that it was impossible. The main house was surrounded by Croix's followers, and more were moving in that direction—probably to witness whatever ceremony or ritual marked the beginning of a new transformation. Getting inside would mean fighting our way through dozens of vampires.

"There must be fifty of them between us and that house," I said, hating every word. "We'd never make it past the front door."

"We can't just leave her."

"Going in there now would be suicide. And dead, we can't help anyone."

We withdrew from the gardens and made our way back to the car in silence. Behind us, the lights of the Gothic mansion blazed against the Hollywood Hills, and somewhere inside that house, Zelda Kettleton was beginning a conversation she believed would change her life.

The drive back to Los Angeles was all silence and self-recrimination. Every red light felt like another nail in Zelda's coffin.

Irene broke the silence around one in the morning, when we were passing through the outskirts of the city. "We can't save everyone."

"I know." But knowing it and accepting it were two different things. I'd watched Zelda disappear into that Gothic mansion like she was walking into a dream, convinced she was finally getting the artistic recognition she deserved.

I remembered what Mrs. Walker had told me about Margaret's last weeks. The staying out all night, the weird new friends, the way she'd started looking through her mother instead of at her.

"And then?"

"And then she'll come back. Changed. Probably convinced that her transformation is the best thing that ever happened to her, eager to share her new perspective with the people who were closest to her before."

"People like us," I said.

Julian Croix didn't just collect artists. He made them into weapons, sent them back to recruit the people who'd tried to save them.

After what I'd just done to Zelda, I liked my odds.

"What happens now?" Irene finally asked as we pulled into my neighborhood.

I thought about Margaret Walker, about how Dorothy Walker had described her daughter's transformation. The gradual changes, the nocturnal habits, the way she'd talked about different kinds of hunger.

"Now we wait," I said. "And we get ready."

The Tragedy of Zelda Kettleton

We didn't have to wait long.

Four days after watching Zelda disappear into Julian Croix's Gothic mansion, she came back to us. But the woman who knocked on my apartment door that Thursday evening wasn't the frustrated researcher who'd walked away from our table at Musso & Frank's with desperate determination in her eyes.

This was something else entirely.

I'd been cleaning Pops when the knock came—three soft raps on my door, polite and patient, like someone who had all the time in the world. Irene was curled up on my couch, trying to read a book but mostly staring at the same page she'd been on for twenty minutes. We'd both been waiting for this visit, dreading it, preparing for it without really knowing how to prepare for the return of a friend who was no longer human.

The knock came again. Still patient. Still polite.

"Ellie? Irene? I know you're in there. I can hear your heartbeats."

Zelda's voice, but different. Calmer, more confident, with an undertone of amusement that crawled across my skin.

I caught Irene's eye and nodded toward the bedroom, where we'd agreed she should go if this moment came. She shook her head stubbornly, but I pointed again and mouthed the word "please." After a moment's hesitation, she slipped quietly away from the living room.

I checked Pops' magazine—six bullets, three of them silver—and slipped it into my jacket pocket. Pop would have lectured me about keeping a round chambered, but then Pop never faced vampires.

The silver stiletto was in my boot, sharp and ready. A wooden stake carved from the same chair leg I'd used against vampires before sat on my kitchen counter, within easy reach. Detective Miller's rosary was sitting in my office desk drawer, where I'd stupidly left it. Just nerves, maybe, or the weight of knowing a friend was coming to kill us, disrupting my usual preparation routine.

All the weapons in the world wouldn't ease this burden.

"I'm not going anywhere, Ellie," Zelda called through the door. "And I'm not here to hurt anyone. I just want to talk. To share something wonderful that's happened to me."

I walked to the door and looked through the peephole. What I saw caught my breath in my throat.

Zelda was white as fresh porcelain, and just as cold-looking. Her dark hair hung in perfect waves that didn't move in the hallway breeze, and her eyes were dead-calm—the same look I'd seen on corpses before the mortician got to them.

She was beautiful in a way that crawled across my skin. Like someone took the tired newspaper researcher I'd known and painted over all the human parts.

She was also completely, obviously, no longer human.

"You look lovely tonight, by the way," she said, and I realized the door probably wasn't hiding much from those new eyes of hers. "That blue dress really brings out your eyes. Though I have to say, the gun in your pocket is a rather unfriendly touch for a reunion between old friends."

I unlocked the door and opened it, keeping my hand close to Pops. "Hello, Zelda."

"Hello, darling." She smiled, and it was the most beautiful and terrifying expression I'd ever seen. "Aren't you going to invite me in? I've brought wine." She held up a bottle of what looked like expensive French wine. "Something to celebrate with."

"Celebrate what?"

"My new life. Being dead was just the first step. Now I can really live." She tilted her head, studying me with eyes that saw everything. "Julian said you'd be stubborn about this. Most people are, until they see what they're really getting."

Julian Croix told her about me. Which meant he knew exactly who I was, what I'd been doing, and that I was a threat to his operation. The ouroboros pin wasn't a random signature after all—it was bait, meant to draw me deeper into his web.

"May I come in?" Zelda asked again. "I promise I'm not here to force anything on anyone. I just want to talk. To explain. To help you understand what I've discovered."

Every instinct told me to slam the door and keep it locked. But Zelda was Irene's friend, and maybe—just maybe—there was enough of her left to be saved. And if she was here to recruit us, I needed to know what Julian Croix planned.

"Come in," I said, stepping back from the doorway.

Zelda moved into my apartment like she was floating an inch off the ground. Her grace turned me into a bull in a china shop. She looked around my apartment like she was visiting a zoo. Studying the way the natives lived.

"I'd forgotten how charming these little places could be," she said, setting the wine bottle on my kitchen counter. "So... intimate. So wonderfully human in scale." She turned to face me, and her smile was radiant. "Where's Irene? Hiding in the bedroom? You can come out, darling. I'm not going to bite."

She laughed at her own joke. It sounded like wind chimes made of bone.

Irene emerged from the bedroom, moving carefully like she was approaching a dangerous animal. Which, I supposed, she was.

"Hello, Zelda," she said, her voice carefully neutral.

"Hello, darling." Zelda's smile widened. "You look tired. Have you been sleeping well? I haven't slept in four days, and I've never been better in my life."

"What happened to you?" Irene asked.

"Everything." Zelda moved to my couch and settled into it with the kind of grace I'd never seen her possess before. "Everything changed, and I finally understand what I was missing all those years I spent struggling to be a writer."

"And what was that?"

"Time." She said it like it was the answer to every question anyone could ever ask. "Unlimited time to write, to revise, to perfect my craft. No more worrying about rent or deadlines or whether I'm wasting my youth chasing a dream that will never come true. I have eternity now. All the time in the world to become the writer I always knew I could be."

I thought about the recruitment pitch Julian Croix gave Margaret Walker, the promises about transcending human limitations and achieving artistic perfection. It was the same line he'd used on all his victims, tailored to each person's specific desires.

For Margaret, it was fame and recognition. For Zelda, it was time and freedom from the pressures that crushed her for years.

"What did it cost you?" I asked.

Zelda's perfect smile faltered for just a moment. "What do you mean?"

"To get all this time, this perfect creative freedom—what did you have to give up?"

"Nothing important. Just... limitations. The need for sleep, for food, for all the little human inconveniences that waste so much of our lives." She leaned forward, and her eyes held an intensity that was almost hypnotic. "Don't you see, Ellie? Humanity's just a cage. Mortality's just a disease. Why would you want to stay sick?"

"The way he cured you?"

"Yes." Her smile returned, radiant and terrible. "The way he saved me from a life of frustration and failure and endless, pointless struggle. Do you know what I've written in four days? Three chapters of the most beautiful work I've ever done. Words that'll outlast everything."

"What about the cost?"

"What cost?"

I gestured toward her perfect, pale, inhuman beauty. "The feeding. The killing. The fact that you're not alive anymore."

For the first time since she'd walked through my door, Zelda's mask slipped. Something hungry flickered behind her eyes—like a cat playing with a mouse that suddenly bit back.

Then the mask slipped back into place, but it didn't fit quite as perfectly as before.

"Feeding isn't killing, Ellie. It's sharing. They give me what I need, I give them something beautiful." But her voice carried an edge now, and her perfect posture shifted slightly. She was starting to look less like a Renaissance madonna and more like a predator trying to be patient but running out of reasons to stay polite.

"Show me," I said.

"What?"

"Show me this beautiful transaction. Feed on me. Right now. Let me experience this communion you're talking about."

For a moment, the only sound in the apartment was the ticking of my kitchen clock and the distant hum of traffic from the street below.

Then she began to laugh.

It started as a soft chuckle, but it built quickly into something that had nothing to do with humor. Her perfect features twisted into an expression of rage and hunger that turned her into a Renaissance painting of a demon rather than a saint.

"Oh, Ellie," she said, and her voice changed completely. No more gentle persuasion, no more maternal warmth. This was the voice of something that was never human, that saw people as nothing more than sources of food and entertainment. "You really don't understand, do you?"

She moved faster than anything human has a right to move, crossing my small living room in a blur of motion that ended with her standing directly in front of me, close enough that I could see the hunger burning in her eyes.

"I'm not here to make you a deal," she said, her beautiful face contorted with rage. "I'm here to collect you. Julian wants you specifically, Ellie. You and Irene both. He's very interested in adding a detective and a journalist to his collection—thinks you might be useful for certain projects he has in mind."

I went for Pops, but she was faster. Her hand closed around my wrist with strength that could have crushed bone, stopping my draw before it started.

"The feeding," she continued, her voice now a predatory purr, "is just a pleasant side effect. The real purpose is to break you down, to weaken you and prepare you for transformation. Julian likes his new acquisitions to be properly prepared."

She squeezed my wrist, and I felt the bones grind together. Pain shot up my arm, but I forced myself not to cry out.

"As for communion," she said, leaning closer so that her breath touched my cheek, "there's nothing consensual about it. I hold them down and I drain them slowly, savoring every moment of their terror and pain. Because the fear sweetens the blood, and Julian taught me to appreciate the artistry in a victim's suffering."

The beautiful mask was gone completely now. What stood in my living room wasn't my friend Zelda anymore—it was a monster wearing her face, speaking with her voice, but driven by hungers that bore no relation to human needs or desires.

"Irene, run," I managed to gasp through the pain in my wrist.

But when I looked toward the chair where she'd been sitting, it was empty. Irene vanished, probably slipped into the bedroom or the kitchen while Zelda was focused on me.

Zelda noticed too, and her grip on my wrist tightened. "Where did she go?"

"I don't know."

"Don't lie to me." She twisted my wrist, and this time I couldn't hold back a gasp of pain. "I can hear your hearts from across the room. I can taste fear on the air, smell blood moving under skin. Your girlfriend's hiding somewhere close, thinking she can wait until I'm distracted."

She leaned closer, and I could see that her teeth changed. They were still perfectly white, but they were also sharp and pointed, designed for tearing flesh and finding arteries.

"Here's what's going to happen, Ellie. I'm going to find your little girlfriend, and I'm going to feed on her while you watch. Slowly. Carefully. Ensuring she stays conscious for as long as possible. And then, when she's weak and broken and begging for death, I'm going to start on you."

That's when I heard the soft footstep behind her.

Zelda spun around, faster than human reflexes should have allowed, but not fast enough. Irene swung the wooden stake I'd left on my kitchen counter like a baseball bat, connecting with the side of Zelda's head with a wet thunk that sent her staggering sideways.

She didn't go down—whatever Julian Croix did to her strengthened and toughened her beyond any human—but the blow loosened her grip on my wrist enough for me to tear free.

I went for Pops again, but Zelda recovered faster than I'd expected. She backhanded Irene across the face with casual strength, sending her crashing into my bookshelf in an explosion of falling books and splintered wood.

"Stupid little bitch," Zelda snarled, her voice now completely inhuman. "I was going to do this quickly for you, but now I think I'll take my time."

She started toward Irene, who was trying to pull herself upright from the wreckage of my bookshelf. Blood ran from her nose, and she moved like someone who'd just taken a serious blow to the head.

I had Pops out now, the silver bullets ready, but I hesitated for just a moment. This was still Zelda—or was Zelda—and some part of me didn't want to believe that the woman who'd shared coffee and conversation with us just a week ago was truly gone.

That moment of hesitation nearly cost Irene her life.

Zelda reached her before I could fire, grabbing a handful of Irene's hair and jerking her head back to expose her throat. I could see the points of her teeth, see the hunger in her eyes, see her preparing to feed.

I put a silver bullet through her left shoulder.

The impact spun her around and threw her against my kitchen wall, but it didn't put her down. She looked at the hole in her shoulder with more irritation than pain, then looked at me with the kind of rage I'd only seen in the eyes of cornered predators.

"Silver bullets," she said, her voice thick with fury. "How wonderfully prepared of you. But it will take more than that to stop me."

She came at me like a hurricane, moving faster than my eyes could track. I got off another shot, but she was already too close. Her shoulder slammed into my chest, driving the air from my lungs and sending me crashing backward over my coffee table.

Pops went flying, skittering across my hardwood floor to end up somewhere near the front door. I tried to roll away, but she was on top of me before I could move, straddling my chest with her knees pinning my arms to the floor.

"I'm going to enjoy this," she said, her beautiful face twisted with savage hunger. "Julian wanted me to bring you back alive, but I think

I'll tell him you resisted too much. That I drained you completely to subdue you."

She leaned down toward my throat, and I could feel the unnatural heat radiating from her skin. Her teeth were fully extended now, more like fangs than anything human, and I could see the predatory intelligence in her eyes as she chose exactly where to bite.

That's when I remembered the silver stiletto in my boot.

It took every bit of strength I possessed to work my foot up far enough to reach the handle. Zelda was so focused on positioning herself for the perfect bite that she didn't notice the movement until it was too late.

I drove six inches of blessed silver up through her ribs and into her heart.

The effect was immediate and devastating. Silver might not kill a vampire instantly, but it disrupted whatever unnatural forces kept them animated. Zelda convulsed, her back arching in agony, her perfect features contorting as the blessed metal burned her from the inside.

But she still wasn't dead.

She rolled off me, clawing at the stiletto handle, trying to pull it out. Black blood—not the red blood of the living, but something dark and thick and wrong—seeped around the blade and stained her perfect skin.

"You... bitch," she gasped, her voice no longer beautiful or commanding. Now she just sounded like a dying animal. "Do you have any idea... what you've done?"

I struggled to my feet, my chest aching where she'd tackled me. "I've stopped a monster."

"I was... perfect. Eternal. I could have... given you everything..." She managed to get her fingers around the stiletto handle, but when she tried to pull it out, the silver burned her palms. She screamed, a sound that had nothing human in it.

"You were dead," I said. "Julian Croix killed you and turned you into his puppet. Whatever you think you've become, it's not life."

"It's... better than life." But even as she said it, I could see the light beginning to fade from her eyes. The stiletto was doing its work, the blessed silver disrupting whatever dark magic kept her animated.

"Ellie," Irene called from across the room. She was still sitting in the wreckage of my bookshelf, blood on her face and her voice shaky, but she was alive. "Is she...?"

"Dying," I said. "Finally."

But as I watched Zelda struggle with the silver in her heart, I realized that killing her—really killing her, ensuring she stayed dead—was going to require more than just stabbing her with blessed metal.

The vampire lore I'd read was clear about that. Silver could hurt them, could disrupt their unnatural existence, but permanent death required decapitation or a wooden stake through the heart or direct sunlight.

The wooden stake was somewhere on the floor, probably broken when Irene used it as a weapon. The sun set hours ago. Which left only one option.

I looked around my destroyed living room and found what I needed—a heavy kitchen knife that got knocked off my counter during the fight. It wasn't ideal, wasn't designed for what I was about to do, but it was sharp and it was available.

Zelda saw me pick it up, and her eyes went wide with understanding. "No," she whispered. "Please. I'm... I'm still me. Still your friend. This isn't... it doesn't have to..."

But even as she tried to plead, I could see the hunger still burning in her eyes. The thing Julian Croix created might wear Zelda's face and speak with her voice, but it wasn't her. It was a predator that would kill Irene and me and dozens of other innocent people if I let it live.

I knelt down beside her and positioned the kitchen knife at her throat. "I'm sorry, Zelda," I said, and I meant it. "I'm sorry I couldn't save you."

What followed was nothing like the clean, quick decapitations you see in movies. Cutting through a human neck—even an undead one—required sawing through skin and muscle and cartilage and bone. It was messy and difficult and took longer than anyone should ever have to experience.

Zelda fought me every inch of the way, even weakened by the silver in her heart. Her hands clawed at my arms, leaving scratches that burned like acid. She tried to bite, tried to scream, tried everything she could to stop me from finishing what I'd started.

But I kept cutting, kept sawing through tissue that was tougher than it should have been, kept working until the knife finally scraped against her spine. Then I angled the blade and worked it between vertebrae, twisting and prying until I felt the connection finally give way.

The whole process took nearly five minutes. Five minutes of the most intimate and horrifying violence I'd ever experienced, worsened by the fact that the face contorting in pain and rage belonged to someone who'd been my friend.

When it was finally over, when Zelda's head rolled away from her body and the unnatural light finally died from her eyes, I sat back on my heels and stared at what I'd done.

My hands were covered in black blood. My clothes were soaked with it. The smell filled my apartment—not the copper scent of human blood, but something fouler, like flowers left too long in stagnant water.

"Ellie." Irene's voice came from very far away. "Ellie, it's over. She's dead."

I looked across the room to where she was slowly pulling herself upright. There was concern in her eyes, and something else—the kind of careful wariness you'd show to someone who might not be entirely stable.

"Are you hurt?" I asked, my voice coming out hoarse and strange.

"Bruised. Maybe a mild concussion. Nothing that won't heal." She took a tentative step toward me, then stopped when she saw how much blood covered my hands and clothes. "What about you?"

I looked down at myself, at the evidence of what I'd just done. "I killed her. I killed Zelda."

"You killed a vampire," Irene corrected gently. "Zelda was already dead. Julian Croix killed her days ago."

I knew she was right, intellectually. But emotionally, it was like I'd just murdered someone who'd trusted me enough to come to my apartment alone. Someone who'd brought wine and wanted to share good news and died on my living room floor with my knife at her throat.

"We need to clean this up," I said, because focusing on practical matters was easier than thinking about what I'd just done. "And we need to get rid of the body."

"Ellie—"

"She came here to recruit us. That means Julian Croix will be expecting her back with news about whether we're willing to join his collection voluntarily." I forced myself to stand up, to start thinking like a detective instead of someone who'd just killed a friend. "When she doesn't return, he'll know something went wrong. He'll know we're a threat."

Irene nodded slowly. "What do you want to do?"

I looked around my destroyed apartment, at the black blood soaking into my hardwood floors, at the severed head that once belonged to someone I'd cared about.

"We clean up this mess," I said. "We dispose of the evidence. And then we plan our war against Julian Croix."

"War?"

"He turned Zelda into a monster and sent her to kill us. He's been collecting artists for months, maybe years, turning them into predators and using them to hunt more victims. He murdered Margaret Walker when her transformation failed, and he'll murder more people if we don't stop him." I wiped black blood off my hands with a kitchen towel, trying not to think about how it got there. "This isn't just about solving a case anymore. It's personal."

We spent the next four hours cleaning my apartment. Scrubbing blood off walls and floors, gathering up the pieces of what was once Zelda Kettleton, wrapping everything in plastic and old sheets. The head went into a canvas bag I'd used for laundry. The body required two large garbage bags and most of my masking tape.

By dawn, there was no evidence that a vampire died in my living room. No evidence except for the scratches on my arms that burned like chemical burns, the bruises on Irene's face, and the memory of what I was forced to do.

We loaded the remains into my car and drove out to the mountains east of Los Angeles, to a place where the coyotes and vultures would dispose of anything we left behind. By the time we dumped the last of the bags into a ravine that would be inaccessible to anyone without serious climbing equipment, the sun was fully up and Los Angeles was waking up to another perfect day.

"What happens now?" Irene asked as we drove back toward the city.

I thought about Julian Croix, sleeping in his Gothic mansion in the Hills, probably expecting a report from Zelda about whether she'd been successful in recruiting two new additions to his collection. When that report didn't come, he'd know that we were no longer potential victims—we were active enemies.

That endangered us, but it also endangered us more. He'd killed Margaret Walker for being unsuitable. What would he do to people who'd killed one of his transformed followers?

"Now we prepare," I said. "We gather allies, we learn everything we can about how to fight vampires, and we plan an assault on his operation that will put him down permanently."

"And if we can't? If he's too strong, or too well-protected, or too smart for us to beat?"

I touched the scratches on my arm, feeling the acid burn where Zelda's claws opened my skin. Somewhere in those marks was the memory of cutting through her throat with a kitchen knife, of the way she'd looked at me in the final moments before the light died in her eyes.

"Then we'll die trying," I said. "Because the alternative is letting him continue collecting artists, continue turning people like Zelda into monsters, continue killing anyone who doesn't fit into his perfect immortal collection."

We drove the rest of the way back to my apartment in silence, both of us lost in our own thoughts. By the time we climbed the stairs to my floor, I'd reached a decision that would define everything that came after.

Julian Croix declared war when he transformed Zelda and sent her to recruit us. He turned it personal when he forced me to kill someone I'd considered a friend.

Now it was my turn to show him what war really looks like.

The silver stiletto was still on my kitchen counter where I'd left it after cleaning Zelda's blood off the blade. I picked it up and tested its weight in my hand, thinking about everything I'd learned about fighting monsters over the past eight months.

Silver could hurt them. Cut off their heads or stake them through the heart, and they stayed dead. Holy water worked too. They were strong and fast, but not bulletproof.

Most importantly, they got cocky. Started thinking they were invincible. That was when you could get them. Julian Croix screwed up royally. Turning it personal was the last thing he should have done.

After what just happened to Zelda, I liked my odds.

PART TWO
THE BLOOD KISS

In the Archives

The grief hit me in waves at first—hot tears burning my cheeks while I scrubbed Zelda's blood from the kitchen floor, violent sobs that doubled me over while Irene held me in the shower afterward. But by Friday morning's light, something harder had crystallized in my chest. Something cold, sharp, and hungry for payback.

Julian Croix had turned my friend into a monster, then sent her to kill me. He'd made me cut through her throat with a kitchen knife while she clawed at my face with fingers that had once typed research notes and book reviews. He'd turned an act of survival into an intimate horror that would wake me up screaming for the rest of my life.

Now it was my turn to return the favor.

I sat at my rebuilt kitchen table—the old one had been destroyed in the fight—staring at the silver ouroboros pin I'd taken from Margaret Walker's body. Detective Miller's rosary lay beside it, along with three spare clips for Pops and a list of phone numbers I'd been avoiding for the past six months.

It was time to call in some favors from my time dealing with the Crescent Club.

"You sure about this?" Irene asked. She stood by the window, looking out at Spring Street with the careful attention of someone who'd learned that monsters could arrive in broad daylight wearing friendly faces. The bruises on her cheek had darkened overnight, purple and yellow reminders of how close we'd both come to joining Julian Croix's collection.

"I'm sure." I picked up the phone and dialed a number from memory. "Bill Kowalski saved Benjamin Finch's research from the bookstore fire. If anyone knows how to fight supernatural predators, it's him."

The phone rang four times before a familiar voice answered.

"Kowalski."

"Bill, it's Eleanor Vance."

A pause. "Jesus, Ellie. I wondered when you'd call. Been hearing some strange stories around town—young artists disappearing, suicide cases that don't add up. Figured you might be working something supernatural again."

"Vampires this time. European one with delusions of artistic grandeur. He's been collecting Hollywood talent like they're paintbrushes."

"How many?"

"At least thirty transformed followers that I've seen, probably more. And he's expanding his operation." I looked at the silver pin, thinking about Margaret Walker's staged death and the careful way Croix had positioned her body. "He killed a young actress named Margaret Walker when her transformation failed. Last night he sent one of his converts to recruit me and Irene. It didn't go well for her."

Bill was quiet for a moment. "You kill her?"

"Had to. She was going to drain Irene while I watched." The memory of cutting through Zelda's throat made my hands shake. "Bill, this isn't like the werewolves. This bastard turns his recruitment process into performance art. He makes his victims want to become monsters."

"Where do you want to meet?"

"Somewhere secure. Somewhere we can spread out maps and research without worrying about who might be listening."

"I've got a warehouse in the garment district. Industrial building, multiple exits, good sight lines. Nobody goes there except me, and I sweep it for surveillance equipment every week." He gave me an address on Mateo Street. "One hour."

I hung up and looked at Irene, who was still watching the street like she expected vampires to come marching up Spring Street in broad daylight.

"Pack everything we have on Julian Croix," I said. "And grab that bottle of holy water from the bathroom cabinet. If we're going to fight, we might as well do it right."

The warehouse Bill had chosen sat in a row of similar buildings that served the garment manufacturers clustered around downtown Los Angeles. From the outside it looked like any other industrial space—loading docks, small windows set high in concrete walls, the kind of place where people minded their own business and didn't ask questions about strange visitors.

Inside, it was something else entirely.

Bill Kowalski had turned the main floor into a research center that would have impressed the FBI. Long tables held maps of Los Angeles marked with colored pins and string connections. File cabinets lined the walls, labeled with dates going back to the 1890s. And in the center of it all, spread across what had once been a cutting table, were the materials he'd saved from Alistair Finch's burning bookstore.

"Welcome to the war room," Bill said, looking older and more tired than he had during the werewolf crisis. "Been working out of here since October, trying to figure out what other supernatural threats might be operating in the city."

He was a solid man in his fifties, built like someone who'd spent years working construction but smart enough to have survived forty years of hunting monsters. His work clothes were clean but worn, and his hands showed the scars that came from handling silver weapons on a regular basis.

"Find anything?" Irene asked, looking around at the organized chaos with professional interest.

"More than I wanted to," Bill replied. "Turns out werewolves weren't the only predators using Los Angeles as a hunting ground. I've got files on at least three other supernatural operations that were active during the Crescent Club's reign. Most of them scattered when Marcus Grayson's pack fell, but some stuck around."

He led us to a section of the warehouse where photographs were pinned to a large bulletin board. I recognized some of the faces—young actors and writers who'd made minor headlines when they'd disappeared or died under suspicious circumstances.

"These are all connected to your European director," Bill continued. "Started showing up in missing persons reports about eight months ago. Always the same pattern: struggling artist, recent contact with mysterious benefactor, sudden change in behavior, then disappearance or death."

I studied the photographs, counting at least twenty faces. All young, all attractive, all with the kind of desperate hunger for success that Julian Croix seemed to specialize in exploiting.

"How did you connect them to Croix?"

"Property records, mostly." Bill walked to another table covered with legal documents and city permits. "Your friend has been busy acquiring real estate under a network of shell corporations. Companies that exist only on paper, all traced back to a single bank account in Nevada that gets regular wire transfers from somewhere in Europe."

He spread out a map of Los Angeles County marked with red circles. "Safe houses in the Hills, warehouses near the docks, even a ranch in Malibu County. All purchased in the past year, all paid for in cash through dummy corporations."

The scope of it was staggering. Julian Croix wasn't just running a recruitment operation—he was building an empire. Properties scattered across the county, each one probably serving a different function in his grand design for immortal artistry.

"There's more," Bill said, pulling out a thick folder labeled "Financial Records." "The European bank transfers aren't random. They come in regular installments, always the same amount, always timed to coincide with major art sales in London and Paris."

"Art sales?"

"Paintings, sculptures, rare manuscripts. All attributed to unknown artists, all sold through private collectors who don't ask too many questions about provenance." Bill opened the folder and showed us auction records and sales receipts. "Someone's been flooding the European art market with works supposedly created by mysterious masters who shun publicity."

Irene and I exchanged glances. "He's selling the work his converts create," she said. "Croix transforms artists, makes them produce new pieces, then sells the results to fund his operations."

It was brilliant in the worst possible way. Julian Croix had turned vampire recruitment into a self-funding artistic enterprise. He collected artists, transformed them into immortal creatures with unlimited time to create, then sold their work to finance the acquisition of more artists. A perfect closed loop that could run indefinitely as long as there were desperate people willing to believe his promises about transcending human limitations.

"What about the research Finch saved?" I asked. "Anything useful for fighting vampires?"

Bill led us to the center of the warehouse, where Benjamin Finch's salvaged materials were laid out in careful organization. Leather-bound journals dating back to the 1890s, maps showing supernatural activity across Los Angeles, and weapons that looked like they belonged in a museum but were still sharp enough to kill.

"Finch's father was thorough," Bill said, opening one of the journals. "Vampires, werewolves, demons, things I can't even pronounce. But the vampire section is extensive."

I leaned over the journal, reading entries written in careful script about creatures that fed on human blood and turned their victims into willing servants. The research was comprehensive—methods of killing, ways to detect them, psychological profiles of their typical hunting patterns.

"According to this," I said, running my finger down a page of notes, "vampires are master manipulators who often pose as artists, philosophers, or religious leaders. They use their apparent immortality and supernatural abilities to inspire fanatical devotion in their victims."

"That matches what we've seen with Croix," Irene said. "He's not just hunting random victims—he's specifically targeting people who feel like failures, who are desperate for validation and willing to believe that their lack of success is proof of their artistic superiority rather than evidence that they need to work harder."

Bill nodded grimly. "Perfect psychological profile for conversion. People who are already convinced that ordinary human existence isn't good enough, who want to believe there's some higher form of being they can achieve."

I kept reading, looking for practical information about how to fight creatures like Julian Croix. The silver stiletto in my boot had wounded the vampire in Croix's garden, but it hadn't killed her. Zelda had required decapitation to finally die, and even that had been messy and difficult.

"Here," I said, finding a passage about vampire vulnerabilities. "Silver causes them pain and disrupts their supernatural abilities, but it doesn't kill them permanently. For that, you need either decapitation, a wooden stake through the heart, or direct sunlight. Stakes are lethal—death takes a few minutes, but it's certain."

"What about holy water and religious symbols?"

"Effective against younger vampires or those with weak will. Older ones, especially those with strong philosophical frameworks to justify their existence, are harder to affect with religious items." I looked up at Bill and Irene. "Julian Croix has probably been a vampire for decades, maybe centuries. And he's built an entire artistic philosophy to justify what he's become. Holy water might slow him down, but it won't stop him."

While Bill and I worked through the supernatural research, Irene had claimed a corner of the warehouse for her own investigation. She'd brought files from the Los Angeles Times archives, along with a list of contacts she'd developed during her years covering crime in the city.

"I've been tracking what Croix calls 'The Velvet Coterie,'" she said, looking up from a stack of newspaper clippings and handwritten notes. "That's what his transformed followers call themselves—artists who've been elevated to a higher form of existence."

She'd created her own bulletin board, with photographs and brief biographies of people who'd disappeared from Los Angeles' artistic community over the past year. Actors, writers, directors, even a few musicians and painters. All young, all talented, all desperate enough for success that they'd been willing to listen to Julian Croix's promises about transcending human limitations.

"The pattern is consistent," Irene continued. "Each victim goes through a period of increasing isolation from their former friends and colleagues. They stop showing up for auditions or meetings, quit their day jobs, cut contact with family members who don't understand their new artistic vision."

"Then what?"

"Then they resurface about a week later, but different. Pale, nocturnal, moving carefully like they're not entirely comfortable in their own bodies. Their old friends describe them as changed—more confident, more arrogant, but also somehow empty. Like they've lost something essential about what made them human."

I thought about Zelda's transformation, the way her beautiful face had hidden something hungry and predatory. She'd claimed to be more alive than ever, but there had been nothing alive about the way she'd looked at Irene and me. We'd been food to her, nothing more.

"According to my sources," Irene continued, "several of these transformed artists have been spotted at exclusive Hollywood parties, always moving in packs, always hunting for new recruits for Croix's artistic community. They work like a pyramid scheme for immortality."

"Have any of them tried to contact former friends or colleagues?"

Irene's expression grew troubled. "More than a dozen, according to the people I've interviewed. They show up at apartments or offices, claiming they want to share wonderful news about their artistic breakthrough. Always after dark, always alone, always focused on people who were close to them before their transformation."

Just like Zelda had done with us. I felt a chill thinking about how many other friendships Julian Croix had corrupted, how many former victims he'd sent back to recruit the people who'd once cared about them.

"The worst part," Irene added, "is that some of the recruitment attempts are successful. I found at least six cases where someone disappeared after being visited by a former friend who'd recently undergone Croix's transformation process."

The scope of Julian Croix's operation was becoming clearer, and it was more horrifying than I'd imagined. He wasn't just collecting individual artists—he was turning them into predators who could expand his operation by recruiting from their own social networks. Every person he transformed became a node in an ever-expanding web of supernatural corruption.

"How many total conversions are we looking at?" Bill asked.

Irene checked her notes. "Confirmed disappearances over the past eight months: forty-seven people. But that's just the ones where family or friends reported them missing. If Croix is targeting people who are already isolated, people who wouldn't be missed right away..."

She didn't need to finish the sentence. We were looking at potentially hundreds of people who'd been transformed from struggling artists into immortal predators, all of them convinced they'd achieved everything they'd ever wanted.

I walked back to the research table where Benjamin Finch's journals lay open, looking for information about vampire covens and how to disrupt them. What I found made my blood run cold.

"According to this research," I said, "vampires who create large numbers of converts often use them for mass recruitment events. Gatherings where dozens of potential victims are exposed to the vampire's influence simultaneously, making the conversion process more efficient."

"Like the parties we observed at Croix's estate," Bill said.

"Exactly. But there's something else." I found the relevant passage and read it aloud. "Vampire covens that reach a certain size often attempt to reveal themselves publicly, believing that their supernatural advantages will allow them to dominate human society openly rather than operating from the shadows."

The implications were staggering. If Julian Croix had been building toward some kind of public revelation, if he planned to announce the existence of his immortal artistic community to the world, the results could be catastrophic. Not just for Los Angeles, but for anywhere his philosophy of supernatural artistic superiority might spread.

"We need to stop him before he reaches that point," I said. "Before he decides that hiding in the shadows isn't good enough anymore."

Bill nodded grimly. "What's our timeline?"

I thought about everything we'd learned. Croix's expanding network of properties, his growing collection of transformed artists, the systematic way he'd been building his operation over the past year.

"Based on the pattern of disappearances," I said, "he's been accelerating his recruitment recently. More people vanishing, larger gatherings at his estate. My guess is that he's building toward something big—a culminating event that will either establish his control over Los Angeles' artistic community or announce his presence to the wider world."

"How long do we have?"

I looked around the warehouse at the evidence of Julian Croix's ambitions. Maps showing his properties across the county. Financial records proving his international connections. Photographs of dozens of young artists who'd believed his promises about transcending human limitations.

"Weeks, maybe less. We need to start hitting his operation now, before he's ready for whatever he's planning."

Irene stood up from her research corner, her expression determined despite the bruises on her face. "What's our first target?"

I thought about the careful way Julian Croix had built his network, the multiple properties and shell corporations Bill had identified. Going after Croix himself would be nearly impossible—his estate was too well defended, and he'd be expecting retaliation after Zelda's death.

But his operation depended on a steady stream of new recruits, and those recruits had to come from somewhere. If we could disrupt his recruitment network, cut off his supply of new victims, we might be able to force him into the open where we could get at him.

"We start with his lieutenants," I said. "The transformed artists he's using to recruit new victims. We identify them, track them down, and put them out of commission permanently."

"You mean kill them," Bill said. It wasn't a question.

"I mean stop them from turning more people into monsters. Whatever that takes." I picked up the silver ouroboros pin, feeling its weight in my palm. "Julian Croix started a this when he transformed Zelda and sent her to kill us. Now we finish it."

We spent the rest of the afternoon planning our campaign against the Velvet Coterie. Bill would continue tracking Croix's financial networks and property holdings, looking for patterns that might reveal his ultimate plans. Irene would use her newspaper contacts to identify specific individuals who'd been transformed, focusing on those who were actively recruiting new victims.

I would handle the direct action—hunting down Croix's lieutenants and putting them down before they could convert more innocent people into predators.

It wasn't going to be easy. Fighting vampires required specific weapons, careful timing, and the kind of intimate violence that would mark me for the rest of my life. But after what I'd been forced to do to Zelda, after watching Julian Croix turn friendship into a weapon designed to destroy me, I was ready for that kind of fight.

By the time we left the warehouse, the sun was setting over Los Angeles, painting the sky in shades of orange and red that reminded me of dried blood. Somewhere in the Hills, Julian Croix was probably waking up for another night of artistic recruitment, adding new names to his collection of immortal predators.

But this time, he'd find someone hunting back.

I touched the silver stiletto in my boot and started planning which of his lieutenants would die first. The confict between us had escalated beyond personal vendetta now—it was about stopping a monster who thought he could turn all of Los Angeles into his personal art gallery, populated by creatures who'd given up their humanity for the promise of eternal creativity.

Julian Croix had made his opening moves. Margaret Walker's staged death, Zelda's corrupted recruitment visit, the careful psychological warfare designed to break me down and make me vulnerable to his influence.

Now it was my turn to show him what a real fight looked like.

After what I'd done to Zelda, after five minutes of cutting through her throat while she clawed at my face, I knew I could handle whatever Julian Croix threw at me.

The Stakeout at the Velvet Vesper

Irene found me at my office Saturday evening, hunched over maps of Julian Croix's property network while cleaning Pops for the third time that day. The familiar ritual of breaking down the gun, checking each component, and reassembling it kept my hands busy while my mind worked through the problem. Pop had taught me that a clean weapon was a reliable weapon, and right now I needed all the reliability I could get. I was about to hunt vampires who were expecting retaliation.

"I found one," she said, settling into the client chair across from my desk. She looked tired but determined, the bruises on her face from Zelda's attack fading to yellow and green. "One of his lieutenants. Someone we can get to."

I looked up from Pops, interested. "Tell me."

She pulled out a manila folder thick with newspaper clippings and handwritten notes. "His name is Vincent Ashford. Former screenwriter, disappeared from his apartment in West Hollywood about six weeks ago. Friends reported him missing after he failed to show up for a meeting with a potential producer."

"And now?"

"Now he's been spotted at the Velvet Vesper, an exclusive nightclub on Sunset Strip. High-end place that caters to Hollywood types with unusual tastes." Irene opened the folder and showed me photographs taken with a telephoto lens—grainy images of a pale, thin man in an expensive suit. "My source says he shows up every Friday night, always alone, always hunting."

I studied the photographs. Vincent Ashford looked like he'd been handsome before his transformation, the kind of clean-cut features that would have served him well in Hollywood's social circles. But the camera had caught something predatory in his posture, the way he stood too still while scanning a crowd of potential victims.

"What kind of hunting?"

"The recruiting kind. According to the club's staff, he targets young women who are new to the city, particularly ones who mention wanting to break into pictures or modeling. He buys them expensive drinks, talks about connections in the industry, then suggests private meetings to discuss their careers."

It was exactly the pattern we'd identified in Julian Croix's operation. Find vulnerable people with artistic ambitions, offer them validation and opportunity, then gradually introduce them to increasingly dangerous ideas about transcending human limitations.

"How many?"

"At least four in the past month, according to the bartender I spoke with. Young women who left the club with Ashford and were never seen again." Irene's expression hardened. "He's working his way through Hollywood's newest arrivals, picking off the ones who don't have family or friends to miss them immediately."

I finished reassembling Pops and slid it into my shoulder holster. "When's he due back?"

"Tonight. He keeps a regular schedule—shows up around ten, works the crowd until midnight, then either leaves alone or with company." She checked her watch. "It's eight-thirty now. If we move fast, we can be in position before he arrives."

The Velvet Vesper sat on a stretch of Sunset Strip that catered to Los Angeles' more adventurous nightlife. From the outside, it looked like any other upscale nightclub—neon sign, velvet rope, doorman in a tuxedo checking names against a guest list. But there was something about the place that set my teeth on edge, a feeling that the people going inside were looking for experiences they couldn't find at more conventional establishments.

"How do we get in?" I asked, watching well-dressed couples disappear through the club's entrance.

"Press credentials," Irene replied, pulling two cards from her purse. "I'm covering Hollywood nightlife for the Times, you're my photographer. The manager thinks we're doing a feature story about exclusive entertainment venues."

The credentials got us past the doorman and into a world that felt like it had been designed by someone who'd read too many Gothic novels. The main room was all dark wood and red velvet, lit by candelabras that threw dancing shadows on the walls. A jazz trio played in one corner while couples danced on a floor that seemed too small for the number of people trying to use it.

But it was the clientele that caught my attention. They looked like Hollywood types—well-dressed, attractive, confident in the way that came from money and success. But there was something predatory about the way they moved through the crowd, the careful attention they paid to newcomers, the way conversations seemed to have an underlying tension that had nothing to do with normal social interaction.

"How many of them do you think are human?" I murmured to Irene as we found seats at a corner table with good sight lines.

"Not enough," she replied, scanning the room with professional interest. "Look at the way they're clustering around certain individuals. It's like watching sharks circle bait."

She was right. The club's regulars—the pale, careful ones who moved like they were uncomfortable in their own bodies—had arranged themselves around a handful of newcomers. Young men and women who looked excited to be in such an exclusive place, who didn't notice that their new friends never seemed to eat or drink anything, who were too flattered by the attention to ask why everyone was so interested in their personal stories.

A feeding ground. Julian Croix had turned the Velvet Vesper into a recruitment center where his transformed followers could hunt for new victims while maintaining the pretense of normal social interaction.

"There," Irene said, nodding toward the entrance. "Ten-fifteen, right on schedule."

Vincent Ashford glided through the crowd like he owned the place, nodding to the pale regulars while his eyes searched for fresh targets. He'd chosen his hunting ground well—the Velvet Vesper's atmosphere of exclusivity and sophistication would make potential victims feel special, chosen, ready to believe promises about unlimited opportunities in exchange for small favors.

I watched him work. The practiced smile, sliding up to the bar to cut off her view of the room. Classic isolation technique. Five minutes later they were at a corner table, her hanging on every word while he spun stories about the career waiting for her if she just knew the right people.

"He's got her," Irene said quietly. "Whatever he's promising, she's buying it."

I stood up, checking that the silver stiletto was secure in my boot. "Time to interrupt their conversation."

"What about the other vampires? If you attack him here, they'll all converge on us."

I counted at least a dozen pale faces in the crowd. She was right—starting something here would be suicide. We needed to get Ashford away from his backup, somewhere we could deal with him without worrying about reinforcements.

"We follow them," I decided. "He'll want privacy to complete his recruitment pitch. Once they're alone, we make our move."

The blonde woman—I'd heard Ashford call her Susan—was completely under his spell by the time they left the club together around midnight. She walked beside him with the kind of dreamy excitement that suggested she was already imagining her name in lights, already convinced that Vincent Ashford was going to change her life forever.

She had no idea how right she was.

They took Ashford's car, a black Cadillac that screamed expensive but not flashy, and drove north into the Hollywood Hills. Irene and I followed at a distance, using side streets and parallel routes to avoid being spotted. Ashford took his time, winding through scenic routes. More time to work on his mark.

"Where do you think he's taking her?" Irene asked.

"Somewhere private. Somewhere he can finish what he started." I thought about the safe houses Bill had found, properties Croix owned under fake names. "One of Croix's bolt-holes, probably. A place where screaming won't attract attention."

The Cadillac finally stopped at a modernist house perched on a hillside with commanding views of the city below. Perfect spot for a screenwriter before his transformation—expensive but not ostentatious, designed for privacy rather than display.

I parked where we could watch the house without being seen, then checked my weapons one more time: Pops with its nine rounds, three of them silver, the silver stiletto, sharp and blessed, and Detective Miller's rosary that hung around my neck, though I wasn't sure how much good it would do against an older vampire like Ashford.

"How do we play this?" Irene asked.

"Carefully. Vampires are stronger and faster than humans, but they're not invulnerable. Silver causes them pain, disrupts their supernatural abilities. If I can get close enough to wound him seriously, it might level the playing field."

"What about the girl?"

I thought about Susan's excited expression as she'd left the club with her new benefactor, convinced she was about to get everything she'd ever wanted. By now, Ashford would be explaining his philosophy, making transformation sound like the chance of a lifetime instead of a one-way ticket to hell.

"If we're lucky, he's still in recruitment mode. That means he'll want her willing participation, which gives us time." I checked my watch. "But not much. Once he starts the actual transformation process, we might not be able to save her."

We approached the house from the back, using landscaping and architectural features for cover. The windows glowed with warm light, and I could hear voices from inside—Ashford's cultured tones and Susan's animated responses. She sounded excited, intrigued, completely unaware that she was being prepared for something worse than death.

"There," Irene whispered, pointing to a set of French doors that opened onto a patio. "We can see into what looks like the living room."

We crept closer, staying low and moving carefully. The view through the French doors confirmed my worst fears. Susan sat on an expensive sofa, a glass of wine in her hand, listening with rapt attention while Vincent Ashford paced in front of her. Full sales pitch mode, gesturing while he talked about how mortality held back real artists, how the brave ones could transcend all that.

"He's getting ready to make his offer," I whispered to Irene. "Once she agrees to the transformation, we won't have another chance."

I tried the French doors and found them unlocked—probably Ashford's confidence that no one would be foolish enough to interrupt his work. I eased the door open just enough to slip inside, the silver stiletto already in my hand.

Ashford sensed me before he saw me. His head whipped around, and I was looking into predator's eyes—the kind I'd learned to recognize. His handsome features twisted into something hungry and dangerous.

"Well, well," he said in that smooth voice that screamed money and education. "Eleanor Vance, I presume. Julian said you might show up eventually."

Susan looked confused, her wine glass frozen halfway to her lips. "Vincent? Who is this woman?"

"Someone who doesn't understand what I'm offering you, my dear," Ashford replied, not taking his eyes off me. "Someone who thinks that mortality is something worth preserving."

I kept the silver stiletto ready, noting the distance between us and the way he'd positioned himself between me and Susan. "Let the girl go, Ashford. Your quarrel is with me."

He laughed. "Oh, but she's so perfect for what we do. Young, talented, desperate enough to buy the line that her failures prove she's better than this world instead of just not good enough." His gaze shifted briefly to Susan. "You want to be immortal, don't you, dear? You want all the time in the world to perfect your craft?"

Susan's eyes went wide, but not with fear. With desire. "You're serious? You can really do that?"

"Vincent here is a vampire," I said, hoping to break through whatever psychological manipulation he'd been using on her. "He feeds on human blood, and he wants to turn you into the same kind of monster he's become."

But instead of running, Susan looked back at Ashford with something that might have been hope. "Is that true? Are you really immortal?"

Ashford smiled, showing teeth that were too sharp to be entirely human. "Every word. And I can share that gift with you, if you're brave enough to accept it."

That's when I realized I was too late. Whatever promises he'd been making, whatever philosophy he'd been spouting, Susan was already convinced. She wanted what he was offering, even knowing what it really was.

"Last chance, Ashford," I said, raising the silver stiletto. "Let her go."

"I'm afraid that's not possible," he replied, and then he moved.

He was fast—faster than anything human had a right to be—but I'd been fighting supernatural predators for six months. I rolled sideways as his claws raked the air where my throat had been, came up with the stiletto ready, and managed to slice across his forearm before he could recover his balance.

The effect of the silver was immediate and devastating. Ashford screamed, a sound that had nothing human in it, and staggered backward. Smoke rose from the wound on his arm, and I could see the metal burning him from the inside.

But he didn't go down.

"Silver," he hissed, looking at me with eyes that blazed with inhuman fury. "Clever little detective. But it will take more than that to stop me."

Susan screamed from somewhere behind me, but I couldn't spare the attention to look at her. Ashford was circling now, moving with the kind of predatory patience that suggested he was done underestimating me.

"Julian told me about what you did to poor Zelda," he said, his voice thick with rage. "How you butchered her with a kitchen knife while she tried to save you from your own limitations."

The mention of Zelda hit me like a physical blow. I felt the familiar weight of guilt settle in my chest—the knowledge that I'd been forced to kill someone I'd once considered a friend.

"She wasn't trying to save me," I said, keeping the silver stiletto between us. "She was trying to drain me while making me watch her kill Irene."

"She was trying to show you the beauty of transcendence," Ashford corrected. "The glory of abandoning mortal concerns for something infinitely more rewarding."

He feinted left, then came at me from the right. I got the stiletto up in time to block his claws, but the force of his attack drove me backward into a coffee table. Wood splintered under the impact, and I felt something sharp dig into my back.

Ashford was on top of me before I could roll away, his hands closing around my throat with strength that could have crushed my windpipe. I could see his fangs extending, see the hunger burning in his eyes as he prepared to feed.

That's when my groping hand found what had been digging into my back—a broken leg from the coffee table, splintered into a sharp point by our collision.

I drove six inches of jagged wood up through Vincent Ashford's chest and into his heart.

The effect was instant. His body went rigid, back arching, hands falling away from my throat. He collapsed with the stake jutting from his chest like a flag.

But he wasn't dead. Not yet.

From Finch's notes, a stake through the heart didn't kill them—just paralyzed them. Helpless but awake, trapped in their own bodies. I could see the awareness in Ashford's eyes, the rage and terror as he realized what had happened to him.

His mouth opened and closed soundlessly, trying to speak or scream. His fingers twitched as he tried to reach for the stake, but his body wouldn't obey his commands. He was completely, utterly helpless.

"Jesus Christ," Susan breathed from somewhere behind me. "What did you do to him?"

I struggled to my feet, my throat sore where Ashford's fingers had dug in. "I stopped him from turning you into a monster."

But when I looked at her, what I saw was worse than Ashford's strength. Disappointment. Susan was staring at the paralyzed vampire like I'd just killed her dreams.

"You killed him," she said, her voice hollow with loss. "He was going to make me immortal, and you killed him."

I thought about explaining what immortality really meant in Croix's world—hunting, feeding, losing your soul piece by piece. But the look in her eyes told me she wouldn't listen. Ashford had done his work too well.

"He would have murdered you," I said instead. "Turned you into something that feeds on innocent people."

"He would have made me perfect," she said, backing toward the door. "All the time in the world to create. Everything I ever wanted."

She ran before I could stop her, leaving me alone with Vincent Ashford's paralyzed form.

As I caught my breath, something caught my eye—a small camera mounted in the corner near the ceiling, its lens pointed directly at where Ashford had fallen. Modern equipment, out of place in the vintage house. A small red light blinked steadily. Croix had been watching.

I realized my mistake immediately—Susan knew where Croix's estate was. She'd been there during recruitment. And she was desperate enough to trade information about what happened here for another chance at transformation.

I found the recording equipment in a locked closet—professional surveillance gear connected to a remote feed. Croix hadn't just been watching; he'd been recording. I smashed the equipment, but the damage was done. He'd seen everything.

Ashford stared up at me with eyes full of hatred and terror, still conscious, still aware, but unable to move or speak or do anything but experience the agony of having a wooden stake driven through his undead heart.

I knelt beside him and looked into those hate-filled eyes. "This is for every innocent person you've recruited for Julian Croix's collection."

Then I used the silver stiletto to cut off his head.

Messier than Zelda had been—vampires were tougher, even staked ones—but I'd learned. I knew the angles now, how to work between vertebrae, how to keep sawing even when my arms burned and the blood—too dark, too thick—made everything slippery.

When it was finally over, when Vincent Ashford's head rolled away from his body and the unnatural light finally died from his eyes, I sat back on my heels and stared at what I'd done.

Another friend of Julian Croix's, permanently removed from his collection. Another predator who would never again hunt innocent people with promises of artistic immortality.

But also another five minutes of the most intimate and brutal violence imaginable, another memory that would wake me up screaming for the rest of my life.

I heard footsteps outside and turned to see Irene approaching cautiously through the French doors. She took one look at the blood covering my hands and clothes, at Vincent Ashford's severed head, and immediately understood what had happened.

"Did the stake work?" she asked.

"It killed him. Took about three minutes, but he's dead." I wiped blood off my hands with a rag from Ashford's kitchen. "That's two confirmed methods for killing vampires—decapitation and wooden stakes through the heart. Both effective, both brutal."

"What about the girl?"

"She ran. And from the look in her eyes, she's going to try to find another one of Croix's lieutenants to complete what Ashford started." I thought about Susan's disappointed expression, the way she'd stared at the paralyzed vampire like I'd just destroyed her dreams rather than saved her life. "Julian Croix has done his work too well. He's convinced people that becoming a monster is the same as achieving artistic perfection."

We spent the next hour cleaning up the evidence of what had happened in Vincent Ashford's hillside house. The body went into several garbage bags, along with blood-soaked furniture and anything else that might connect the scene to our visit. The head required special handling—vampires had a way of coming back if you didn't dispose of them properly, and I wasn't taking any chances.

By dawn, there was no trace that Vincent Ashford had ever existed, except for the memory of his paralyzed eyes staring up at me while I sawed through his throat with a silver blade.

"One down," I said as we drove back toward the city through the early morning light. "How many more lieutenants does Croix have?"

Irene consulted her notes. "At least a dozen that I've been able to identify, probably more. We're looking at months of this kind of work—tracking them down one by one, getting close enough to kill them without alerting the others."

I thought about the methodical campaign we'd have to wage. Weeks or months of hunting vampires through Los Angeles' nightlife, each confrontation as brutal as what I'd just experienced with Vincent Ashford.

But as we reached downtown Los Angeles and the morning commuters began filling the streets with normal human activity, I felt something that surprised me.

Satisfaction.

Vincent Ashford had been recruiting innocent people, turning them into predators who would spend eternity hunting others. Now he was dead, permanently removed from the equation. One less monster prowling the city's nightclubs.

"We can do this," I said, more to myself than to Irene. "One lieutenant at a time, we can dismantle his entire operation."

"And when we've eliminated all his followers?"

I touched the silver stiletto in my boot, thinking about Julian Croix sleeping in his Gothic mansion in the Hills, probably unaware that he'd just lost one of his most effective recruiters.

"Then we go after the master himself."

This wasn't just personal anymore. It was about stopping a monster who thought he could turn all of Los Angeles into his personal hunting ground, full of creatures who'd traded their souls for pretty promises.

Vincent Ashford had been the first casualty of that war. He wouldn't be the last.

After what I'd just done with a broken coffee table leg and a silver stiletto, after confirming that wooden stakes worked as well as the old stories claimed, I was more confident than ever that Julian Croix could be beaten.

It would just require more violence, more brutality, and more bloody work that would mark me for the rest of my life.

But after watching Ashford work on Susan, after seeing her disappointment when I saved her from becoming a monster, I was ready for the fight.

Some monsters needed to be killed, no matter what it cost the person doing the killing.

The Artist's Message

I didn't sleep much Sunday morning. Every time I closed my eyes, I saw Vincent Ashford convulsing around the wooden stake I'd driven through his heart, watched the light drain from his eyes as whatever dark magic kept him animated finally let go. Three minutes of watching a monster die, and every second was burned into my memory.

By noon, I gave up on rest and headed to the office. Spring Street was quiet on Sunday, most of the downtown businesses closed, which made the package waiting outside my door even more conspicuous.

It sat propped against the frosted glass that read "Vance Investigations," wrapped in brown paper and tied with black silk ribbon. No delivery markings, no postal stamps, nothing to show how it had gotten there or who had left it. Just my name written across the top in elegant script that looked like it belonged on a museum placard.

I drew Pops and checked the hallway before approaching the package. Empty. Whoever had delivered this had come and gone without being seen, probably sometime after midnight when the building was deserted.

I unlocked my office door and carried the package inside, setting it on Pop's old desk while I checked the windows and made sure I was alone. Then I cut the ribbon with the silver stiletto and unwrapped what Julian Croix had sent me.

The frame was expensive—dark wood with gold inlay, the kind of craftsmanship that probably cost more than most people made in a month. Behind glass so clear it seemed to disappear entirely was a charcoal sketch drawn with museum-quality skill.

It showed Vincent Ashford in his final moments.

Every detail was perfect, rendered with an artist's eye for composition and dramatic effect. Ashford's face, twisted in agony as the wooden stake pierced his heart. His hands, clawed and reaching for something just out of frame. The way his expensive suit had rumpled around the wound, the spreading stain of black blood across the carpet.

But it was more than just a reproduction of what I'd witnessed. The artist had caught something deeper, something that turned brutal killing into a moment of dark beauty. The play of light and shadow across Ashford's features. The elegant curve of his spine as his body arched around the stake. The way his hair had fallen across his forehead, making him look almost peaceful despite the violence of his death.

It was exquisite. It was horrible. And it was signed in the lower right corner with a flowing signature: "J. Croix."

Attached to the back of the frame was an envelope with my name written in the same elegant script. Inside, a single sheet of expensive paper covered with handwriting that looked like calligraphy.

My Dear Miss Vance,

I hope you will accept this small token of my appreciation for your remarkable performance last evening. I confess myself quite moved by the raw power of your artistic vision—the improvised use of found materials, the intimate nature of the engagement, the way you transformed a simple act of violence into something approaching transcendence.

Your technique with the wooden stake was particularly inspired. The angle of penetration, the force of the thrust, the way you held Vincent's gaze as life left his eyes—these are the hallmarks of a true artist working in the medium of mortality itself. Most practitioners of your craft lack such... aesthetic sensibility.

I find myself curious about your other works. How did you dispatch poor Zelda? Was there the same attention to visual composition, the same understanding that death can be rendered beautiful when approached with the proper artistic vision? I suspect there was. You have the eye for such things, the natural talent that cannot be taught.

Please know that I bear you no ill will for your recent activities. On the contrary, I consider myself fortunate to have discovered an artist of your caliber operating in my city. Los Angeles has such a shortage of individuals who understand that violence, properly executed, is indistinguishable from performance art.

I look forward to your next exhibition. May I suggest a more public venue? Your work deserves a larger audience.

With sincere admiration for your brutal aesthetic,

Julian Croix

P.S. - I do hope you kept the wooden stake. The best artists always sign their work.

I read the letter three times, each pass making my skin crawl worse than the last. Julian Croix wasn't just acknowledging that I'd killed one of his lieutenants—he was praising me for it. Treating Vincent Ashford's death like a piece of performance art, critiquing my technique as if I were some kind of avant-garde sculptor working in blood and terror.

The worst part was how he'd managed to make it sound reasonable. The careful way he'd described the fight, turning my desperate struggle for survival into something calculated and aesthetic. The way he'd reframed brutal necessity as artistic choice, as if I'd driven that stake through Ashford's heart because I was creating something beautiful rather than because the bastard was trying to kill me.

I set the letter down and looked at the sketch again, trying to see it as just a drawing instead of evidence that Julian Croix had been watching while I fought for my life. But the detail was too precise, too accurate. He'd either been there personally or had gotten a report from someone who had been.

Which meant that every move I made, every action I took against his operation, was being observed and evaluated. Not by an enemy seeking tactical advantage, but by a critic reviewing my performance.

The phone rang, cutting through my analysis of Julian Croix's psychological warfare. I picked it up on the second ring, my voice coming out harsher than I'd intended.

"Vance Investigations."

"Ellie? You sound terrible." Irene's concerned voice was exactly what I needed to hear. "Did you get any sleep?"

"Some. Listen, can you come to the office? Julian Croix sent me a present, and I want you to see it before I decide what to do about it."

"What kind of present?"

I looked at the sketch again, noting the way Croix had captured the exact moment when Vincent Ashford realized he was going to die. "The kind that makes me want to burn this building down and start over somewhere else."

Irene arrived twenty minutes later, still wearing the same clothes from yesterday and looking like she'd gotten about as much sleep as I had. She took one look at the framed sketch on my desk and went very still.

"Jesus Christ, Ellie. When did this arrive?"

"Found it outside my door this morning. Along with a note that's even worse than the picture."

She read Julian Croix's letter in silence, her expression growing more troubled with each paragraph. When she finished, she set it down carefully and looked at me with something that might have been fear.

"He's trying to mess with your head."

"It's working." I picked up the letter and read the postscript again. "Look at this—he's treating what happened to Vincent Ashford like it was some kind of art exhibition. Like I killed him because I was making a statement about death and beauty instead of because he was trying to drain an innocent girl."

"But you know that's not true."

"Do I?" I thought about the three minutes I'd spent watching Ashford die, the way I'd felt when the light finally went out of his eyes. Relief, yes. Satisfaction that another of Croix's predators was permanently removed from the equation. But there had been something else too, something I didn't want to examine too closely. "What if he's right? What if I'm starting to enjoy this?"

Irene walked around the desk and put her hands on my shoulders, forcing me to look at her. "Eleanor Vance, you are not a killer. You're someone who's been forced to kill in order to protect innocent people. There's a difference."

"Is there? Because right now it doesn't feel like there's much of a difference at all."

I thought about Zelda's transformation, the way her beautiful face had hidden something hungry and predatory. About Vincent Ashford's recruitment speech, the promises of artistic immortality he'd been making to Susan before I'd interrupted. About Margaret Walker, found dead in Griffith Park with her body positioned like a work of art.

Julian Croix was turning everything into art. Murder, transformation, even my attempts to stop him—it was all just raw material for his aesthetic vision. And by sending me this sketch, by praising my "brutal aesthetic" and "raw talent," he was trying to make me complicit in that vision.

He was trying to turn me into another one of his artists.

"Look at the signature," I said, pointing to the corner of the sketch. "He didn't just draw this—he signed it. Like he's proud of what he created. Like Vincent Ashford's death was something worth celebrating."

"It's psychological warfare," Irene said. "He's trying to make you doubt yourself, trying to corrupt the way you think about what you're doing. Don't let him."

But even as she said it, I could feel the doubt taking root in my mind. What if Julian Croix was right about me? What if I had some kind of natural talent for violence, some aesthetic appreciation for death that I'd never recognized before? What if the only difference between us was that he'd embraced what he was while I was still pretending to be something else?

The sketch seemed to mock me from its expensive frame, showing Vincent Ashford's final moments rendered with the kind of artistic skill that transformed brutality into beauty. I'd been there, I'd watched him die, and I had to admit that there had been something almost graceful about the way he'd fallen, something poetic about the contrast between his pale skin and the dark blood spreading across the carpet.

Julian Croix had seen that too. He'd seen it and captured it and turned it into art.

"What am I supposed to do with this?" I asked, gesturing toward the sketch. "Keep it? Burn it? Hang it on my wall?"

"You're supposed to remember that it's a weapon," Irene replied. "A tool designed to make you think of yourself as something you're not. Julian Croix is trying to turn you into one of his collection, Ellie. Not by transforming you into a vampire, but by convincing you that you're already an artist working in the same medium he is."

I knew she was right. Intellectually, I understood exactly what Julian Croix was trying to accomplish with his gift. He was reframing my actions, changing the context, trying to make me see myself through his eyes instead of my own.

But the sketch was so beautifully done, so technically perfect, that it was hard not to appreciate the skill involved. And the letter was so perceptive, so accurate in its assessment of what had happened during the fight, that it was difficult to dismiss entirely.

Maybe I did have an aesthetic appreciation for violence. Maybe there was something about the way I approached killing that went beyond simple necessity. Maybe Julian Croix had seen something in me that I'd never recognized in myself.

"He wants a response," I said, reading through the letter one more time. "He's treating this like the opening move in some kind of artistic dialogue. He shows me his work, critiques mine, suggests improvements for next time."

"And?"

I thought about that. Julian Croix had sent me a masterpiece—a sketch so technically accomplished and aesthetically striking that it belonged in a gallery. He'd praised my technique, complimented my artistic vision, positioned himself as a mentor figure offering guidance to a promising student.

But underneath all the cultured sophistication, all the artistic appreciation and aesthetic theory, was a simple truth: he was a monster who fed on human blood and turned innocent people into predators. The sketch might be beautiful, but it commemorated the death of someone who'd been recruiting victims for Julian Croix's collection of immortal artists.

Vincent Ashford had died because he'd been trying to transform Susan into another vampire. I'd killed him to save her life, not because I was making some statement about death and beauty.

That was the difference between Julian Croix and me. He saw everything through the lens of artistic vision, treating human life as raw material for his aesthetic projects. I saw monsters that needed to be stopped before they could hurt more innocent people.

The fact that killing them might be beautiful didn't change why it was necessary.

"I'm going to burn it," I decided. "The sketch, the letter, the whole thing. I'm not playing his game."

"Good." Irene nodded approvingly. "Don't let him get in your head."

But even as I said it, I found myself looking at the sketch one more time. Julian Croix had captured something in Vincent Ashford's final moments that I'd missed during the actual fight—a quality of tragic beauty that transformed the scene from simple violence into something approaching art.

Maybe there was something to be learned from that perspective. Maybe understanding how Julian Croix saw the world would help me anticipate his next moves, predict what he was likely to deploy against me.

Maybe keeping the sketch wasn't about accepting his view of me as an artist. Maybe it was about understanding my enemy well enough to defeat him.

"On second thought," I said, "I think I'll keep it."

"Ellie—"

"Not because I agree with what he's saying. But because it tells me something about how his mind works, how he processes violence and death and the things he does to innocent people." I picked up the sketch and studied Julian Croix's signature, noting the confident flourishes that suggested an ego the size of Los Angeles. "If I'm going to beat him, I need to understand him. And this is the clearest window into his psychology I'm likely to get."

Irene looked skeptical, but she didn't argue. "Just promise me you won't start seeing yourself the way he wants you to."

I thought about that promise, about whether I could honestly make it. Julian Croix's letter had already planted seeds of doubt in my mind, questions about my motivations and methods that I'd never considered before. The sketch had shown me aspects of Vincent Ashford's death that I'd missed in the moment, details that suggested there might be beauty in violence if you knew how to look for it.

But understanding Julian Croix's perspective didn't mean accepting it. Seeing the artistic elements in what I'd done didn't mean I'd done it for artistic reasons. And acknowledging that there might be beauty in death didn't mean I had to start killing for aesthetic purposes rather than practical ones.

"I promise," I said. "I know who I am and why I'm doing this. Julian Croix can try to reframe it however he wants, but I'm not fighting monsters because I'm an artist. I'm fighting them because they're monsters."

I locked the sketch in my desk drawer, next to Detective Miller's rosary and the silver bullets for Pops. Tomorrow, I'd show it to Bill Kowalski, get his opinion on what Julian Croix was trying to accomplish.

But tonight, I was going to try to forget about artistic vision and aesthetic appreciation and brutal beauty. Tonight, I was going to focus on the simple, practical question of how to kill more vampires without losing my soul in the process.

Julian Croix wanted to turn me into one of his artists. He'd sent me a masterpiece designed to show me how beautiful violence could be when approached with the proper aesthetic sensibility.

What he didn't understand was that I already knew how beautiful violence could be. I'd known it since the first time I'd put a silver bullet through a werewolf's heart, since the moment I'd watched the life drain out of Marcus Grayson's eyes in the basement of the abandoned Crescent Club meeting hall.

The difference between Julian Croix and me wasn't that he saw beauty in death while I saw only necessity. The difference was that he created death for the sake of beauty, while I created beauty in the service of stopping death.

He was an artist who happened to be a killer. I was a killer who happened to have an eye for art.

And that distinction, no matter how subtle it might seem, was what was going to let me destroy him without becoming him.

The sketch could stay in my desk drawer, a reminder of how sophisticated and dangerous my enemy really was. But it wasn't going to change who I was or why I was fighting.

Some monsters needed to be killed, no matter how beautifully they died.

And Julian Croix was about to learn that some private investigators didn't change their methods just because someone sent them a fancy drawing with a note.

The Ghost on the Wire

Monday morning found me back at Bill Kowalski's warehouse, staring at Julian Croix's sketch while trying to figure out how a vampire had managed to witness Vincent Ashford's death without me spotting him. The charcoal drawing was too accurate, too detailed, for someone who hadn't been there personally or gotten a damn thorough report from someone who had been.

"He's got eyes on us," Bill said, studying the elegant signature in the corner of the frame. "Question is whether he was there himself or has people following your movements."

"People," Irene corrected from her position at a table covered with financial documents. "Vampires. And I think I know how he's tracking us."

She'd been working since dawn, following the paper trail Bill had started on Julian Croix's business network. Bank records, property transfers, corporate filings—all the bureaucratic debris that got left behind when someone built a criminal empire in plain sight.

"Show me," I said.

Irene spread out a map of Los Angeles County marked with colored pins. Red for properties Croix owned directly, blue for shell corporations, yellow for businesses that might be connected to his operation.

"I found the pattern," she said, pointing to a cluster of yellow pins near the harbor. "Croix doesn't just own real estate—he owns shipping companies, trucking firms, warehouses near the docks. All the infrastructure you'd need to move large quantities of cargo without attracting official attention."

Bill frowned at the map. "What kind of cargo requires that much secrecy?"

"The kind that's still breathing when it gets loaded," I replied, thinking about the recruitment parties I'd observed at Croix's estate. "He's been collecting artists for months. Question is, what's he doing with them after they're transformed?"

Irene pulled out a shipping manifest she'd obtained through her contacts at the Los Angeles Times. "Pacific Coast Transport, one of his shell companies, has been booking regular cargo shipments to San Francisco, Seattle, and Portland. Always the same specifications—custom wooden crates, special handling requirements, overnight delivery."

"How often?"

"Twice a month for the past six months. Always scheduled around the new moon, always departing just before dawn." She looked up from the manifest with troubled eyes. "Ellie, I think he's been exporting his operation. Building vampire networks in other cities, using Los Angeles as his recruiting and training center."

The implications hit me like a kick to the gut. Julian Croix wasn't just building a collection of immortal artists in Los Angeles—he was creating a franchise operation. Transforming desperate people into vampires, then shipping them to other cities where they could establish their own recruiting networks.

It was brilliant in the worst way possible.

The call came from LAPD Wednesday morning. Another body in Griffith Park, staged like Margaret Walker's had been. Detective Torres sounded tired.

"Same M.O. as your missing actress case," he said. "Young woman, exsanguinated, two puncture wounds on the neck that the M.E. says look like animal bites. ID in her purse says Susan Martinez, twenty-three, aspiring actress from Pasadena."

I felt cold. Susan had gotten what she wanted.

"When?" I asked.

"Coroner says sometime Monday night. She'd been dead about thirty-six hours when the body was found."

Monday night—three days after she'd run from Ashford's house, desperate to find another vampire who'd complete her transformation. She'd found one. And discovered too late that Croix's promises of eternal artistic achievement were just pretty words wrapped around murder.

"Thanks for letting me know," I said.

After I hung up, I sat at my desk and thought about the look in Susan's eyes when I'd killed Ashford. Disappointment. Loss. Like I'd stolen her dreams instead of saved her life.

Some people couldn't be saved from themselves.

Instead of trying to control a single city, he was building a national network of vampire cells, all of them following his artistic philosophy about transcending human limitations. Each new city would become another hunting ground, another source of victims who could be transformed and shipped elsewhere.

"How many cities?" Bill asked.

Irene consulted her notes. "Based on the shipping records I could access, at least eight major cities along the West Coast. But there could be more—these are just the shipments going through this one company."

I studied the map, thinking about dozens of young artists disappearing from Los Angeles only to resurface in San Francisco or Seattle, ready to begin the same recruitment process that had claimed Margaret Walker and Zelda Kettleton. Each transformed vampire would carry Julian Croix's philosophy to a new hunting ground, spreading his influence like a plague.

"Where's the staging area?" I asked. "He'd need somewhere to prepare shipments, keep the transformed vampires ready for transport."

Irene pointed to a warehouse district near Terminal Island. "Pacific Coast Transport operates out of a facility here. According to the records, they've been taking delivery of custom wooden containers for the past three months. Special orders, paid for in cash."

"Coffins," Bill said grimly. "He's shipping them in coffins filled with their native soil."

The vampire lore Benjamin Finch had collected was specific about that requirement. Vampires needed to rest in earth from their place of transformation, especially during long journeys. Julian Croix would have to provide each of his exports with a traveling coffin filled with soil from Los Angeles.

"We need to see that warehouse," I said. "If Croix is really running an export operation, there should be evidence of how many vampires he's shipped and where they've gone."

Bill checked his watch. "Middle of the day, most of his people will be sleeping. Best time to take a look without running into resistance."

An hour later, we were driving through the industrial maze that surrounded Los Angeles Harbor, following Irene's directions toward Pacific Coast Transport's warehouse facility. The area was a sprawling collection of loading docks, freight yards, and storage buildings that served the cargo ships arriving daily from ports around the Pacific. Perfect cover for someone who needed to move unusual shipments without attracting attention.

The Pacific Coast Transport warehouse sat at the end of a dead-end street, surrounded by other industrial buildings that looked largely abandoned during daylight hours. It was bigger than I'd expected—a concrete and steel structure that could have housed several freight trains, with loading docks designed for heavy cargo and multiple truck bays for local delivery.

"No guards visible," Bill observed, scanning the building through binoculars. "But that doesn't mean it's undefended."

We parked three blocks away and approached on foot, using other buildings for cover. The main entrance was secured with heavy chains and industrial padlocks, but Bill had brought tools from his construction work that made short work of the security measures.

"Company locks," he explained as the chains fell away. "Same type I deal with on job sites every day."

The warehouse interior was dark and cavernous, filled with the kind of echoing silence that suggested recent activity but current emptiness. Emergency lighting cast long shadows between rows of shipping containers and wooden crates, making the space feel like a cathedral built for the devil's work.

But it was the smell that hit me first—earth and wood and something faintly metallic that reminded me of dried blood.

"Jesus," Irene whispered as our eyes adjusted to the dim lighting.

The warehouse floor was arranged like a factory assembly line, with workstations positioned along a path that led from the main entrance to the loading docks. The first station held stacks of expensive hardwood—mahogany and oak cut to precise specifications. The second station contained metalworking equipment for crafting hinges and latches. The third station was where it all came together.

Coffins. Dozens of them, in various stages of completion.

They weren't the simple pine boxes used for pauper burials or the ornate caskets favored by funeral homes. These were custom-built traveling containers, designed to be both elegant and functional. Each coffin was lined with rich fabric and fitted with ventilation systems that would allow the occupant to breathe during transport. The craftsmanship was museum-quality, the kind of work that belonged in European cathedrals rather than Los Angeles warehouses.

"How many?" Bill asked, walking between the rows of completed coffins.

I counted quickly, noting that each coffin was labeled with a destination and shipping date. "Forty-three finished, maybe a dozen more in various stages of construction."

"That's not the worst part," Irene said from deeper in the warehouse. "Look at this."

She was standing beside a large industrial scale surrounded by bags of dark soil. Not the sandy earth of Los Angeles, but rich, black dirt that looked like it had been imported from somewhere with more fertile growing conditions.

"He's not using local soil," she continued. "This is coming from somewhere else, somewhere that's been... prepared."

Bill knelt beside one of the soil bags and cut it open with a pocket knife. The earth that spilled out was so dark it was almost black, and it carried a smell that was wrong in ways I couldn't put my finger on. Not decay, exactly, but something older and more basic.

"This isn't natural soil," he said, letting the earth run through his fingers. "It's been treated with something, processed somehow."

I was about to respond when I heard the sound of vehicles approaching the warehouse. Multiple engines, moving fast, coming at us from different directions.

"Company," I said, drawing Pops. "Back door?"

Bill pointed toward the loading docks. "Through there, but we'll have to cross open ground to reach the street."

The sound of car doors slamming echoed from outside the main entrance, followed by voices calling out instructions. They were coordinating their approach, surrounding the building to cut off our escape.

"How many?" Irene asked.

I listened to the voices, trying to count distinct speakers. At least six, probably more. All of them moving with the kind of disciplined coordination that suggested military or law enforcement training.

"Too many to fight," I decided. "We need to get out of here before they complete their perimeter."

We made our way toward the loading docks, staying low and using the rows of coffins for cover. But as we reached the back of the warehouse, I could see more vehicles pulling up outside the rear entrance. Julian Croix's people had anticipated the possibility that intruders might try to escape through the loading area.

We were trapped.

"Windows?" Bill suggested.

I looked up at the small windows set high in the warehouse walls, designed for ventilation rather than access. They might be large enough to squeeze through, but reaching them would require climbing equipment we didn't have.

"Wait," Irene said, studying the layout of the warehouse. "What about those shipping containers? If we can get on top of them, we might be able to reach the roof."

She was right. A stack of metal shipping containers sat against the east wall, creating a makeshift staircase that led to within a few feet of the ceiling. From there, we might be able to break through to the roof and escape across the tops of adjacent buildings.

The sound of the main entrance being forced open made the decision for us. We climbed quickly, using the corrugated surfaces of the shipping containers for handholds, trying to stay quiet despite the urgency of our situation.

Behind us, flashlight beams began sweeping through the warehouse as Julian Croix's people spread out to search for intruders. I could hear their voices calling out positions, coordinating their hunt with professional efficiency.

"There," one of them said. "Fresh marks in the dust near the coffin assembly area. They were here recently."

We reached the top of the shipping container stack just as the searchers began moving in our direction. Bill had brought a small crowbar that he used to pry open an access panel in the warehouse roof, creating an opening large enough for us to squeeze through.

"Ladies first," he whispered.

Irene went through the opening, followed by me, then Bill. We found ourselves on the flat roof of the warehouse, surrounded by similar buildings that stretched toward the harbor. The late afternoon sun was blinding after the darkness inside, but it also meant we could see clearly in all directions.

And what I saw made my blood turn cold.

The warehouse wasn't the only building in Julian Croix's shipping operation. The entire block was under his control, with vehicles positioned around every building and men moving between them in coordinated patrols. We weren't just trapped in a single warehouse—we were in the middle of a fortified compound.

"How many people does he have?" Irene asked, studying the tactical deployment below us.

I counted vehicles and estimated personnel. "At least twenty, maybe thirty. All of them human, from what I can tell."

"Human?"

"Daylight operation," Bill explained. "Vampires would be sleeping during the day. These are probably contractors, mercenaries hired to provide security for his shipping business."

That was both good news and bad news. Good because it meant we were dealing with human reflexes and limitations rather than supernatural speed and strength. Bad because it meant Julian Croix had the resources to hire professional security teams, which suggested his operation was much larger and more profitable than we'd realized.

"Movement below," Irene warned.

Through the access panel we'd created, I could see flashlight beams moving systematically through the warehouse. The search team was being thorough, checking every possible hiding place, following our trail toward the shipping containers.

"They'll figure out how we got out," I said. "We need to move before they get up here."

We made our way across the warehouse roof, using ventilation equipment and utility structures for cover. The adjacent building was separated by a gap of about eight feet—jumpable, but not without risk.

Bill went first, landing hard but safely on the next roof. Irene followed, and I brought up the rear, trying not to think about the three-story drop to the concrete below.

From the second building, we could see our car parked three blocks away. But between us and freedom were several more rooftops, at least two more jumps, and the very real possibility that Julian Croix's security team would figure out our escape route before we could reach street level.

"There," Irene pointed toward a fire escape on the far side of the building complex. "If we can reach that, we can get down to the alley."

We moved as quickly as stealth would allow, staying low and avoiding the skylights that might reveal our position to anyone inside the buildings below. Behind us, I could hear shouting from the warehouse as the search team discovered our escape route.

The fire escape was old and rusty, but it held our weight as we climbed down to the alley. From there, it was a three-block run through industrial back streets to reach our car, staying in cover and hoping that Julian Croix's people wouldn't expand their search perimeter quickly enough to catch us.

We made it to the car without being spotted, but I could hear vehicles starting up back at the warehouse complex. They'd be conducting a systematic search of the area, looking for anyone who might have been inside their facility.

"Drive," I told Bill as we climbed into his truck. "Fast, but not fast enough to attract attention."

We made our way out of the harbor district using side streets and parallel routes, putting distance between ourselves and Julian Croix's shipping operation. It wasn't until we'd reached downtown Los Angeles that I felt safe enough to start thinking about what we'd discovered.

"Fifty-five coffins," I said, going over the numbers in my head. "Custom-built, ready for shipment. That's fifty-five vampires Julian Croix is planning to export to other cities."

"Or has already exported," Irene corrected. "Some of those coffins might have been for shipments that already went out."

Bill nodded grimly. "The shipping manifests showed regular departures over the past six months. Could be dozens of vampires already operating in other cities, all of them following Croix's artistic philosophy."

The scope of it was staggering. Julian Croix wasn't just building a vampire coven in Los Angeles—he was creating a national network of immortal artists, each one capable of establishing their own recruitment operation in a new city. San Francisco, Seattle, Portland, and God knew how many other cities could already have active vampire cells targeting their local artistic communities.

"We need to warn people," Irene said. "Contact the authorities in those other cities, let them know what they're dealing with."

"And tell them what?" I asked. "That vampires are real and they're running recruitment operations targeting struggling artists? They'll think we're insane."

"Some of them will," Bill agreed. "But not all. There are people in other cities who've seen things they can't explain, who've been wondering why so many young artists have been disappearing. They might be willing to listen."

I thought about Agent Reynolds, the federal operative who'd helped us during the werewolf crisis. He'd understood the reality of supernatural threats operating in American cities, and he'd hinted that there were others in the government who shared that understanding.

"I might know someone," I said. "Federal contact who's dealt with supernatural threats before. If anyone can get warnings to the right people in other cities, it would be him."

"What about the shipping operation?" Irene asked. "Do we try to shut it down?"

I considered that. The warehouse complex was heavily guarded, and Julian Croix's people now knew that someone had been investigating their operation. Any future approach would be met with much stronger resistance.

But the evidence we'd seen suggested that the shipping operation was the key to Julian Croix's entire strategy. If he couldn't transport his transformed vampires to other cities, his expansion plans would collapse. He'd be limited to building a single coven in Los Angeles, which would be much easier to contain and eliminate.

"We come back," I decided. "But not until we've figured out a way to hit them hard enough to shut down the entire operation permanently."

"When?"

I thought about the shipping manifests Irene had obtained, the regular pattern of departures timed around the new moon. "Next shipment is scheduled for Thursday night. That gives us three days to plan an approach that will put Julian Croix's export business out of commission permanently."

"And if we can't?"

I looked back toward the harbor district, where Julian Croix's shipping operation was probably already implementing new security measures to prevent future intrusions. Somewhere in those warehouses, dozens of custom-built coffins were waiting to transport transformed vampires to cities across the West Coast.

Each coffin represented innocent people who would be hunted, recruited, and transformed into predators. Each shipment would plant the seeds of new vampire covens that would spread Julian Croix's artistic philosophy to communities that had no idea what was coming for them.

"Then Julian Croix wins," I said. "And Los Angeles becomes the headquarters for a vampire network that could eventually spread across the entire country."

The war between us had just escalated beyond anything I'd imagined. It wasn't enough to stop Julian Croix's recruitment operation in Los Angeles—we had to prevent him from exporting his methodology to other cities where it could take root and grow.

Thursday night's shipment couldn't be allowed to leave the harbor.

Whatever it took, however dangerous it might be, we had to find a way to shut down Julian Croix's expansion plans before they metastasized beyond our ability to contain them.

Some battles were won through patient intelligence gathering and careful tactical planning but this was going to require the kind of direct action that either ended the threat permanently or got everyone involved killed trying.

After what I'd seen in that warehouse, after counting fifty-five coffins ready to ship vampires across the country, I was ready for that kind of fight.

Julian Croix thought he was building an artistic empire. What he was really building was his own destruction.

Thursday night would prove which one of us was right.

A Warning in Silver

The phone yanked me out of sleep at seven Tuesday morning. I'd been up until dawn staring at maps of Croix's shipping setup, trying to figure angles. I grabbed the receiver on the third ring, my voice coming out rougher than I'd intended.

"Vance Investigations."

"Ellie, it's me." Bill Kowalski's voice was tight with pain and something that might have been fear. "I need you to come to Good Samaritan Hospital. Now."

I sat up in the bed I'd made on my office couch, instantly alert. "What happened?"

"They found me. Croix's people. Came at me on the job site around six this morning." A pause filled with the sound of hospital equipment in the background. "I'm alive, but it was close. Too damn close."

"How bad?"

"Bad enough that I'm talking to you from a hospital bed instead of the war room. But not so bad that I can't tell you what I learned about how much vampires hate silver." His voice carried the kind of grim satisfaction that came from surviving something that should have killed you. "They really, really hate silver."

I was already pulling on clothes, checking my weapons out of habit. "I'll be there in twenty minutes. Don't talk to anyone else until I arrive."

"Wasn't planning on it. Room 314. And Ellie? Watch your back. If they came after me this fast, they know exactly who's been hitting their operation."

The line went dead, leaving me staring at the receiver while my mind raced through the implications. Either Croix had supernatural watchers, or he was paying human eyes to track us. Either way, we were blown.

Either way, the gloves were off. Croix was playing for keeps now.

Good Samaritan Hospital squatted in downtown LA like a brick fortress---been patching up the city's wounded since before the first world war. I'd been there before---bullet wounds and broken bones were occupational hazards for private investigators who specialized in cases involving violent criminals.

But I'd never been there to visit someone who'd survived a vampire attack.

Room 314---surgical wing. That told me everything about how close Bill had come to not making this call. I found him propped up in a hospital bed, his chest wrapped in bandages and his left arm in a sling. His face was pale but alert, and his eyes held the kind of hard focus that came from someone who'd been in life-or-death situations before.

"You look like hell," I said, settling into the visitor's chair beside his bed.

"You should see the other guys." He gestured toward a water pitcher on the bedside table. "Pour me some of that, would you? Talking hurts, but the morphine's wearing off and I need to tell you what happened while I remember the details."

I poured water into a paper cup and handed it to him, noting the way his right hand shook slightly as he brought it to his lips. Whatever had happened on that construction site, it had been violent enough to leave Bill Kowalski---a man who'd survived fighting werewolves---genuinely shaken.

"Start from the beginning," I said.

Bill took a careful sip of water and leaned back against his pillows. "I was working the Bryson Hotel renovation project downtown. Big job, eight stories, lots of structural work. Started at five-thirty like always, checking the equipment and making sure the site was secure before the crews showed up."

The Bryson Hotel. I knew the place---an old building from the 1920s that had seen better days, the kind of renovation project that kept construction workers busy for months. The perfect place for someone to have an accident that would look like workplace negligence rather than supernatural violence.

"Who else was there?"

"Nobody. That was the point---I always get there early to make sure everything's ready for the day shift. Usually takes me an hour to check all the floors, test the equipment, make sure nobody's stolen anything overnight." He shifted in the bed, wincing as the movement pulled at his bandages. "I was on the fifth floor checking the electrical work when I heard something that didn't belong."

"What kind of something?"

"Footsteps. Wrong somehow---too light, too deliberate. Like someone trying not to be heard but didn't quite understand how sound carried in an empty building." Bill's expression hardened. "I knew immediately it wasn't one of my guys. They make noise when they walk, talk to each other, act like normal people. This was different."

I thought about Vincent Ashford's unnatural movement patterns, the way transformed vampires carried themselves like they weren't entirely comfortable in their own bodies. "How many?"

"Two, from what I could tell. Moving together but not talking, coordinating without verbal communication. Professional." He took another sip of water, his hand steadier this time. "I grabbed my crowbar and started toward the stairwell, figuring I could get down to the street level and call for help."

"But they were waiting for you."

"Smart bastards had split up. One came up the main stairs, the other used the freight elevator. Pinned me between the fifth and sixth floors with nowhere to run except up." Bill's voice dropped to a whisper. "That's when I saw what we're really dealing with."

He reached toward the bedside table with his good arm, pulling out a small cloth bag that clinked when he moved it. "The crowbar I was carrying? I had it silver-plated last year, after the werewolf business. Figured it couldn't hurt to be prepared for the next supernatural crisis."

The bag contained metal shavings that gleamed like captured starlight. Silver, scraped from whatever Bill had hit hard enough to leave these remnants behind.

"Show me," I said.

Bill unwrapped the bandages around his left arm carefully, revealing wounds that looked like they'd been made by claws. Four parallel gouges ran from his elbow to his wrist, deep enough to require stitches but not quite deep enough to hit bone. But it was the pattern around the wounds that caught my attention---burned flesh, as if the vampire's claws had been dipped in acid.

"Son of a bitch grabbed my arm while I was swinging the crowbar," Bill explained. "Got his claws into me good, would have ripped my arm off if I hadn't connected with his chest on the backswing."

"What happened when you hit him?"

Bill's expression shifted to something that might have been satisfaction mixed with remembered horror. "He screamed. Not like a human scream---like metal being torn apart, like something fundamental breaking inside him. And the smell..." He shuddered. "Burning meat and sulfur, like he was cooking from the inside out."

I studied the silver shavings, thinking about the implications. We'd known that silver caused vampires pain, but Bill's experience suggested it was much more than simple discomfort. The vampire who'd attacked him had been hurt badly enough to retreat, despite having him outnumbered and isolated.

"How did you get away?"

"The one I hit with the crowbar went down hard, thrashing around on the floor like he was having some kind of seizure. Gave me enough time to get past him and make for the stairs." Bill gestured toward his chest bandages. "But the second one was waiting for me on the fourth floor. Faster than anything human had a right to be."

"More claws?"

"Worse. He didn't just want to hurt me---he wanted to send a message." Bill's voice dropped to barely above a whisper. "He carved something into my chest. Three letters. VEL."

I felt my blood turn cold. "The Velvet Coterie."

"Had to be. He was very careful about it, very precise. Made sure each letter was deep enough to scar, but not deep enough to kill me immediately." Bill looked at me with eyes that had seen too much violence. "He wanted me to live long enough to tell you what happened."

Croix wasn't just hitting back---he was making a point. The carved letters, the timing, the way they'd pulled back once their message was delivered---all of it designed to show us we were marked.

"How did you survive?"

Bill reached under his pillow and pulled out what remained of his silver-plated crowbar. The tool had been bent almost in half, and the silver plating was gone from the business end, scraped away by repeated impacts. But there were dark stains along the metal that looked too thick to be entirely human blood.

"Turns out vampires bleed when you hit them hard enough with silver," he said. "First one I knocked down, second one I fought room to room down four flights of stairs. Every time he'd get close enough to use those claws, I'd catch him with the crowbar."

"And the silver kept him from healing?"

"More than that. It seemed to weaken him, slow him down. By the time we reached the ground floor, he was moving like a regular human instead of some kind of supernatural predator." Bill hefted the destroyed crowbar, noting its weight distribution. "That's when I knew I could hurt him bad enough to make him retreat."

"What happened then?"

"I got lucky. Or maybe he got orders to pull back. He was standing over me, ready to finish the job, when he suddenly went very still. Like he was listening to something I couldn't hear." Bill's expression grew troubled. "Then he just... left. Walked out of the building like nothing had happened, leaving me bleeding on the floor."

I thought about that. Vampires didn't typically retreat from fights they were winning unless they had compelling reasons. Julian Croix might have called off the attack once his message had been delivered, or perhaps he'd wanted Bill alive to spread word about what happened to people who interfered with Coterie operations.

"How did you get to the hospital?"

"First construction worker showed up at seven, found me unconscious in the lobby. Figured I'd had an accident with some equipment, called an ambulance." Bill gestured toward his bandages. "Doctors think I fell through a window and got cut up by the glass. They couldn't explain the burn patterns around the wounds, but they did a good job patching me up."

I studied the silver shavings again, thinking about the tactical implications of what Bill had learned. Silver weapons were more than just effective against vampires---they were devastatingly effective. A silver-plated crowbar had been enough to fight off two supernatural predators, even when Bill was outnumbered and trapped.

"We need to get you more silver weapons," I said. "And we need to warn Irene. If they came after you this fast, she could be next."

"Already thought of that." Bill reached toward the bedside table again, pulling out a small address book. "Called her from the payphone downstairs while the doctors were arguing about my treatment. She's safe at the Times building, but she's not leaving until one of us comes to get her."

"Smart woman."

"Smart enough to know that Julian Croix doesn't make empty threats." Bill looked at me with the kind of seriousness that came from someone who'd just survived something that should have killed him. "This wasn't random, Ellie. They knew exactly where to find me, exactly when I'd be alone. That suggests surveillance we haven't detected or intelligence sources we don't know about."

I thought about the professional security teams we'd encountered at the warehouse, the sophisticated way Julian Croix had built his shipping operation. He had the resources to hire human intelligence networks, people who could track our movements and report our patterns without ever showing up on our supernatural radar.

"We're going to have to change our approach," I said. "No more predictable schedules, no more working alone. From now on, we operate like we're at war."

"We are at war." Bill gestured toward his chest wounds. "The question is whether we're prepared to fight the kind of battle Julian Croix has in mind."

I thought about that as I made arrangements with the hospital staff. The doctors wanted to keep Bill for observation---internal injuries, severe blood loss, the possibility of infection from whatever had caused those unusual burn patterns around his wounds. They were talking about keeping him another two days minimum, possibly longer if complications developed.

Bill argued, but the head nurse was having none of it. "Mr. Kowalski, you lost nearly a third of your blood volume. You have deep tissue injuries that need time to heal properly. And those chest wounds..." She glanced at the bandages covering the carved letters. "Whatever caused those requires careful monitoring to prevent infection."

"How long?" Bill asked, defeat creeping into his voice.

"Wednesday afternoon at the earliest, assuming your condition remains stable and we don't see signs of infection." She softened slightly. "You're lucky to be alive, Mr. Kowalski. A few hours more and you would have bled out on that construction site."

I stayed with Bill for another hour, going over what his attack revealed about Julian Croix's capabilities and intentions. We discussed the surveillance implications, the professional execution of the ambush, and most importantly, the devastating effectiveness of silver weapons against vampire physiology.

"I need to contact Irene," I said finally. "And then I need to figure out our next move. Thursday night shipping---we have less than two days to stop it."

"Be careful, Ellie. If they could find me at a construction site, they can find you anywhere."

"Let them try." I touched the silver stiletto in my boot, thinking about the way Bill's silver-plated crowbar had sent two vampires retreating in agony. "After what you learned about how much they hate silver, I'm looking forward to the next encounter."

I spent Tuesday afternoon and evening coordinating with Irene at the Times building, analyzing what Bill's attack revealed about Julian Croix's operation. We couldn't visit Bill again---the hospital had strict visiting hours, and we couldn't risk leading Croix's watchers back to someone who was already vulnerable.

Instead, we focused on arming ourselves properly. Irene had already started the process, purchasing a silver-plated baseball bat from a sporting goods store and researching metalworking shops that could silver-plate weapons on short notice. By Tuesday evening, we'd identified three facilities that could handle rush orders.

Wednesday morning, I returned to Good Samaritan Hospital. Bill looked better---color returning to his face, moving with less obvious pain. The doctors were pleased with his recovery, attributing it to his exceptional physical condition and previous combat experience. They didn't know that experience came from fighting werewolves, not human enemies.

"They're letting me out this afternoon," Bill reported when I arrived at his room. "Wound healing is progressing faster than expected, no signs of infection. I'll need to take it easy for a few days, but I can function."

"That's good, because we need you." I pulled out the silver-plated weapons Irene and I had collected. "Baseball bat, crowbar, two combat knives, and a set of brass knuckles. All silver-plated, all ready for vampire hunting."

Bill hefted the crowbar, testing its weight and balance. "Better than the one I destroyed. Good work."

At three o'clock Wednesday afternoon, I checked Bill out of Good Samaritan Hospital against continued medical advice. The doctors insisted he needed more recovery time, more monitoring, more bed rest. Bill signed the discharge papers and walked out with his new arsenal of silver weapons.

"Where to now?" Bill asked as we left the hospital and headed toward my car.

"The war room. We need to contact Irene and plan our next move." Thursday night shipping---less than twenty-four hours to stop it. "And we need to figure out how to get close enough to that warehouse complex to shut down the export operation permanently."

"What about more attacks? If they came after me, they'll come after you and Irene too."

I touched the silver stiletto in my boot, thinking about the weapons cache we'd been building. "Let them come. After what you learned about how much vampires hate silver, I'm looking forward to the next encounter."

The drive to Bill's warehouse took twenty minutes through downtown Los Angeles traffic, with both of us constantly checking mirrors and side streets for signs of surveillance. But the city looked normal---businessmen hurrying to office buildings, shoppers heading toward department stores, the usual mixture of human activity that had nothing to do with supernatural warfare.

That was the most disturbing part. Julian Croix's operation existed in the shadows of ordinary life, hidden behind legitimate businesses and normal social interactions. The vampires who'd attacked Bill had probably disappeared back into their daytime hiding places, indistinguishable from any other nocturnal predators seeking shelter from the sun.

"There," Bill said, pointing toward a black sedan that had been following us for the past six blocks. "Same car, maintaining distance, professional surveillance."

I checked the rearview mirror and saw what he meant. The sedan was hanging back far enough to avoid detection by amateur observers, but close enough to maintain visual contact. The driver was good---probably ex-military or ex-law enforcement, someone with training in urban surveillance techniques.

"Human or vampire?"

"Human, from the way he's handling the daylight. But that doesn't make him less dangerous." Bill checked his watch. "Nine-thirty in the morning. If they're using human assets for daytime surveillance, that suggests a much larger operation than we realized."

I made a series of random turns, testing whether the sedan would follow. It did, maintaining the same professional distance, confirming that we were being actively tracked. Julian Croix wasn't just retaliating for the warehouse intrusion---he was gathering intelligence for future operations.

"We need to lose him before we reach the war room," I said.

"I know a place."

Bill directed me toward the garment district, where narrow streets and heavy truck traffic would make surveillance difficult to maintain. We led the sedan through a maze of loading docks and industrial alleys, using delivery trucks for cover and sudden turns to break visual contact.

By the time we reached the warehouse on Mateo Street, we'd lost our tail. But the experience had driven home how much the tactical situation had changed since Monday's infiltration. Julian Croix was no longer simply defending his operations---he was actively hunting the people who threatened them.

The war room looked exactly as we'd left it Monday afternoon, except for one addition. A silver-plated baseball bat leaned against the main research table, along with a note written in Irene's precise handwriting: "Went to the sporting goods store yesterday. Figured we needed better weapons. Back by noon. -I"

"Smart woman," Bill said, hefting the bat with his good arm. "Silver plating over aluminum. Light enough to swing fast, heavy enough to do serious damage."

I found similar modifications throughout the warehouse. Silver-plated tools, improvised weapons with silver components, even a crossbow that someone had fitted with silver-tipped bolts. Irene had spent Tuesday turning Bill's workshop into an armory specifically designed for fighting vampires.

"She's been busy," I observed.

"She's been scared. And fear makes people do stupid things or brilliant things, depending on their personality." Bill settled into a chair at the research table, favoring his injured chest. "In Irene's case, it makes her prepare for a fight."

We spent the next hour analyzing what Bill's attack revealed about Julian Croix's capabilities and intentions. Either Croix had supernatural watchers, or he was paying human eyes to track us. Either way, we were blown. The precision of the attack---targeting Bill specifically, at a location where he was isolated and vulnerable---indicated detailed knowledge of our team members and their daily routines.

Most importantly, the decision to let Bill survive sent a clear message about Julian Croix's strategic priorities. He wasn't trying to eliminate threats to his operation---he was trying to terrorize them into submission. The carved letters on Bill's chest, the careful timing of the attack, the way the vampires had retreated once their message was delivered---it was all designed to demonstrate the Coterie's reach and ruthlessness.

"He wants us to know we're being hunted," I said, studying the silver shavings Bill had scraped from his crowbar. "Every move we make, every place we go, every person we contact---he wants us to wonder if we're walking into another ambush."

"Psychological warfare," Bill agreed. "But it works both ways. What I learned about silver weapons gives us a significant tactical advantage. Those vampires weren't just hurt---they were crippled. Silver doesn't just cause them pain; it disrupts their supernatural abilities."

Ashford was faster and stronger than any of us, but my silver blade dropped him quick enough. The vampire who'd attacked Irene and me in our apartment had backed down when confronted with silver weapons, despite having us outnumbered.

"We need to arm everyone with silver weapons," I decided. "Not just silver bullets, but silver blades, silver-plated clubs, anything that can get close enough to disrupt their abilities."

"I can handle that," Bill said. "Got contacts at metalworking shops all over the city. Give me a day, I can have enough silver weapons to outfit a small army."

"Do it. And make sure Irene knows what happened here. If Julian Croix is escalating to direct attacks on our team, she needs to be prepared for anything."

Bill nodded grimly. "What about you? Where will you be while I'm collecting an arsenal?"

Thursday night shipping---less than twenty-four hours to stop it. Julian Croix's export operation was the key to his entire strategy, the foundation of his plan to build a national network of vampire cells. If we could destroy those fifty-five coffins, prevent that shipment from leaving Los Angeles, we might be able to contain his operation to a single city.

But the warehouse complex was heavily defended, and Julian Croix now knew that someone was actively working to sabotage his plans. Any approach to the shipping facility would be met with overwhelming resistance.

"I'm going to contact Agent Reynolds," I said. "The federal government needs to know about the national scope of this threat. And I'm going to find out if there are any other resources we can bring to bear against Julian Croix's operation."

"Federal resources?"

"Military, police, anyone with guns and badges who can shut down a vampire shipping operation." I looked at the maps of Julian

Croix's property network, thinking about the scale of what we were facing. "We can't fight this alone, Bill. Not anymore."

He nodded slowly, understanding the implications. That changed everything. This wasn't detective work anymore---this was survival.

"Be careful, Ellie. If they could find me at a construction site, they can find you anywhere."

"Let them try." I touched the silver stiletto in my boot, thinking about the way Bill's silver-plated crowbar had sent two vampires retreating in agony. "After what you learned about how much they hate silver, I'm looking forward to the next encounter."

Driving back downtown, I checked every car, every face, every shadow that might be hiding watchers. Croix had turned LA into a hunting ground. Vampires and humans stalking each other through the city's normal face.

But he'd also made a crucial mistake. By attacking Bill, by demonstrating the Coterie's willingness to use violence against anyone who threatened their operations, he'd shown me exactly what kind of evil we were really fighting.

This wasn't good versus evil. This was predator versus prey---whoever hit hardest would walk away.

Julian Croix thought he was the predator in this relationship. The silver shavings in my pocket suggested he was about to learn otherwise.

Before I left, Bill showed me something else Father Rodriguez had provided—a vial of blessed water meant for internal consumption rather than combat use.

"The Father said it wouldn't heal me completely, but it would speed things up. Vampires hate the stuff, but it's supposed to help humans recover from supernatural injuries." He drank half the vial while I watched. "Tastes like copper."

I watched him grimace, then nod. "Already feels better. Like drinking hot soup when you're sick—works from the inside out."

Father Rodriguez, it seemed, had been preparing for this kind of fight longer than any of us realized. The Church knew about vampires, had known for centuries. They'd developed tools not just for fighting them, but for helping their victims survive.

Some private dicks folded when things got personal. But some of us had learned to kill monsters---learned that sometimes you fight fire with fire.

Julian Croix was about to discover which category I belonged to.

The House on the Hill

After dropping Bill at the warehouse Wednesday afternoon, I did something that would have made my old patrol sergeant laugh himself sick. I was going to hit the books before I hit the streets.

Seeing Bill carved up like that had rattled me. We were fighting blind, throwing punches in the dark.

Julian Croix made the werewolves from last year look like street punks. This was organized crime with fangs.

Bill looked better than he had any right to, the holy water having worked some kind of miracle on his injuries. The deepest wounds had closed overnight, and while his ribs still hurt, the pain was manageable.

"Not fully healed," he admitted, "but functional. That's all we need."

I called Irene from the payphone outside Bill's place, pumping nickels into the thing while trucks rumbled past hauling who-knows-what to the docks.

"How's Bill?" No hello, no small talk.

"He was released from the hospital today. Should make a full recovery, but he needs to take it easy for a few days." I looked around the industrial street, noting how normal everything appeared despite the supernatural conflict brewing beneath the surface. "Irene, we need to understand what we're really fighting. I'm going to the Central Library to research that mansion. Can you hit the Times archives and see what you can dig up about Julian Croix's background?"

"Already heading there. This whole setup's got me thinking---Croix isn't running some nickel-and-dime bloodsucker operation." Static crackled across the line. "The money, the organization, the way he gets inside people's heads---this isn't amateur hour."

"What are you thinking?"

"Croix learned this somewhere else. You don't get this good at mind games without practice." I could hear papers rustling in the background. "I'm going to trace his history, see if I can find any European connections or previous operations that match his current methods."

"Good. I'll focus on the mansion itself---the architecture, the history, anything that might explain why he chose that specific location." I checked my watch. "Let's meet back at your apartment around six. That should give us both enough time to dig deep."

"Be careful, Ellie. If we're right about his sophistication, he's probably monitoring us more closely than we realize."

The Central Library looked like a cross between a cathedral and a fortress, all gray stone and narrow windows that made you feel small just walking up the steps. I'd used the place before, chasing down deadbeat dads and insurance cheats. But this was different. This was hunting monsters with a library card.

The research librarian was a middle-aged woman with steel-rimmed glasses who looked like she'd been working there since the building opened. She listened to my request for information about properties on Mulholland Drive with the patient expression of someone who'd heard stranger questions.

"Mulholland Drive was mostly undeveloped until the 1920s," she explained, leading me to a section of the archives dedicated to Los Angeles real estate development. "But that particular property---1864 Mulholland---has an interesting history. There are several folders in our collection relating to the site."

Interesting was an understatement.

The first documents I found dated back to the 1890s, when the property had been part of the Rancho Santa Monica land grant. Spanish colonial records described it as "tierra maldita"---cursed land---that indigenous peoples had avoided for generations. The records cited "psychological disturbances" affecting anyone who spent extended periods near certain stone formations on the property.

An 1897 survey commissioned by a development company included notes from workers who'd reported "unusual sensations" and "mental distress" while examining the land. The survey had been abandoned after three workers had suffered what the supervising engineer described as "nervous breakdowns of mysterious origin."

In 1912, an archaeological expedition from USC had studied the stone circles that gave the property its reputation. Professor Edward Whitman's report was clinical and skeptical, but even he couldn't entirely dismiss what his team had experienced.

"The stone formations appear to be naturally occurring geological features that have been modified by human hands," Whitman had written. "Local indigenous oral traditions claim these circles served ritual purposes, though the specific nature of those rituals remains unclear."

But buried in the report's appendices were worker testimonies that told a different story. Construction laborers clearing brush from the site had reported vivid dreams, heightened emotional states, and periods of dissociation that ceased immediately upon leaving the property.

"The workers' reports, while scientifically inadmissible, suggest that the site continues to produce psychological effects similar to those described in indigenous oral traditions," Whitman had concluded. "Whether these effects result from geological factors, archaeological significance, or psychological suggestion remains to be determined."

The stone circles were still there in 1923, according to the next set of documents I found. But by then, they'd been incorporated into the foundation of a mansion built by a wealthy businessman named Theodore Fairchild.

Fairchild's architectural plans were unlike anything I'd seen in residential construction. Every measurement was specified to the quarter-inch, every material chosen according to criteria that went far beyond normal building requirements. The foundation work alone had required imported limestone from specific quarries in New Mexico, metal components fabricated from custom alloys, and construction techniques designed to enhance rather than simply accommodate the existing stone circles.

The specifications included detailed chemical analyses of soil composition, magnetic field measurements taken at various points throughout the property, and even astronomical calculations showing the relationship between the building's orientation and seasonal celestial events. This wasn't just a house---it was a precision instrument designed to interact with forces that conventional architecture ignored entirely.

Most disturbing were the handwritten notes scattered throughout the margins of the architectural drawings. Theodore Fairchild had apparently been intimately involved in every aspect of the design process, adding modifications and refinements that pushed the project far beyond the original architect's plans.

"Resonant materials as specified by consultant," read one note. "Amplitude effect confirmed in preliminary tests. Dr. H. advises maximum power achievable through geometric precision."

"Foundation stones must align with existing circle formations within 0.5 degrees," read another. "Any deviation will compromise the harmonic relationships essential to proper function."

"Basement level to incorporate acoustic chambers positioned at nodes of maximum field strength. Consultation with Dr. H. indicates this will triple effective range."

Dr. H. I spent the next hour tracking down references to Fairchild's mysterious consultant.

The name that eventually surfaced was Dr. Cornelius Hayworth, a professor of archaeology at USC who'd specialized in pre-Columbian cultures. His academic career had been brief but intense, producing a series of papers in the early 1920s that had challenged conventional understanding of indigenous technological capabilities.

Hayworth's research was housed in the library's collection of discredited academic work---papers that had been professionally rejected but preserved for historical completeness. His theories about indigenous electromagnetic manipulation had been dismissed as pseudoscience by his peers, but reading his work with fresh eyes, I began to understand why Theodore Fairchild had hired him.

Hayworth claimed that certain Native American cultures had possessed sophisticated understanding of what he called "natural electromagnetic resonance systems"---arrangements of stones and metal that could focus and amplify subtle energy fields. According to his research, indigenous peoples had built these arrays at specific geographical locations where geological conditions enhanced the effects.

"The stone circles are not primitive religious structures," Hayworth had written in a 1921 paper. "They are precision instruments designed to interact with naturally occurring electromagnetic phenomena. Proper reconstruction of the amplification arrays, using materials and geometric relationships specified in surviving rock art, could produce effects of unprecedented scope and intensity."

Reading further, I found papers describing Hayworth's experimental work. He'd built scale models of indigenous stone circles, testing various configurations and materials to verify his theories about electromagnetic amplification. The results he'd documented were both fascinating and terrifying.

"Subject testing confirms that properly tuned arrays can induce altered states of consciousness in 97% of individuals exposed to field effects for periods exceeding ten minutes," he'd noted in a 1922 paper. "Subjects report enhanced receptivity to suggestion, decreased critical thinking capacity, and in some cases, temporary episodes of dissociation during which they claim to receive 'instructions' from external sources."

Hayworth's research had been discredited by his academic peers, who'd dismissed his work as pseudoscience. The university had quietly encouraged his resignation in 1925 after colleagues complained that his experiments were "ethically questionable" and "potentially dangerous to student volunteers."

But not before he'd consulted on at least three construction projects in the Los Angeles area.

I found references to the other projects in city planning records. The first had been a private residence in Beverly Hills, built in 1924 for a railroad executive named Charles Henley. Henley had lived in the house for less than a year before selling it at a significant loss, claiming that the building was "psychologically disturbing" to both family and visitors.

The second project had been a spiritual retreat center in the San Fernando Valley, constructed in 1925 for a religious group that had disbanded within six months of moving into the facility. Members had reported that the building "amplified negative emotions" and made meditation or prayer impossible.

Both structures had been demolished by subsequent owners who'd complained of the same phenomena that had plagued the Mulholland Drive property for decades.

But Theodore Fairchild had been different. Instead of running from the supernatural effects, he'd tried to harness and control them.

I found extensive documentation of Fairchild's experiments in a folder labeled "Personal Papers - Donated by Family Estate." These weren't official records, but private notes and journals that had been donated to the library after Fairchild's death.

Fairchild had been tweaking his supernatural radio station for months. Moving copper plates, rebuilding basement rooms, testing different setups. The man was obsessed with getting the signal just right.

"Moved the copper in the east wall. People are more agreeable now. Effect lasts about forty-five minutes." September 1925.

"Installation of additional resonance chambers in sub-basement level creates interference patterns in northwest quadrant," read another entry. "Dr. H. advises repositioning tertiary elements to eliminate dead zones and maximize coverage area."

The journals documented a systematic campaign to turn the mansion into what Fairchild called "a mechanism for influencing human consciousness on an unprecedented scale." He'd hosted regular gatherings of Los Angeles social elite, using his enhanced home to experiment with mass suggestion and psychological manipulation.

"Evening gathering of 47 guests," Fairchild had written in October 1925. "Field effects at maximum intensity. Successfully induced unanimous agreement to investment proposal that would have been rejected under normal circumstances. Subjects retained no memory of decision-making process, expressing surprise at their own choices when contacted the following day."

But the system had been unstable. Fairchild's later journal entries documented increasing problems as he'd pushed the amplification array beyond its design limits. The electromagnetic fields that enhanced his ability to influence others had begun affecting him as well.

"Experiencing auditory phenomena during extended exposure periods," he'd noted in a January 1926 entry. "Voices emanating from the stone formations, speaking in mathematical formulas rather than words. Dr. H. advises reducing field intensity, but effects too valuable to abandon."

"Sleep patterns disrupted," read a February entry. "Dreams consist entirely of geometric calculations and architectural modifications. Waking hours increasingly devoted to refining the array configurations. Margaret expresses concern about my behavior, but she cannot understand the importance of the work."

The final entries were barely legible, filled with mathematical equations and geometric diagrams rather than coherent sentences. Fairchild had apparently spent his last months obsessed with perfecting calculations that would maximize the array's power, working through the night on formulas that his family later described as "incomprehensible gibberish."

"The voices are clearer now," read one of the last coherent entries, dated September 1926. "They speak of harmonics that transcend human limitations, of consciousness unbound by mortal constraints. The array is nearly complete. Soon I will achieve the transformation they promise."

Theodore Fairchild had been found in his study on October 15, 1926, catatonic and surrounded by walls covered with mathematical calculations. His family had committed him to an asylum, where he'd died six months later without ever recovering his sanity.

The mansion had sat empty for twenty-three years before Julian Croix had leased it six months ago through his shell corporation. But Croix's interest in Hayworth's work went back much further—Agent Reynolds's intelligence suggested he'd been studying Hayworth's papers since the 1930s, spending decades understanding the theory before finally implementing it at this location.

Looking at all the evidence spread across my table, I began to understand the true scope of what we were facing. Julian Croix hadn't just chosen the Mulholland Drive property at random---he'd inherited a supernatural weapon that had been under development for decades. Theodore Fairchild had done the experimental work, building and testing an amplification system that could influence human consciousness on a massive scale.

Julian Croix had simply moved in and put that system to use for his own purposes.

The mansion wasn't just a vampire's lair---it was a precision instrument designed to break down human psychological resistance. No wonder his victims walked willingly into transformation. By the time they reached his estate, their mental defenses had already been worn down by forces they couldn't detect or understand.

But Hayworth's papers also revealed crucial information about the system's vulnerabilities.

According to his calculations, the amplification array depended on precise geometric relationships between the foundation stones and the metal components in the walls. Disrupting those relationships---by removing key stones or damaging specific wall sections---could cause the entire system to lose coherence.

"Think of them like radio transmitters," Hayworth had written. "Tune them right, and you get beautiful music. Push them too hard, and they blow up in your face."

More importantly, Hayworth had noted that the system became unstable during periods of maximum activity. When large amounts of electromagnetic energy were being channeled through the mansion, the structural stress on the focusing elements increased dramatically.

"Overload conditions produce catastrophic resonance failure," he'd warned in his technical notes. "The arrays can be forced beyond design capacity deliberately, but the resulting energy release would destroy the installation and likely cause significant structural damage to the surrounding building."

I was copying down equations when the hair on my neck stood up. The guy in the expensive suit near the door---he'd been watching me for the past ten minutes.

Our eyes met, and he smiled like we were old friends. Like he knew exactly what I was reading and why it should worry me.

Julian Croix. Even twenty feet away, even in the dim library light, I knew that face from Irene's photos.

He stood and walked toward the exit with the unhurried confidence of someone who knew exactly how rattled his target was becoming.

As he passed my table on his way to the exit, he paused just long enough to lean down and speak quietly.

"Fascinating reading, Miss Vance. Hayworth was a brilliant man." European accent, old money smooth. The kind of voice that could talk you into anything. "I do hope you're finding the technical specifications useful. Building codes can be so... illuminating when one understands their true purpose."

He straightened and continued toward the exit, but paused near the door to add, "Please give my regards to Miss Stout. I trust her own research is proving equally educational."

Then he was gone, leaving me staring at the space where he'd been standing while my heart hammered against my ribs.

Julian Croix knew exactly what I was researching. More than that, he knew that Irene was conducting her own investigation at the Times archives. He was monitoring both of us, staying informed about our discoveries, probably planning his next moves based on what we learned.

I gathered my materials and left the library as quickly as possible without running, checking constantly for surveillance. The encounter had been brief, but it had accomplished exactly what Julian Croix had intended---letting me know that he was watching, that he was always one step ahead, that he was confident enough in his superiority to approach me directly in a public place.

The drive back to Irene's apartment took forty minutes through downtown traffic, with me using every evasive technique I'd learned from Pop to make sure I wasn't being followed. By the time I reached her building, I was reasonably certain I'd lost any surveillance, but the encounter with Julian Croix had left me deeply unsettled.

I found Irene exactly where I'd expected---surrounded by newspapers, file folders, and handwritten notes that covered every surface of her kitchen table. But the expression on her face when I entered told me that her research had been as disturbing as mine.

"You look like you've seen a ghost," she said, stubbing out a cigarette.

"Worse. I ran into Julian Croix at the library. He knew exactly what I was researching, and he made sure I knew that he's been watching both of us." I dropped into the chair across from her and pulled out my notes. "But I found what we needed, Irene. I know how his amplification system works, and I know how to destroy it."

"Good, because I found out why he's so interested in expanding his operation rapidly." Irene lit another cigarette and gestured toward the papers covering her table. "Julian Croix isn't just building a vampire coven, Ellie. He's been doing this for decades. Moving from city to city, building networks, then disappearing before anyone realizes what he's done. Paris in 1903, Vienna in 1911, Berlin in 1923. Same pattern every time---artistic recruitment, mysterious disappearances, then he vanishes and pops up somewhere else."

She pushed a folder toward me filled with newspaper clippings from European cities, all describing similar phenomena to what we'd been investigating in Los Angeles. Young artists disappearing after attending exclusive gatherings. Suicides among the creative community. Unexplained shipping operations moving mysterious cargo.

"Twenty-six years to perfect what Hayworth only dreamed about."

Looking at the evidence spread between us---Hayworth's technical specifications on one side, Irene's documented history of Julian Croix's operations on the other---I began to see the complete picture.

Julian Croix had been building vampire networks across Europe for decades, using the same psychological manipulation techniques each time. But Los Angeles was different. Here, he'd found a supernatural amplification system that magnified his abilities beyond anything he'd achieved in previous cities. The mansion on Mulholland Drive had transformed him from a successful recruiter into something far more dangerous---a vampire who could break down human resistance on an industrial scale.

"So we need to get invited to one of his gatherings. Get close enough to plant explosives at these structural weak points while he's distracted by his recruitment efforts."

"Exactly. And I think I know how we're going to get that invitation." I thought about Julian Croix's smile in the library, the way he'd spoken to me as if we were old acquaintances engaged in an intellectual game. "He wants us to come. This whole escalation---attacking Bill, calling you directly, monitoring our research---it's all designed to draw us into a final confrontation."

"Why would he want that?"

I thought about the sketch he'd sent me after Vincent Ashford's death, the way he'd praised my "brutal aesthetic" and artistic vision. Julian Croix didn't just want to defeat us---he wanted to convert us. Turn us into masterpieces that would validate his philosophy about transcending human limitations.

"Because he thinks he can win," I said. "He thinks his amplification system makes him invulnerable, that we'll walk into his mansion and be overwhelmed by psychic influence just like every other victim."

"But we know better now."

"We know better now." I looked at the technical specifications that showed exactly where Julian Croix's supernatural fortress was weakest. "He's built his empire on stolen power amplified through ancient ritual sites. We're going to tear it down with good old-fashioned detective work and precisely applied violence."

"What's our next move?" Irene asked.

I thought about the Thursday night shipping deadline, now less than twelve hours away. We had to stop that shipment from leaving Los Angeles, but we also had to destroy the source of Julian Croix's power permanently.

"First, we get this information to Bill tomorrow morning and make sure he's recovered enough to help with tactical planning. Then we contact Agent Reynolds and tell him about the national scope of this threat." I gathered up the architectural drawings, studying the placement of vulnerable points in Julian Croix's amplification system. "And then we wait for Julian Croix to send us that invitation I know is coming."

The conflict between us was escalating rapidly, and I could feel the final confrontation approaching. Julian Croix had made his stronghold from centuries-old supernatural energy focused through architectural mastery. But every weapon had a weakness, and now we knew exactly where to find his.

The werewolves had taught me something: humans with guns and guts could beat monsters with claws and magic. Croix had his ancient mumbo-jumbo.

We had dynamite and bullets.

He was about to find out how dangerous cornered humans could be.

The Critic

Thursday morning brought crisp April air to Los Angeles, the kind of weather that reminded you this was actually a city and not just orange groves with delusions of grandeur. I was making coffee when the phone rang, sharp as a gunshot in the morning quiet.

"Miss Vance?" The voice was clipped, professional, with just enough authority to make me reach for the notepad I kept by the phone. "Agent Reynolds, Federal Bureau of Investigation. We met last October during the Crescent Club investigation."

My blood chilled, then heated. Agent Reynolds was the federal agent I met after defeating the werewolves of the Crescent Club, the man who'd confirmed that somewhere in Washington, people knew monsters were real. If he was calling now, Julian Croix's vampire empire had attracted the wrong kind of attention.

"I remember," I said, checking the locks on my front door by reflex. "What can I do for you, Agent Reynolds?"

"We need to meet. Developments in your current case require federal coordination." His tone carried measured urgency—the kind that suggested he was calling from an office where other people might be listening. "Are you familiar with Clifton's Cafeteria on Broadway?"

"I can find it."

"One hour. Come alone, but bring any research materials you've gathered on your subject. And Miss Vance?" He paused, and I could hear papers rustling in the background. "Be very careful. The individual you're investigating has attracted attention from sources operating considerably above local law enforcement."

The line went dead, leaving me staring at the receiver while coffee percolated on the stove. Federal attention meant Julian Croix's operation had grown beyond anything I'd imagined, but it also meant I might finally have access to resources that could match his supernatural advantages.

I gathered the architectural drawings from Theodore Fairchild's mansion, Dr. Hayworth's technical specifications, and the shipping manifests Irene had obtained from her newspaper contacts. Whatever Agent Reynolds wanted to discuss, he'd need to understand the full scope of what we were facing.

Clifton's Cafeteria occupied a prominent Broadway corner, a massive art deco establishment that had been feeding downtown workers since 1935. The place looked like someone had crossed a restaurant with a museum, murals of California history covering every wall.

I found Agent Reynolds at a corner table near the back, where he could watch both entrances while maintaining the appearance of a businessman grabbing lunch between meetings. Agent Reynolds looked exactly as I remembered from October—middle-aged, well-dressed, with patient alertness suggesting years of dealing with situations that didn't officially exist.

"Miss Vance," he said, standing to shake hands with the formal courtesy of someone who'd been trained to maintain professional demeanor under any circumstances. "Thank you for coming. I trust your investigation has been... educational."

"Educational isn't the word I'd use." I sat across from him, noting the federal briefcase positioned where he could reach it quickly if necessary. "Try terrifying. Julian Croix is running a vampire export operation that could go national in a matter of hours."

Agent Reynolds nodded slowly, confirming what I'd suspected—the federal government already knew about Julian Croix's shipping network. "We've been monitoring unusual disappearances in multiple West Coast cities. Young artists, writers, musicians. All talented, all struggling financially, all vanishing without traces local police can follow."

"How long have you been watching?"

"Since August. Our attention was initially drawn by suicide rates among Hollywood's creative community—specifically, the number of prominent individuals who'd taken their own lives after producing what critics described as their finest work." Reynolds opened his briefcase and withdrew a folder thick with newspaper clippings and death certificates. "Seventeen confirmed cases over the past eight months. All of them involving artists who'd recently completed projects that exceeded their previous capabilities."

I thought about Margaret Walker's final painting, the masterpiece that had captured something essential about human vulnerability while demonstrating technical skill she'd never possessed before. Julian Croix had been turning his victims into artistic prodigies before destroying them, using their enhanced creativity to validate his philosophy while eliminating witnesses to his methodology.

"But that's not why you called me," I said.

"No. We called you because our European contacts have provided intelligence about Julian Croix's background that changes the tactical situation considerably." Reynolds pulled out a thick dossier bound in official government folders. "What do you know about vampire hierarchies, Miss Vance?"

"Beyond the basic folklore? Not much."

"Vampire covens operate according to complex social structures that date back centuries. Older vampires command younger ones, established territories are respected by newcomers, and deviation from traditional practices is discouraged through methods that make human warfare look civilized."

Reynolds opened the dossier, revealing surveillance photographs, diplomatic cables, and what appeared to be translated documents written in multiple European languages. The photographs showed Julian Croix at various social gatherings, but these weren't his Hollywood recruitment parties. These were formal affairs in elaborate European settings, with individuals whose clothing and bearing suggested centuries of aristocratic authority.

"Julian Croix's real name is Julian Beaumont," Reynolds continued. "He's approximately four hundred years old, originally transformed in France during the reign of Louis XIV. For three centuries, he operated according to established vampire traditions—feeding discretely, avoiding public attention, maintaining the secrecy that allows vampire society to coexist with human civilization."

"What changed?"

"His artistic philosophy. During the late nineteenth century, he became obsessed with the idea that vampires were superior beings who should reveal themselves to humanity rather than hiding in shadows. He began recruiting artists, writers, and musicians, transforming them into what he called 'eternal devotees of beauty.' The goal was to create vampire artists whose work would be so magnificent that human society would willingly accept supernatural rule in exchange for access to transcendent art."

The scope of Julian Croix's ambitions was even more staggering than I'd realized. He wasn't just building a network of vampire cells—he was planning to overthrow the fundamental relationship between human and supernatural society.

"European vampire covens viewed this as blasphemy," Reynolds explained. "Vampire survival depends on secrecy, on maintaining the illusion that they're nothing more than folklore and superstition. Julian Croix's plan threatened to expose the entire supernatural community to human scrutiny and potential retaliation."

"So they exiled him."

"In 1923. Stripped of his territorial rights, forbidden from returning to any European city, and marked for destruction if he attempted to implement his artistic revelation philosophy anywhere under European vampire jurisdiction."

"Which is why he came to Los Angeles."

Reynolds nodded grimly. "American territories weren't subject to European vampire law. He could establish his operation here without interference from traditional covens, building toward the public revelation that European vampires had specifically forbidden."

I thought about the shipping manifests showing vampires being exported to cities across the West Coast. Julian Croix wasn't just hiding from European authority—he was building an American vampire empire that would be powerful enough to challenge European traditions directly.

"But here's the crucial intelligence," Reynolds continued. "European covens are now aware of his activities in Los Angeles. They've been monitoring his operation through their own intelligence networks, and they're becoming increasingly concerned about the potential for exposure."

"Concerned enough to intervene?"

"Concerned enough to authorize direct action. Three vampires left London last week with travel documents that show Los Angeles as their destination. They're not coming to join Julian Croix's operation—they're coming to eliminate it."

The tactical situation had just become exponentially more complex. Julian Croix was planning his largest vampire export operation for tonight, while European vampire assassins were en route to destroy his entire network. Los Angeles was about to become a battleground between competing factions of immortal predators.

"When will they arrive?"

"Our immigration contacts suggest tomorrow at the earliest, possibly as late as Saturday. Ship travel takes time, even for vampires with diplomatic resources." Reynolds closed the dossier, his expression grim. "But Miss Vance, you need to understand what European vampire elimination operations involve. They don't just kill the target—they destroy everyone associated with the target's activities. Every human who's had contact with Julian Croix's operation, every potential witness to vampire activity, every possible source of future exposure."

"Including us."

"Including everyone who's investigated Julian Croix's activities, learned about vampire society, or gathered evidence that could compromise supernatural secrecy. The European vampires will view you, Miss Stout, and Mr. Kowalski as security risks that require permanent elimination."

I thought about Irene's newspaper research, Bill's surveillance network, my own investigation into the mansion's supernatural amplification system. We'd gathered enough evidence to prove vampire society's existence to any rational observer, which made us targets for anyone committed to maintaining supernatural secrecy.

"What are you suggesting?"

"That you have a very narrow window to resolve this situation before it escalates beyond anyone's ability to control. Julian Croix's Thursday night shipment represents his final major expansion effort—if you can disrupt it, you'll cripple his operation sufficiently that the European vampires might consider the threat neutralized."

"And if we can't?"

Reynolds's expression grew cold. "Then Los Angeles becomes the site of a vampire war between Julian Croix's American network and European elimination specialists. The collateral damage would be... significant."

I thought about the Thursday night shipping deadline, now less than twelve hours away. We'd planned to wait for Julian Croix's invitation to his mansion, but if European vampires were coming to eliminate all witnesses, waiting might mean dying before we could complete our mission.

"Is there any way the federal government can intervene directly?"

"Officially, the federal government doesn't acknowledge that vampires exist. Unofficially, we maintain intelligence-sharing agreements with European vampire authorities that prevent our supernatural monitoring from escalating into territorial conflicts." Reynolds leaned forward, his voice dropping to levels that wouldn't carry beyond our table. "We can't act against Julian Croix without violating treaties that have kept supernatural warfare off American soil for decades."

"But you can provide intelligence support."

"Limited intelligence support. Resources that might prove useful to private citizens conducting their own investigations into criminal activities that happen to involve supernatural elements."

Reynolds reached into his briefcase and withdrew a manila envelope sealed with federal tape. "Building permit applications are public records, Miss Vance. Anyone can request copies of architectural documents filed with city planning departments."

"Original blueprints for Julian Croix's estate?"

"Complete structural drawings, including basement levels and utility access points not shown in the abbreviated plans available through normal research channels. An anonymous tip suggested that these documents might prove relevant to your investigation."

I accepted the envelope, feeling the weight of detailed architectural plans that would show exactly where Dr. Hayworth's amplification chambers were located within the mansion's structure. With these blueprints, we could target the specific points where explosive charges would cause maximum damage to Julian Croix's supernatural weapon.

"Agent Reynolds, I need to ask you directly—if we succeed in destroying Julian Croix's operation, will the federal government protect us from European vampire retaliation?"

He was quiet for a long moment, considering implications that extended far beyond my personal survival. "If Julian Croix's threat is eliminated before European vampires arrive in Los Angeles, there would be no evidence of exposure requiring cleanup. Mysterious disappearances, unexplained suicides, and criminal shipping operations could all be attributed to conventional criminal activity."

"Plausible deniability."

"For everyone involved. The European vampires return to their territories, the federal government maintains its supernatural intelligence agreements, and private citizens who happened to investigate criminal activities continue their normal lives without official acknowledgment of what they discovered."

It was as close to a promise of protection as Agent Reynolds could offer without compromising federal policy. Stop Julian Croix before the European vampires arrived, and we might survive the cleanup efforts that would follow. Fail, and we'd be eliminated along with everyone else who knew too much about vampire society.

"There's one more thing," Reynolds said, pulling out a smaller envelope marked with the kind of official seals that suggested it contained resources unavailable to normal citizens. "Anonymous intelligence indicates that certain religious institutions maintain archives of materials relevant to combating supernatural threats. Father Rodriguez at Saint Vibiana's Cathedral has been... cooperative... with federal investigations in the past."

The second envelope contained what appeared to be a letter of introduction to a Catholic priest who understood the reality of supernatural warfare. Another resource for our final assault on Julian Croix's operation, assuming we survived long enough to use it.

"Agent Reynolds, I have to ask—why is the federal government helping us? Why not just wait for the European vampires to handle the situation?"

His smile held no warmth. "Because European vampire elimination operations don't distinguish between guilty and innocent, Miss Vance. Julian Croix has been recruiting from Los Angeles' artistic community for over a year. Hundreds of young artists have attended his parties, heard his philosophical presentations, been exposed to his recruitment methods. European vampires would consider all of them potential security risks."

"Mass elimination."

"The European approach prioritizes certainty over precision. They would systematically hunt down everyone who'd had contact with Julian Croix's operation, ensuring that no witnesses remained to compromise vampire secrecy. Young artists who'd merely attended parties, journalists who'd written about mysterious disappearances, even family members who'd asked too many questions about missing relatives."

The scope of the potential slaughter was staggering. Julian Croix's recruitment network had touched hundreds of lives throughout Los Angeles' creative community. European vampire assassins would treat all of them as targets requiring elimination.

"How much time do we have?"

"European vampires typically conduct elimination operations during the new moon period, when darkness provides maximum tactical advantage. The new moon is Saturday night—they'll likely move then, assuming they arrive in time to conduct proper reconnaissance."

Less than forty-eight hours to stop Julian Croix's export operation and destroy his network before European vampires turned Los Angeles into a hunting ground for supernatural cleanup specialists.

"Miss Vance, I want to be absolutely clear about the federal government's position," Reynolds said, closing his briefcase with the precise motions of someone ending an official meeting. "We have no knowledge of your investigation, no record of this conversation, and no official interest in your activities. If you succeed in disrupting criminal operations that happen to involve supernatural elements, any evidence you gather will be treated as the product of private investigation into conventional crimes."

"And if we fail?"

"The federal government will express appropriate regret about the tragic criminal violence that claimed the lives of several Los Angeles residents during a gang war between international smuggling operations."

Agent Reynolds stood, leaving cash on the table to pay for the coffee he'd barely touched. "Good luck, Miss Vance. For what it's worth, I hope you prove that human determination can outmatch supernatural advantages."

I watched him leave through the cafeteria's main entrance, disappearing into the afternoon crowd of downtown shoppers and office workers. The meeting had lasted less than an hour, but it had fundamentally changed the tactical situation we were facing.

We weren't just fighting Julian Croix's vampire network anymore. We were racing against European vampire assassins who would kill everyone in Los Angeles who'd been exposed to supernatural truth. Success meant destroying Julian Croix's operation before the cleanup specialists arrived. Failure meant mass murder on a scale that would dwarf anything Julian Croix had planned.

I opened the envelope containing the original blueprints for the mansion on Mulholland Drive, spreading them across the cafeteria table. The detailed architectural drawings showed everything Agent Reynolds had promised—basement levels, utility access points, and most importantly, the exact locations where Dr. Hayworth's amplification chambers had been installed within the building's structure.

The technical specifications were precise enough for someone with demolitions experience to place charges at points where structural damage would collapse the entire supernatural amplification system. Bill Kowalski's military background included engineering training crucial for calculating the explosives needed to bring down Julian Croix's most powerful weapon.

But first, we had to survive Thursday night's shipping operation.

I left Clifton's Cafeteria and drove directly to Bill's warehouse on Mateo Street, using surveillance detection techniques to ensure I wasn't being followed by either Julian Croix's people or federal agents monitoring my activities. The architectural blueprints represented intelligence that could determine the outcome of our fight against the vampire network, and I couldn't afford to compromise them through careless security.

I found Bill exactly where I'd expected—standing over maps of Julian Croix's property holdings while checking the loads in half a dozen silver-filled magazines for his military surplus rifles. The bruises from Tuesday's vampire attack had faded, but his movements still favored the ribs where Julian Croix's people had worked him over with supernatural strength.

"Federal contact came through," I announced, spreading Agent Reynolds's blueprints across the planning table. "Original architectural drawings for the mansion, including the amplification chambers we need to destroy."

Bill studied the technical specifications with the focused attention of someone who'd spent years analyzing enemy fortifications for vulnerable points. His finger traced the building's structural elements, noting load-bearing walls, utility connections, and the geometric relationships between Dr. Hayworth's resonance chambers.

"This is comprehensive," he said after several minutes of careful study. "Detailed enough for precision demolitions work. If we can get explosive charges to these six locations, the entire amplification system will collapse."

"How much explosives would we need?"

"For a building this size, with reinforced construction designed to channel electromagnetic energy? Significant amounts. Military-grade materials, not the kind of charges you can manufacture from household supplies." Bill looked up from the blueprints, his expression grim. "We'd need federal resources or military connections to acquire sufficient materials."

"Agent Reynolds might be able to help with that, but it would require more federal involvement than his current authorization allows. What about alternative approaches?"

Bill returned to the architectural drawings, studying the mansion's electrical and water systems. "The amplification chambers depend on precise metal components built into the walls and foundations. We don't necessarily need to demolish the entire building—just disrupt the geometric relationships that make the system function."

"Targeted sabotage instead of wholesale destruction."

"Exactly. Remove or damage specific focusing elements, and the entire array becomes unstable. According to these technical notes, Dr. Hayworth warned that disrupting key components could cause catastrophic resonance failures."

I thought about Hayworth's papers describing how the amplification system could be overloaded during periods of maximum energy flow. Julian Croix's recruitment parties weren't just opportunities to influence victims—they were windows of vulnerability when his supernatural weapon was operating at dangerous levels.

"What about overloading the system during a recruitment party?" I asked. "Force it beyond safe operating parameters until it destroys itself?"

Bill studied Hayworth's calculations, noting the warnings about cascade failures and permanent damage to the foundational elements. "Possible, but extremely dangerous. We'd need to be inside the mansion when the system collapsed, and there's no way to predict exactly how the failure would manifest."

"Electromagnetic explosion? Structural collapse?"

"Could be either, or both. Dr. Hayworth's notes suggest that cascade failures produce massive releases of the energy that's been stored in the amplification chambers. Anyone in the building when that happens would be exposed to electromagnetic fields powerful enough to disrupt human neurological function."

"Meaning what, exactly?"

"Meaning we could end up catatonic like Theodore Fairchild, if we're lucky. If we're unlucky, the electromagnetic release could stop our hearts or scramble our brain chemistry beyond recovery."

The risks were staggering, but the alternative was allowing Julian Croix's vampire network to export to eight cities while European assassins prepared to eliminate everyone who'd learned about supernatural society.

"Bill, we're out of time and options. Thursday night's shipment happens whether we're ready or not, and European vampires are coming to clean up loose ends regardless of what we've discovered. If we're going to stop this, it has to be tonight."

He nodded slowly, understanding the tactical realities as clearly as I did. "Then we plan for a suicide mission that might have a chance of success rather than certain failure if we do nothing."

"What would we need?"

"Silver weapons for dealing with Julian Croix's transformed followers. Explosives for targeted sabotage of the amplification system's focusing elements. And most importantly, some way to get invited to tonight's recruitment party so we can access the mansion when the amplification system is operating at maximum capacity."

I thought about Julian Croix's approach at the library, the way he'd spoken to me as if we were engaged in an intellectual competition. He wanted to convert me, to prove that his artistic philosophy could transform even someone who'd been hunting him into a willing follower.

"I think I know how to get that invitation," I said. "But it's going to require putting myself directly in Julian Croix's hands, trusting that his ego will make him overconfident enough to give us the opening we need."

"Ellie, that's incredibly dangerous. Once you're inside his amplification field, your psychological resistance will be compromised. He'll be able to influence your thinking in ways you won't even notice."

"I know. But someone has to get close enough to plant charges at those structural weak points, and it has to be someone he wants to recruit rather than simply kill."

Bill was quiet for several minutes, studying the architectural blueprints and considering the tactical challenges we were facing. Finally, he looked up with the expression of someone who'd accepted an impossible mission because it was the only option available.

"All right. If we're doing this, we do it properly. Military precision, redundant backup plans, and enough firepower to fight our way out if the recruitment approach fails."

"What do you need?"

"Time to acquire explosives and additional silver ammunition. Coordination with Irene to ensure she has backup documentation of everything we've discovered, in case we don't survive to present evidence to federal authorities. And most importantly, confirmation that Agent Reynolds can protect her if European vampires arrive before we've eliminated the threat."

I thought about Irene waiting at her apartment, probably researching additional details about Julian Croix's international network while we planned an assault that might get everyone killed. She deserved to know about the European vampire threat, but she also deserved the chance to escape Los Angeles before elimination specialists arrived.

"I'll call her and explain the situation. Give her the choice of staying to help or leaving town until this is resolved."

"And if she chooses to stay?"

"Then we plan for three people instead of two, and hope that extra intelligence support makes the difference between success and getting everyone killed."

The conflict between human and supernatural was escalating toward a final confrontation determining whether Julian Croix's vampire network spread across America or died in the ruins of his amplified mansion. We had less than twelve hours to prepare for a mission requiring perfect execution under impossible circumstances.

But I'd learned dealing with the Crescent Club was that human determination, applied with sufficient knowledge and careful planning, could overcome supernatural advantages. Julian Croix had built his empire on stolen power amplified through ancient ritual sites. We were going to tear it down with modern weapons and precise violence winning a world war.

Some monsters thought superior firepower guaranteed victory. They were about to learn that humans fought best when they had nothing left to lose.

The invitation to Julian Croix's final recruitment party was coming. When it arrived, we'd be ready.

An Invitation to the Premiere

Thursday evening brought smog-thick darkness that made Los Angeles feel like a city under siege. I'd spent the afternoon at Bill's warehouse, going over Agent Reynolds's blueprints until we could identify every structural weak point in Julian Croix's supernatural amplification system. The federal intelligence had been comprehensive, but it had also confirmed what I'd suspected---we were planning an assault on a building designed to be an impregnable fortress for creatures already transcending human limitations.

By six o'clock, we'd developed three separate approaches for destroying the mansion's psychic amplification chambers, each one requiring different resources and carrying different risks. But all of them depended on getting inside the estate during one of Julian Croix's recruitment parties, when the electromagnetic systems would be operating at maximum capacity and therefore most vulnerable to catastrophic overload.

The invitation we'd been waiting for was probably already on its way.

I was driving back to my office when the radio crackled with news that made my blood turn cold. The evening report mentioned a shipping delay at San Pedro Harbor---customs inspectors conducting "routine examinations" of cargo scheduled for departure on various freight vessels. The delays were described as minor administrative issues, but I recognized federal intervention when I heard it.

Agent Reynolds was buying us time, using bureaucratic procedures to prevent Julian Croix's vampire export operation from departing on schedule. It was a temporary measure at best---customs inspectors could only delay shipments for so long before questions would be asked by people who didn't understand the supernatural implications of fifty-seven coffins bound for eight different cities.

But it meant the Thursday night shipping deadline had been pushed back, possibly to Friday evening. We had gained perhaps twenty-four hours before Julian Croix's vampire network went national.

I parked outside my office building on Spring Street, noting how the April shadows seemed deeper than usual, as if something was absorbing light before it could illuminate the normal world. The feeling of being watched had become so constant over the past week that I barely noticed it anymore, but tonight it carried an intensity suggesting the surveillance was more than professional interest.

Julian Croix knew about the federal meeting. He knew about the shipping delays. And he was probably planning his response with the kind of tactical precision that came from four centuries of supernatural instinct.

My office was exactly as I'd left it that morning---doors locked, papers organized, coffee cup still sitting on my desk next to the architectural drawings I'd been studying before meeting Agent Reynolds. But something felt different. Not wrong, exactly, but changed in some way my subconscious recognized even if my rational mind couldn't identify the specific alteration.

It wasn't until I reached for the light switch that I saw the envelope.

It sat in the exact center of my desk, positioned with mathematical precision on top of the blotter where I couldn't possibly miss it. The envelope was thick, cream-colored paper with a weight and texture suggesting European craftsmanship. My name was written across the front in elegant calligraphy done with an antique fountain pen, each letter formed with attention to detail turning simple correspondence into art.

But it was the return address that made my skin crawl. Embossed in gold leaf at the upper left corner was a simple inscription: "Julian Croix, 1864 Mulholland Drive."

He'd been in my office. Walked through my locked door, placed his invitation on my desk, and left without disturbing anything else. The casual violation of what I'd thought was secure space was more unnerving than any direct threat could have been. It demonstrated capabilities I hadn't anticipated and suggested no place in Los Angeles was safe from his influence.

I picked up the envelope, feeling the substantial weight of whatever was enclosed. This wasn't just a simple letter---there were multiple documents inside, thick enough to suggest Julian Croix had something comprehensive to communicate.

The envelope opened with crisp precision from expensive materials properly maintained. Inside were three items: a formal invitation printed on heavy card stock, a smaller envelope sealed with red wax, and a newspaper clipping.

The invitation was a masterpiece of understated elegance. Gold embossing, careful typography, paper thick enough to use as a weapon. But the content was what made my hands shake as I read:

Mr. Julian Croix cordially requests the pleasure of your company at the world premiere of "The Eternal Canvas" Friday, April 9th, 1949 Eight o'clock in the evening 1864 Mulholland Drive Los Angeles, California

Cocktails and hors d'oeuvres will be served Appropriate artistic attire suggested This invitation extends to Miss Irene Stout

R.S.V.P. not required Your attendance is anticipated

The formal language couldn't disguise what this really was---a challenge issued with absolute confidence in the outcome. Julian Croix wasn't just inviting us to his estate; he was summoning us to witness our own transformation or destruction. The phrase "your attendance is anticipated" carried the weight of inevitability, as if our presence at Friday night's premiere was not a request but a foregone conclusion.

But it was the postscript, written in the same elegant handwriting as the envelope address, that revealed the true nature of his intentions:

"Art is the lie that enables us to realize the truth. I trust you will find Friday evening's presentation... illuminating. The canvas awaits completion."

I thought about the sketch he'd sent after Vincent Ashford's death, how he'd praised my "brutal aesthetic" while describing the killing as artistic expression. Julian Croix didn't just want to convert us---he wanted to turn our final confrontation into the climactic scene of whatever artistic statement he was trying to make.

The newspaper clipping was from Thursday morning's Los Angeles Times, specifically a review from the entertainment section. The headline read "UNDERGROUND CINEMA REACHES NEW HEIGHTS OF ARTISTIC ACHIEVEMENT," and the byline belonged to someone I'd never heard of: Harrison Fitzgerald, Film Critic.

I started reading, and immediately understood why Julian Croix had included this particular review:

"The Eternal Canvas" represents a quantum leap forward in cinematic art, a film so revolutionary in its approach to the relationship between mortality and creative expression that it will undoubtedly be studied for decades to come. Director Julian Croix has achieved something unprecedented---a motion picture transcending the medium itself to become a philosophical statement about the nature of artistic immortality.

The film follows a group of struggling artists who discover that true creative expression requires abandoning the limitations imposed by conventional human existence. Through a series of increasingly intense artistic revelations, they learn that mortality is the enemy of genuine artistic achievement, and that only by transcending their humanity can they create works of lasting significance.

What makes "The Eternal Canvas" extraordinary is not just its revolutionary subject matter, but the way Croix has assembled a cast capable of conveying the complex emotional journey from human limitation to artistic transcendence. Each performer brings a depth of understanding to their role that suggests personal experience with the transformation process the film depicts.

This is not cinema for mass consumption. "The Eternal Canvas" demands intellectual engagement, emotional commitment, and a willingness to question fundamental assumptions about the relationship between art and mortality. Audiences seeking conventional entertainment will be disappointed. But for those prepared to encounter a genuine work of art, Friday evening's premiere promises to be a landmark event in the history of American film.

The premiere will be held at Mr. Croix's private estate, with attendance limited to individuals specifically invited based on their demonstrated commitment to serious artistic endeavor. This exclusivity is not pretension but necessity---the film requires an audience capable of appreciating its revolutionary vision.

Rating: Five Stars. Essential viewing for anyone serious about the future of cinematic art.

The review was dated Thursday, April 8th---today. But according to Irene's research on missing persons, Harrison Fitzgerald had disappeared from his apartment seven days ago, leaving behind unpaid bills and a half-finished article about the decline of artistic standards in Hollywood film production. Seven days since his disappearance, but the review was published today. That meant Croix had been keeping him alive—or undead—for a full week, using him like a typewriter that produced perfect critical analysis on demand. How many reviews had Fitzgerald written in that time? How many times had Croix 'preserved' him between sessions?

The review was dated today, but Fitzgerald had disappeared a week ago. A week in Croix's gallery could feel like months to someone experiencing it—the gallery's amplification system distorted time perception for the preserved victims. Seven days of objective time, but potentially months of subjective experience.

Julian Croix had either kept Fitzgerald alive for a week to write this review, or he'd transformed him into a vampire and was using his enhanced abilities to produce sophisticated critical analysis that would attract exactly the sort of people he wanted to recruit. Either way, the review represented evidence of Julian Croix's systematic approach to building public anticipation for his premiere while ensuring only suitable candidates would seek attendance.

The smaller envelope sealed with red wax bore no inscription except my initials embossed in the same gold leaf as the return address. I broke the seal carefully, noting that the wax was still slightly warm to the touch despite having been in my office for who knew how long.

Inside was a single sheet of paper with a brief message written in Julian Croix's distinctive handwriting:

Miss Vance,

By now you understand the scope of what you have chosen to oppose. The federal authorities you consulted today represent institutions that have accommodated supernatural society for decades, maintaining treaties and agreements that ensure conflicts like ours remain contained within acceptable parameters. Their intelligence was accurate but incomplete---I have been preparing for this confrontation considerably longer than they realize.

"Yes, my amplification system can be overloaded. But Dr. Hayworth never considered that someone might want it to overload. I've spent nearly two decades studying his work, understanding the mathematics, preparing for implementation. The six months in this mansion have been merely the culmination of decades of research."

Tomorrow evening's premiere will demonstrate the difference between destruction and transformation. The electromagnetic release that would normally destroy the amplification array will instead be focused through the assembled audience, creating a shared experience of consciousness expansion that will permanently alter everyone present. Your friends will not simply die during the system's collapse---they will be transformed into components of a collective artistic consciousness far more sophisticated than anything they could achieve individually.

You and Miss Stout represent the final elements necessary to complete this transformation. Your investigative skills and her journalistic abilities will be essential for documenting the transcendence process, ensuring that my artistic statement receives the kind of comprehensive analysis it deserves. Your resistance to my influence makes you more valuable, not less---the contrast between human limitation and supernatural capability will provide the dramatic tension that gives the transformation meaning.

The European vampires currently en route to Los Angeles will arrive too late to prevent Friday evening's premiere, though they will undoubtedly attempt to eliminate any witnesses to what they consider my blasphemous violation of traditional vampire secrecy. This urgency should clarify your tactical situation: you must either accept my invitation willingly, or attempt to disrupt my plans through violent intervention that will likely result in your deaths before you can accomplish any meaningful damage to my operation.

I trust you will choose the more interesting option.

Your attendance Friday evening will allow me to complete an artistic statement that has been years in preparation. Your absence will merely delay its completion while guaranteeing that you and your associates become casualties of European elimination efforts rather than participants in genuine artistic transcendence.

The choice, as always, remains yours.

Respectfully, Julian Croix

P.S. - The shipping operation you attempted to disrupt has been rescheduled rather than canceled. Federal intervention can delay but not prevent the export of my artistic philosophy to cities that will prove more receptive to supernatural innovation than Los Angeles has been.

I set the letter down and stared at it for several minutes, trying to process the implications of what Julian Croix had revealed. He knew about Agent Reynolds. He knew about the shipping delays. He knew about the European vampire elimination team. And he was using all of these elements as components in some kind of elaborate artistic statement that would climax with our transformation or destruction.

But more disturbing was his claim about the amplification system. If he was telling the truth about controlled overload, then our plan to destroy his supernatural weapon might actually help him achieve whatever he was planning. We'd been preparing to cause an electromagnetic cascade failure that would collapse the entire amplification array. If Julian Croix had found a way to channel that energy into a mass transformation process, our sabotage efforts would become the instrument of his victory.

The phone rang, cutting through my analysis of tactical impossibilities. I picked it up on the second ring, already knowing who was calling.

"Ellie?" Irene's voice carried controlled tension suggesting she'd received her own invitation. "Please tell me you found what I found in your office."

"Embossed invitation, newspaper review, and a personal letter explaining how we're going to become involuntary participants in Julian Croix's artistic masterpiece?"

"That's the one. Along with some additional materials that make me think he's been planning this specific confrontation for considerably longer than we realized."

"What kind of additional materials?"

"Photographs, Ellie. Surveillance photographs of us taken over the past six months. Pictures of our conversations, our meals together, even shots taken inside my apartment that show he's been monitoring our relationship since long before we started investigating his operation."

The scope of Julian Croix's surveillance was staggering. He hadn't just been watching our investigation---he'd been observing our personal lives, studying our relationship, preparing for a final confrontation that would incorporate elements we'd thought were private. Every conversation we'd had about him, every strategic decision we'd made, had been conducted under his observation.

"Irene, we need to assume that every safe house, every secure location we've identified, has been compromised. If he's been watching us for six months, he knows about Bill's warehouse, Agent Reynolds's contact information, every resource we've developed."

"Agreed. Which means that any planning we do for Friday night has to assume Julian Croix will know our approach in advance."

I thought about the architectural blueprints Agent Reynolds had provided, the detailed specifications showing the exact locations of Dr. Hayworth's amplification chambers. If Julian Croix had been monitoring our investigation, he probably knew we'd acquired the technical information necessary to target his supernatural weapon's vulnerable points.

"Unless that's exactly what he wants," I said slowly, the implications becoming clear. "What if our entire investigation has been carefully guided to ensure we'd develop exactly the kind of attack plan he needs for his controlled overload process?"

"You think he's been manipulating us to attack his amplification system?"

"I think Julian Croix is four hundred years old, Irene. He's had centuries to develop long-term strategic thinking. If he wanted to use an electromagnetic cascade failure as the catalyst for mass transformation, he'd need someone with the technical knowledge and demolitions experience to overload the system precisely. He'd need investigators willing to infiltrate his estate during a recruitment party when the amplification array was operating at maximum capacity."

"He'd need us."

"He'd need us. Our investigation, our federal contacts, our tactical planning---all of it might have been orchestrated to put us in the exact position he needs for Friday night's premiere."

The realization was horrifying. Every decision we'd made, every advantage we'd gained, might have been steps in a dance whose choreography had been determined by Julian Croix from the beginning. Our resistance to his influence had made us valuable not as opponents but as unwitting collaborators in whatever artistic statement he was trying to make.

But even if our investigation had been manipulated, we still had one advantage Julian Croix couldn't control: we knew what he was planning. His letter had revealed too much in his confidence, giving us information about the controlled overload process that we could use to develop countermeasures.

"Irene, can you meet me at Bill's warehouse? We need to warn him about the surveillance and figure out if there's any way to turn Julian Croix's overconfidence against him."

"Already on my way. Ellie, there's something else in my invitation package you need to know about."

"What?"

"A list of names. Everyone who's been invited to Friday night's premiere. It's not just artists and critics---there are federal agents, newspaper editors, even a few city officials. Julian Croix isn't just planning a recruitment party. He's planning to transform everyone in Los Angeles who has any knowledge of supernatural activity."

The scope of Julian Croix's ambitions was even more staggering than I'd imagined. He wasn't just building a vampire empire---he was planning to eliminate every potential witness to supernatural society by transforming them into components of his collective artistic consciousness. Agent Reynolds, the federal agents monitoring vampire activity, journalists who'd written about mysterious disappearances, police officers who'd investigated unusual deaths---all of them would be gathered in one location where they could be permanently silenced through transformation.

"How many names?"

"Eighty-seven. Including us, Bill, Agent Reynolds, and about a dozen other federal operatives whose existence I didn't even know about."

Eighty-seven people who knew enough about vampire society to be considered security risks by European elimination specialists. Julian Croix was planning to transform all of them simultaneously, using the amplification system's controlled overload to create a mass consciousness expansion that would turn federal agents into vampire collaborators and journalists into supernatural propagandists.

"We have to stop him."

"I know. But Ellie, if he's really been manipulating our investigation from the beginning, how do we know that stopping him isn't exactly what he wants us to try to do?"

It was the question I'd been avoiding since reading his letter. If Julian Croix had orchestrated our entire investigation to position us for Friday night's confrontation, then our attempts to sabotage his plans might be the final components necessary for his artistic statement's completion.

But the alternative was allowing him to transform eighty-seven people who represented the sum total of America's knowledge about supernatural threats. Without those federal agents and journalists, European vampire elimination efforts would encounter no organized resistance. Julian Croix's artistic philosophy would spread unchecked, supported by a network of transformed collaborators who would ensure that no future investigations could threaten vampire operations.

"Then we make sure we're the ones controlling the confrontation," I said. "Julian Croix thinks he's been manipulating us, but manipulation works both ways. If he needs us to overload his amplification system, we'll give him exactly what he's asking for---with modifications he won't see coming."

I hung up the phone and gathered the invitation materials, studying them for any details that might reveal weaknesses in Julian Croix's planning. The formal invitation, the newspaper review, the

A HUNGER GROWS IN HOLLYWOOD

personal letter---all of them were designed to demonstrate his complete control of the situation while making our attendance at Friday night's premiere seem inevitable.

But inevitability was a psychological weapon, not a tactical reality. Julian Croix's confidence in his artistic vision might be the very overconfidence that would allow us to turn his own plans against him.

The drive to Bill's warehouse took forty minutes through evening traffic, with me using every surveillance detection technique I'd learned from Pop to ensure I wasn't being followed. If Julian Croix had been monitoring us for six months, he probably knew the location of every safe house and meeting place we'd established. But he might not know exactly when we'd figured out the extent of his surveillance, which gave us a narrow window for tactical planning he couldn't predict.

I found Bill and Irene in the warehouse's main planning room, studying multiple copies of invitation materials spread across several tables. But these weren't just the documents Julian Croix had sent---they were detailed analyses, with notes and diagrams covering every aspect of his written communications.

"He made a mistake," Bill announced without preamble as I entered the room. "The paper, the ink, the printing process---they're all European, but the postmark on the delivery envelope shows local postal processing. He didn't mail these invitations through normal channels."

"Hand delivery?"

"Had to be. Which means he or his people were physically present at every delivery location within the past few hours. If we can identify the timing pattern, we might be able to track his movements and figure out where he's operating from besides the Mulholland Drive estate."

Irene looked up from her own analysis of the newspaper review. "The bigger problem is this Harrison Fitzgerald review. I called the Times---they have no record of anyone by that name ever working for them. But the review appeared in this morning's edition, properly typeset and positioned in the entertainment section where readers would expect to find legitimate film criticism."

"How is that possible?"

"The only explanation is that Julian Croix has sufficient influence at the Times to insert material directly into the printing process. Which means he has allies in positions we haven't identified, people who can manipulate information distribution without attracting attention from newspaper management."

The implications were staggering. If Julian Croix could insert false reviews into major newspapers, he had access to publicity networks that would allow him to promote his artistic philosophy to exactly the audiences he wanted to recruit. The Harrison Fitzgerald review had been designed to attract serious film critics, avant-garde artists, and cultural intellectuals---people whose transformation would lend credibility to whatever statement he was trying to make.

"Bill, what about the technical specifications in his letter? Can we verify his claims about controlled overload?"

"That's where it gets interesting." Bill pulled out Agent Reynolds's architectural blueprints and pointed to several sections he'd marked with red ink. "Dr. Hayworth's original papers include theoretical discussions about channeling electromagnetic releases through geometric configurations. He thought it might be possible to focus amplification failures into specific patterns rather than allowing the energy to dissipate randomly."

"But he never tested the theory?"

"Never had the opportunity. Theodore Fairchild went insane before the experiments could be completed, and the university banned Hayworth's research before he could continue with other projects."

"So Julian Croix has had twenty-six years to perfect techniques that Dr. Hayworth only theorized about."

"Exactly. And if he's been experimenting with controlled overload processes, he might have developed capabilities that our sabotage plans can't account for."

I thought about Julian Croix's letter, the casual confidence with which he'd described turning an electromagnetic cascade failure into a tool for mass transformation. If he really had perfected Dr. Hayworth's theories, then our attempts to destroy his amplification system would become the trigger for exactly the kind of artistic statement he was planning.

"Then we change the approach," I said. "Instead of trying to destroy the amplification system, we figure out how to disrupt the controlled overload process itself."

"How?"

"By giving Julian Croix exactly what he wants, but not in the way he expects it." I spread out the architectural blueprints, studying the geometric relationships between the amplification chambers and the mansion's structural elements. "He needs us to cause an electromagnetic cascade failure during Friday night's premiere. But what if we cause the failure before the premiere starts, when the system isn't configured for controlled overload?"

Irene looked up from her analysis of the invitation materials. "You want to sabotage the amplification system before the guests arrive?"

"I want to sabotage Julian Croix's timeline. If the electromagnetic release happens when he's not prepared to channel it, the energy will dissipate randomly just like Dr. Hayworth predicted. Instead of mass transformation, we get system destruction."

"And Julian Croix?"

"Loses his supernatural weapon and his opportunity for artistic transcendence. The European vampire elimination team arrives to find a powerless exile with no amplification capabilities and no way to threaten vampire secrecy."

Bill studied the blueprints, considering the tactical challenges of early sabotage. "It would require infiltrating the estate hours before the premiere, placing charges at the amplification chambers, and triggering the overload while Julian Croix and his followers are still preparing for the evening's events."

"Which means we'd be attacking during daylight hours, when vampires are at their weakest."

"Assuming they follow traditional limitations. Julian Croix might have found ways to overcome daylight vulnerability, just like he's overcome other vampire restrictions."

I thought about the letter's confident tone, how Julian Croix had described our tactical situation as if he'd anticipated every possible approach we might develop. But confidence could be a weakness as well as a strength. If he was so certain of his control over the situation, he might not have prepared for the possibility that we'd reject his invitation entirely in favor of preemptive action.

"There's only one way to find out," I said. "We conduct reconnaissance of the estate during daylight hours Friday, identify the current security arrangements, and determine whether early sabotage is tactically feasible."

"And if it's not?"

"Then we attend Julian Croix's premiere and find a way to turn his controlled overload process into uncontrolled destruction." I looked at the invitation sitting in the center of the planning table, its elegant typography a mockery of the death trap it represented. "Either way, we make sure Friday night is the end of Julian Croix's artistic empire."

The struggle between human and supernatural was approaching its climax with a precision suggesting both sides had been preparing for this confrontation far longer than either was willing to admit. Julian Croix had spent months positioning us for Friday night's premiere, while we'd spent weeks developing the technical knowledge necessary to destroy his supernatural weapon.

But tomorrow would determine whose preparation had been more thorough, and whose understanding of the tactical situation was more complete. Julian Croix believed his artistic vision made him invulnerable to human resistance. We believed his overconfidence would be the weakness that allowed us to turn his own plans against him.

One of us was about to learn that supernatural power meant nothing when applied against human determination backed by precise knowledge and carefully planned violence.

The invitation to Julian Croix's premiere sat on the table like a challenge carved in elegant typography. Friday evening, we would answer that challenge with the kind of response that had ended a world war and defeated every monster that had ever threatened the people I was sworn to protect.

PART THREE

A BLADE IN THE DARK

Gearing Up

The air in the abandoned auto repair shop smelled of motor oil and rust, but it was the best safe house we could find on twelve hours' notice. When every location you've ever considered secure has been under surveillance for six months, you learn to appreciate places nobody would think to watch---businesses that closed down after the war ended and never reopened.

Bill had found it that morning, using contacts from his construction work to locate a building that had been empty long enough to feel forgotten. The garage bay doors had been padlocked shut since 1946, and the office windows were so thick with grime that even direct sunlight couldn't penetrate to the interior. If Julian Croix's people were monitoring us, they'd have to work considerably harder to observe our preparations.

It was nearly midnight when the three of us finally gathered around the worktable Bill had cleared in the main garage bay. Agent Reynolds's blueprints spread across the oil-stained surface like military maps planning an assault on enemy territory, which, I supposed, they were. The detailed architectural drawings showed every level of the mansion at 1864 Mulholland Drive, including basement chambers that had never appeared on any public documents.

"The amplification system is more extensive than we realized," Bill said, pointing to the geometric patterns that ran beneath the mansion's foundation. "Dr. Hayworth didn't just install electromagnetic resonance chambers in the basement. He built the entire house around a framework designed to channel and focus psychic energy."

I studied the blueprints, noting how the building's load-bearing walls followed precise angles that had nothing to do with conventional architecture. The mansion wasn't just sitting on top of an ancient ritual site---it had been constructed to amplify whatever supernatural forces had been drawing people to this location for centuries.

"What does that mean for our demolitions plan?" Irene asked.

"It means that bringing down the amplification system won't be a matter of placing explosive charges at a few key structural points," Bill replied. "The entire building is the weapon. To destroy Julian Croix's supernatural advantage permanently, we'd have to level the whole mansion."

The scope of destruction required was staggering. We weren't talking about sabotaging a few pieces of equipment hidden in basement chambers. We were planning to destroy a building that had taken decades to construct, using materials and techniques that modern demolitions experts would need weeks to analyze properly.

"How much explosives would that require?" I asked.

"More than we can acquire through normal channels, even with federal assistance. Military-grade materials in quantities that would raise questions we can't answer." Bill leaned back against the workbench, his expression grim. "There might be another approach, though."

He traced his finger along the blueprint's geometric patterns, following lines that connected the basement amplification chambers to structural elements throughout the building. The mansion's supernatural framework was complex, but it was also precisely balanced. Like any engineered system, it had vulnerable points where the right type of damage could cause catastrophic failures.

"If we can overload the amplification system during one of Julian Croix's recruitment parties, when it's operating at maximum capacity, the electromagnetic cascade might be powerful enough to destroy the building from the inside," Bill explained. "We wouldn't need external explosives if we could turn his own weapon against him."

The plan had elegant simplicity, but it also required us to be inside the mansion when the supernatural equivalent of a power plant overload occurred. We'd be triggering a catastrophic failure while standing at ground zero of the explosion.

"How would we survive that?" Irene asked.

"We probably wouldn't," I said, understanding the tactical implications. "This isn't a sabotage mission anymore. It's a suicide attack."

The garage fell silent except for the distant sound of late-night traffic on the industrial streets outside. We'd known since Julian Croix's invitation arrived that Friday night would likely be our last chance to stop his operation before European vampires arrived to eliminate all witnesses. But seeing the tactical requirements laid out in federal blueprints made the hopelessness of our situation impossible to ignore.

Irene reached across the worktable and picked up one of the wooden stakes I'd been preparing. I'd spent the evening breaking apart antique furniture Bill had scavenged from the garage's storage room, using a metal file to sharpen the hardwood into weapons that could penetrate supernatural flesh. The improvised stakes brought back memories of the desperate fight in the nightclub, when I'd driven a broken chair leg through a vampire's heart and learned that classical monster lore sometimes contained more truth than modern skepticism wanted to acknowledge.

"Ellie," Irene said, testing the point of the stake against her thumb, "there's something I need to tell you about traditional vampire defenses."

I looked up from the blueprint I'd been studying, noting the careful tone in her voice---she was about to propose something I wouldn't like.

"What sorts of traditional defenses?"

"I've been researching folklore from across Europe, comparing accounts of vampire encounters from different time periods and geographical regions," she said. "There are protective methods that appear consistently in historical records, techniques that might give us additional advantages against Julian Croix's people."

Bill stopped examining the blueprints and turned his attention to our conversation. His experience during the Crescent Club incident had taught him to take supernatural folklore seriously, especially when it might provide tactical advantages against creatures that exceeded human physical capabilities.

"What sorts of techniques?" he asked.

"Garlic, primarily. Not just eating it or wearing it as decoration, but using it to create barriers that vampires find difficult to cross," Irene explained. "Multiple sources describe braided garlic garlands that were hung across doorways and windows to prevent vampire entry. The accounts are specific enough to suggest this isn't just superstition."

I considered the implications. If garlic could create temporary barriers against vampire movement, we might be able to use it to control access routes within the mansion, forcing Julian Croix's people to approach us through predetermined paths where we'd have tactical advantages.

"How effective would garlic barriers be against vampires as old and powerful as Julian Croix?"

"The folklore suggests that traditional defenses work better against younger vampires who are still strongly connected to their human origins," Irene said. "But even older vampires seem to experience discomfort when confronted with properly prepared protective materials."

It wasn't much of an advantage, but in a situation where we'd be outnumbered thirty to one by creatures with supernatural strength and speed, any tactical benefit might make the difference between success and failure. At worst, garlic barriers would slow down attacking vampires long enough for us to bring silver weapons and wooden stakes into play.

"Where would we acquire enough garlic to create effective barriers?" Bill asked.

"The Grand Central Market downtown has vendors who sell produce in bulk quantities," Irene replied. "I could purchase enough garlic to braid several dozen yards of protective garlands, enough to secure multiple rooms within the mansion."

"And the other traditional defense?" I asked, suspecting there was more to her folklore research than plant-based barriers.

"Holy water." Irene met my eyes with the steady gaze of someone who'd anticipated my skeptical reaction. "Accounts from across centuries describe holy water causing immediate, severe pain when it contacts vampire flesh. The effect is described as similar to acid burns, but with additional supernatural properties that disrupt vampire healing abilities."

My first instinct was to dismiss religious folklore as wishful thinking by people who needed to believe divine intervention could protect them from supernatural threats. But my experience with Detective Miller's rosary had proven that certain blessed objects could affect vampire behavior, even if the mechanism wasn't something I understood.

"You want to visit a church and obtain holy water from a priest," I said.

"Saint Vibiana's Cathedral is less than two miles from here," Irene replied. "The cathedral is open all night for prayer and confession. I could speak with one of the priests and request holy water for blessing a family member who's been ill."

It was a reasonable cover story that wouldn't raise questions about supernatural warfare. Catholic priests blessed holy water regularly for legitimate religious purposes, and they rarely inquired deeply into the specific circumstances that prompted such requests.

"How much holy water would we need for tactical effectiveness?"

"The folklore suggests that small amounts can be highly effective if properly applied," Irene said. "A few drops on wooden stakes would enhance their lethality against vampires. Larger quantities could be used to create temporary barriers similar to garlic garlands, or as weapons during close-quarters combat."

I thought about the practical applications. Holy water that could enhance the effectiveness of our wooden stakes might reduce the time required to kill vampires, allowing us to move through the mansion more quickly. And if it could cause severe pain on contact, it might serve as a backup weapon when silver bullets and stakes weren't immediately available.

"It can't hurt," I said finally, echoing the phrase Irene had used to convince me. "If holy water has even minor effects against vampires, it's worth the risk of acquiring it."

"There's one more thing," Irene said, her voice carrying the hesitation of someone about to suggest something even more controversial. "Some of the folklore mentions specific prayers or incantations that can enhance the effectiveness of traditional vampire defenses. Words that focus the protective power of blessed objects."

Bill looked up from the blueprints, his expression skeptical. "You're talking about magic spells."

"I'm talking about documented historical practices that people used to survive vampire encounters," Irene replied. "Whether the mechanism is supernatural, psychological, or simply a matter of confidence and focus, the results are described consistently across multiple sources."

I considered her argument. Whether or not religious incantations had measurable effects against vampires, they might provide psychological benefits that would improve our performance during combat. Facing supernatural creatures required a level of mental preparation that went beyond normal tactical planning.

"What sorts of prayers are we talking about?"

"Latin phrases requesting divine protection against creatures of darkness," Irene said. "Simple words that can be spoken while applying holy water to weapons or barriers. The folklore suggests that the combination of blessed materials and focused intent creates stronger protective effects than either element alone."

It was an approach that would have seemed ridiculous to me six months ago, before werewolves and vampires had forced me to reconsider the boundaries between rational investigation and supernatural reality. Now it seemed like reasonable preparation for a mission that would require every possible advantage.

"All right," I said. "Tomorrow morning, you visit Saint Vibiana's Cathedral and acquire holy water. While you're doing that, I'll purchase garlic at the Grand Central Market and begin preparing protective garlands. Bill, you study these blueprints and identify the specific locations where we'll need to place charges to trigger an amplification system overload."

"And tomorrow evening?" Bill asked.

"Tomorrow evening, we attend Julian Croix's film premiere and find out whether human determination can outmatch four centuries of supernatural experience."

The garage fell quiet again as each of us contemplated the tactical reality we were facing. We were planning an assault on a fortified position defended by creatures that exceeded human capabilities in every measurable category. Our weapons were improvised, our intelligence was incomplete, and our escape routes were nonexistent.

But we also had advantages that Julian Croix might not have anticipated. We understood his tactical weaknesses, thanks to Agent Reynolds's blueprints. We had weapons that could exploit those weaknesses, enhanced by traditional defenses that might provide additional protection. And we had focused determination that came from fighting for something more important than personal survival.

I picked up one of the sharpened wooden stakes and tested its balance. The hardwood felt solid in my grip, reminiscent of the improvised weapon that had saved my life during the nightclub encounter. These stakes would be more carefully prepared, treated with holy water and wielded with full knowledge of their lethal effectiveness against vampire anatomy.

"Irene," I said, "when you're at the cathedral tomorrow morning, I want you to ask the priest about protective blessings for people who are about to face grave danger."

"What sorts of protective blessings?"

"The sort that might help three people survive a situation where the odds are completely against them." I met her eyes across the worktable, seeing my own grim determination reflected in her expression. "If we're going to do this, we might as well ask for all the help we can get."

Bill folded the blueprints carefully, creating a compact package that could be concealed inside his jacket during tomorrow's preparations. The technical specifications represented months of federal intelligence gathering, information that could determine whether our mission succeeded or failed catastrophically.

"One more thing," he said. "These blueprints show service tunnels that connect the mansion to the surrounding hillside. If we can map those passages, we might have escape routes that Julian Croix's people don't know we've identified."

It was the first hopeful tactical development we'd discussed all evening. Service tunnels would provide alternative access points to the mansion's interior, bypassing the main entrances where security would be heaviest. They might also offer escape routes if our sabotage efforts succeeded and we needed to flee before the building collapsed.

"How extensive are the tunnel systems?" I asked.

"According to these blueprints, they extend several hundred yards into the hills behind the mansion," Bill replied. "Originally built for utility access and emergency evacuation, but they've probably been modified over the decades."

"Can we access them without alerting Julian Croix's security?"

"The tunnel entrances are concealed in drainage culverts and maintenance sheds that look abandoned," Bill said, studying the architectural drawings. "If we approach from the correct angles, we might be able to infiltrate the mansion without triggering perimeter alarms."

The tactical situation was still desperate, but it wasn't entirely hopeless. With proper preparation, traditional vampire defenses, and detailed knowledge of the mansion's vulnerabilities, we might have a chance of disrupting Julian Croix's operation before European vampires arrived to eliminate all witnesses.

I looked at the oil-stained garage around us, noting how the shadows seemed deeper now that we'd committed ourselves to tomorrow night's assault. This abandoned repair shop might be the last safe place any of us would ever know. After tomorrow, we'd either be dead or living in a world where our survival had prevented a supernatural war from spreading across the entire country.

"Get some rest," I told Irene and Bill. "Tomorrow's going to be a long day, and tomorrow night is going to be longer."

They gathered their materials and headed toward the office area where Bill had set up sleeping accommodations. I remained in the garage bay, studying the blueprints by lamplight and thinking about the differences between rational planning and desperate hope.

Somewhere in the hills above Los Angeles, Julian Croix was probably making his own preparations for tomorrow night's confrontation. He had centuries of experience, dozens of supernatural allies, and complete knowledge of our tactical limitations. But he also had something I was beginning to recognize as a crucial weakness.

He thought like an artist, not a soldier. His plans were elaborate performances designed to demonstrate his superiority over human limitations. Our plans were simple, focused on achieving specific objectives regardless of personal cost.

Tomorrow night, we'd find out which approach proved more effective when human determination met supernatural power in a fight that would determine the future of everyone who'd ever learned the truth about the creatures hiding in Hollywood's shadows.

The wooden stake felt balanced in my hand as I tested its weight one final time. Tomorrow, this improvised weapon might be the difference between success and failure, between saving Los Angeles and watching it become a hunting ground for European vampire assassins.

Some fights were worth the risk of everything.

The Deathtrap

Dawn came gray and reluctant over the Hollywood Hills, as if even the sun understood what we were about to attempt. I checked my watch---5:47 AM, April 15th, 1949. In fourteen hours, Julian Croix would host his premiere for "The Eternal Canvas," and by then we'd either have destroyed his supernatural weapon or died trying.

The service tunnel entrance looked exactly as Agent Reynolds's blueprints had indicated---a concrete drainage culvert half-hidden by overgrown brush, designed to blend into the hillside so completely that even maintenance crews would have difficulty locating it without detailed maps. Bill had scouted the approach route twice during the night, confirming that Julian Croix's security focused on the mansion's main entrances rather than these forgotten utility passages.

"Remember," Bill whispered as we crouched beside the culvert opening, "these tunnels were built in the 1920s for emergency evacuation. The architectural drawings show they connect directly to the mansion's basement levels, but we don't know what modifications Julian Croix might have made over the past six months."

I adjusted the leather satchel containing our improvised weapons---wooden stakes treated with holy water, silver bullets for Pops, and Detective Miller's rosary blessed by Father Rodriguez at Saint Vibiana's Cathedral. Irene carried a canvas bag filled with braided garlic garlands, each one prepared according to European folklore specifications she'd researched in the Times archives.

"The holy water worked exactly as described," Irene reported quietly. "Father Rodriguez was very specific about the blessing ritual. He said it would remain effective against supernatural influence for forty-eight hours, long enough for our purposes."

The small glass bottles in my jacket pocket felt reassuring against my ribs. If the folklore proved accurate, holy water would serve as both weapon and defense against Julian Croix's psychic manipulation. But we were about to test centuries-old vampire lore against a creature who'd survived four hundred years by adapting to changing circumstances.

"Last chance to reconsider," I said, meeting both their eyes in the dim morning light. "Once we enter that tunnel, we're committed to seeing this through to whatever end awaits us."

"After what Croix did to Zelda, there's no turning back," Irene replied. "If we don't stop him now, European vampires will eliminate everyone who knows the truth about supernatural activity in Los Angeles. That includes us, regardless of what we do today."

Bill nodded grimly. "The federal intelligence was clear---Saturday night, new moon, optimal conditions for vampire elimination operations. We have perhaps thirty-six hours before foreign operatives arrive to clean up Julian Croix's exposure of vampire society."

I thought about the tactical mathematics. Three humans with improvised weapons against a fortified mansion containing dozens of supernatural creatures, all protected by an electromagnetic amplification system designed to break down human psychological resistance. Our chances of survival were negligible, but our chances of success might be slightly better.

"Then let's find out what we're really made of."

The service tunnel was larger than I'd expected---wide enough for two people to walk side by side, with concrete walls that showed no signs of structural deterioration despite twenty-five years of abandonment. Emergency lighting fixtures hung from the ceiling, though the bulbs had long since burned out or been removed. Our flashlights created moving pools of illumination that revealed a passage extending hundreds of yards into the hillside.

"According to the blueprints, this tunnel connects to three different basement levels," Bill explained as we moved deeper underground.

"The lowest level contains Dr. Hayworth's original amplification chambers. The middle level has storage areas and utility connections. The upper basement opens into the mansion's wine cellar, which provides access to the main house."

"How do we know which level to target first?"

"We don't," I admitted. "But the electromagnetic distortions should be strongest near the amplification chambers. If Julian Croix's supernatural weapon is operating, we'll feel it long before we see it."

Twenty minutes of careful movement brought us to the first branch point, where the tunnel split into three directions according to a junction marker installed during original construction. The left passage sloped upward toward the wine cellar, the center passage continued straight toward utility areas, and the right passage descended toward the amplification chambers.

That's when I felt it---a subtle vibration in the air that made my teeth ache and my vision blur slightly around the edges. The sensation was similar to standing too close to powerful electrical equipment, but with an additional quality that seemed to resonate inside my skull.

"Do you feel that?" Irene asked, pressing her hand against the tunnel wall.

"Electromagnetic field distortion," Bill confirmed. "The amplification system is active, even during daylight hours. Julian Croix must be using it to maintain psychological influence over the transformed vampires while they sleep."

The right passage led us deeper into the mansion's supernatural heart, where Dr. Hayworth's experimental work had created a precision instrument for manipulating human consciousness. The vibration in the air grew stronger with each step, accompanied by a low humming sound that seemed to come from the concrete itself.

But there was something else---whispers at the very edge of hearing, voices speaking words I couldn't quite understand. Not real voices, but psychic impressions transmitted through whatever electromagnetic field the amplification chambers were generating.

"Ellie," Irene said softly, stopping beside a heavy steel door marked with radiation warning symbols from the 1920s. "I'm hearing voices. Are you hearing voices?"

"Psychic interference from the amplification system," I replied, though the whispers were becoming clearer, more insistent. They seemed to know my name, speaking familiar phrases in voices I recognized but couldn't immediately place. "Julian Croix is using the electromagnetic field to project thoughts directly into our minds."

The steel door was unlocked, opening onto a circular chamber lined with metal panels covered in geometric patterns that hurt to look at directly. Banks of electrical equipment hummed along the walls, connected by cables to crystal formations mounted in precise configurations around the room's perimeter. At the center of the chamber stood a chair that looked like a cross between scientific apparatus and medieval torture device.

"This is it," Bill said, studying the amplification equipment with professional attention. "Dr. Hayworth's original consciousness manipulation device, modified and enhanced by Julian Croix over the past six months. No wonder his recruitment parties are so effective---anyone who enters this mansion is exposed to subliminal psychological conditioning."

But I was no longer listening to Bill's technical analysis. The whispers had become clear enough to understand, and they were speaking in Zelda's voice.

Ellie, why did you let me die? I trusted you to save me, but you chose your own survival over mine. Look at what your cowardice has cost.

I knew it was psychic manipulation, but the voice carried emotional weight that bypassed rational analysis. Hearing Zelda's reproach made my chest tighten with guilt I'd been suppressing since the night I'd driven a silver blade through her heart.

"Don't listen to the voices," Irene warned, but her expression showed she was hearing similar psychological attacks. "They're designed to exploit our deepest fears and regrets."

You could have saved her, Ellie. If you'd been faster, smarter, more willing to take risks for people you claimed to care about. Instead, you hesitated, and now she's dead because of your weakness.

The whispers were accompanied by visual distortions---transparent figures moving through the chamber, ghostly projections of Julian Croix's past victims reproaching us for failing to save them.

I recognized some faces from newspaper photographs of missing persons, young artists who'd vanished over the past eight months.

"Garlic," I said, fighting to maintain focus through the psychic assault. "Use the garlic garlands to create barriers against this influence."

Irene opened her canvas bag and began stringing braided garlic across the chamber's entrance, securing the plant material to metal fixtures with techniques she'd learned from European folklore research. The effect was immediate and dramatic---the psychic whispers faded to background noise, and the ghostly projections lost coherence.

"The folklore was accurate," she said with relief. "Garlic disrupts vampire psychic abilities, even when transmitted through electromagnetic amplification."

We worked quickly to establish a protected area within the chamber, using garlic garlands to create barriers around the amplification equipment. The plant material seemed to interfere with the geometric patterns in the metal panels, causing sections of the consciousness manipulation device to flicker and lose power.

But destroying the amplification system completely would require more than garlic barriers. Bill examined the electrical connections, identifying power sources and control mechanisms that regulated the entire supernatural weapon.

"If we disable the wrong components, we might cause an uncontrolled electromagnetic release," he said. "Julian Croix claimed he could channel amplification system failures into controlled overload events. We need to be careful about how we sabotage this equipment."

"What happens if we trigger an uncontrolled release?"

"According to Dr. Hayworth's papers, uncontrolled electromagnetic cascade could cause structural damage throughout the mansion, potentially killing anyone inside the building when it collapses," Bill replied. "But a controlled overload would focus the energy into specific patterns Julian Croix has designed for his own purposes."

I considered our options. We could attempt careful sabotage that would disable the amplification system without causing building collapse, but that approach might take hours we didn't have. Or we could trigger catastrophic failure and hope we could escape before the mansion came down around us.

"There's a third option," Irene said, holding up one of the holy water bottles Father Rodriguez had blessed. "According to the folklore, holy water disrupts vampire psychic abilities at the fundamental level. What if we poured it directly into the amplification equipment?"

The idea had elegant simplicity. If holy water could shatter Julian Croix's mental illusions, it might be able to corrupt the electromagnetic patterns his consciousness manipulation device depended on. We wouldn't be destroying the equipment through conventional sabotage---we'd be poisoning it with substances that were fundamentally incompatible with vampire supernatural abilities.

"Try it on a small section first," I suggested. "Let's see what happens when blessed materials contact electromagnetic amplification circuits."

Irene opened one of the bottles and carefully poured holy water onto a metal panel covered with geometric patterns. The results exceeded our most optimistic expectations. The blessed liquid sizzled like acid against the metal, creating clouds of vapor that smelled of sulfur and ozone. The geometric patterns began to flicker and distort, losing the precise mathematical relationships that Dr. Hayworth had calculated to influence human consciousness.

"It's working," Bill said, watching electrical gauges fluctuate as the amplification system struggled to compensate for the holy water's disruptive effects. "The blessed materials are interfering with the electromagnetic fields on a basic level, corrupting the geometric arrays that focus psychic energy."

But our sabotage efforts had triggered automated alarm systems built into the mansion's security network. Warning lights began flashing throughout the chamber, accompanied by a low-pitched siren that would alert Julian Croix's people to intruders in the amplification chambers.

"Time to go," I announced, shouldering my equipment bag. "We've bought ourselves maybe ten minutes before vampire security arrives to investigate the alarms."

We moved quickly through the tunnel system, using Agent Reynolds's blueprints to navigate toward the upper basement levels where we could access the mansion's main structure. But the electromagnetic distortions caused by our holy water sabotage were having unexpected effects on the building's architecture.

Corridors that should have led to stairwells instead opened onto identical hallways stretching in impossible directions. Doors that the blueprints showed connecting to wine cellars revealed rooms we'd already passed through, as if the mansion's interior had become a maze designed to trap intruders.

"We're walking in circles," Irene observed after we'd passed the same electrical junction box three times. "The building is changing around us, creating false passages that don't match the architectural drawings."

The mansion itself had become our enemy, using whatever supernatural properties Julian Croix had enhanced to prevent us from reaching our objectives. We were trapped in a structure that could alter its internal geometry to frustrate normal navigation methods.

"The holy water," I said, understanding what we needed to do. "If blessed materials can disrupt the amplification system, they might be able to break through architectural illusions as well."

Irene opened another bottle and sprinkled holy water along the corridor walls. The effect was immediate and startling---the false walls began to shimmer and dissolve, revealing the true passages behind Julian Croix's psychic construction. The blessed liquid acted like supernatural acid against vampire illusions, burning away deceptions to expose authentic architecture.

"The looping hallway was a mental trap," Bill realized. "Julian Croix was using the amplification system to project false geometry directly into our minds, making us think we were walking through passages that didn't actually exist."

We followed the true corridors revealed by holy water application, using the blessed liquid to test each door and passage before proceeding. The mansion fought our progress with increasingly sophisticated illusions---rooms that appeared to be on fire when they were actually filled with harmless vapor, staircases that seemed to lead upward but actually descended into basement levels, windows that showed daylight scenes from decades past.

But holy water proved effective against every deception. Each application burned away another layer of Julian Croix's supernatural construction, revealing the 1920s architecture Theodore Fairchild had built around Dr. Hayworth's consciousness manipulation experiments.

"There," Irene said, pointing to a heavy wooden door marked with brass nameplate reading "Wine Cellar - Private Collection." "According to the blueprints, that passage connects to the mansion's main levels."

I tested the door handle with holy water before turning it, watching the blessed liquid sizzle against metal that had been treated with vampire supernatural influence. The wine cellar beyond was exactly as Agent Reynolds's architectural drawings had indicated---rows of storage racks filled with bottles from European vineyards, obviously selected for their connection to Julian Croix's centuries-long history.

But the wine cellar also contained evidence of the mansion's darker purposes. Along the walls hung portraits of young men and women I recognized from missing persons reports, painted with techniques that captured not just their physical appearance but something essential about their personalities. These weren't just artistic representations---they were supernatural trophies, preserving the essence of people Julian Croix had transformed into vampire servants.

"His collection," Bill said grimly. "Everyone who's disappeared over the past eight months, preserved for his artistic appreciation."

The portraits were accompanied by small plaques detailing each victim's background and the circumstances of their transformation. Margaret Walker's painting showed her in 1920s theatrical costume, looking radiantly happy in a way her mother would never see again. Zelda's portrait captured her in the moment of transformation, her expression torn between fear and desperate hope.

Looking at those faces, I understood what we were really fighting. Julian Croix didn't just kill his victims---he collected them, turning human transformation into an artistic statement about the superiority of vampire existence. Each painting represented a life stolen, a family destroyed, a future erased to serve his aesthetic philosophy.

"We need to get upstairs," I said, studying the wine cellar layout. "The main house contains the sleeping chambers where Julian

Croix's transformed followers rest during daylight hours. If we can reach them while they're vulnerable, we might be able to reduce the odds we'll face tonight."

But the mansion had more tricks prepared for us. As we approached the staircase leading to the main house, the wine cellar began to fill with whispers---not psychic projections this time, but actual voices speaking from the portraits themselves.

Why are you here, Ellie? You can't save us. We're part of Julian's collection now, preserved forever in artistic immortality. Join us, and you'll never have to fear death or failure again.

The whispers came from Zelda's portrait, but they carried conviction beyond mere psychological manipulation. Something of her consciousness remained trapped within Julian Croix's supernatural artwork, forced to serve as recruitment bait for other potential victims.

"Don't listen," Irene said, but she was staring at one of the older portraits---a young man whose nameplate identified him as Thomas Fairchild, Theodore's son who had disappeared in 1926 shortly before his father's mental breakdown.

She's right, though, Thomas's portrait whispered: *Julian offered us immortality, unlimited time to perfect our artistic abilities. Look at what we've become---free from human limitations, transcendent beings capable of creating eternal beauty.*

The portraits were working together, creating a chorus of supernatural persuasion designed to weaken our resolve. Each voice spoke with intimate knowledge of our deepest fears and desires, offering solutions that required only submission to Julian Croix's artistic vision.

But I'd heard similar promises before, from Zelda herself on the night I'd been forced to kill her. The seductive appeal of vampire immortality was always the same---eternal time to achieve perfection, freedom from human mortality and limitation. What the promises never mentioned was the price: becoming predators who survived by destroying other people's lives.

"Holy water," I said, approaching Zelda's portrait with a bottle of blessed liquid. "If it can disrupt psychic illusions, it might be able to silence supernatural artwork as well."

I poured holy water across the canvas. The stuff ate through paint and cloth like acid. Zelda's voice stopped immediately. The portraits weren't really them anymore—just psychic impressions, recordings of consciousness captured at the moment of transformation. Destroying them didn't kill anyone; they were already dead. It just released the trapped echoes, letting them finally dissipate instead of being forced to repeat their final moments endlessly.

"Thank you," Zelda's echo whispered as the portrait dissolved into ash. Not gratitude from the real Zelda—she was long gone—but from the psychic remnant that had been trapped in paint and canvas.

We applied holy water to the remaining portraits, watching decades of Julian Croix's artistic collection disappear in clouds of sulfurous vapor. Each destroyed painting released a soul that had been trapped for months or years, forced to serve as recruitment propaganda for vampire transformation.

The wine cellar fell silent except for the distant sound of footsteps echoing through the mansion's upper levels. Julian Croix's security forces had discovered our infiltration and were beginning systematic searches of the building. We had perhaps fifteen minutes before they located us in the basement areas.

"Time to face the main house," I said, checking my weapons one final time. "Whatever's waiting for us upstairs, we're about to find out if human determination can outfight supernatural power."

The staircase leading from the wine cellar opened onto a magnificent entrance hall lined with marble columns and crystal chandeliers. Sunlight streamed through stained glass windows, creating colored patterns on the floor that shifted and moved in ways that defied normal physics. The mansion's main levels were even more thoroughly corrupted by Julian Croix's supernatural influence than the basement areas had been.

But we were no longer the same three people who had entered the service tunnel at dawn. We'd learned to recognize vampire illusions and developed effective countermeasures against psychic manipulation. The mansion might be a supernatural weapon designed to break human psychological resistance, but it was a weapon we now understood how to fight.

I strung garlic garlands across the entrance hall doorways, creating barriers that would prevent vampire movement through the mansion's main passages. Irene prepared additional holy water bottles for combat use, while Bill studied architectural details for structural weak points that could be exploited if we needed to bring the building down.

"Remember," I said as we prepared to advance deeper into Julian Croix's stronghold, "we're not just fighting vampires today. We're fighting for everyone who's ever learned the truth about supernatural activity in Los Angeles. If we fail, European vampire assassins will eliminate hundreds of innocent people to protect their species' secrecy."

The mansion responded to our preparations with increased supernatural hostility. Walls began to bleed, chandeliers flickered with unnatural fire, and mirrors showed reflections of rooms we weren't standing in. But each manifestation dissolved when touched with holy water, proving that Julian Croix's power depended on deception rather than genuine reality alteration.

We were ready to face whatever horrors awaited us in the mansion's upper levels. The real question was whether Julian Croix was ready to face three humans who'd learned to fight supernatural threats with knowledge, preparation, and absolute determination to protect the people they cared about.

The Sleeping Guardians

The staircase from the wine cellar led us into the mansion's main hall, where crystal chandeliers cast dancing shadows across marble floors that seemed to pulse with their own malevolent life. But we were no longer the same three people who had entered through service tunnels at dawn. We'd learned to fight Julian Croix's supernatural illusions, and now we were ready to take the fight directly to his sleeping followers.

"Remember," I whispered as we stood at the base of the grand staircase leading to the upper floors, "stakes through the heart take two to three minutes to kill, but they're completely helpless once the wood penetrates. We go quiet, we go fast, and we finish each one before moving to the next."

The mansion's interior stretched before us like a maze designed by someone who understood human psychology well enough to exploit its weaknesses. Corridors branched in directions that didn't match the architectural blueprints. Doorways opened onto rooms that should have been impossible given the building's exterior dimensions. Even the lighting seemed wrong, coming from sources that cast shadows in multiple directions.

But holy water had proven effective against every supernatural deception we'd encountered. I sprinkled blessed liquid along the walls as we moved, watching false passages shimmer and dissolve to reveal the mansion's true layout. The 1920s architecture Theodore Fairchild had built around Dr. Hayworth's amplification chambers was still there, hidden beneath layers of vampire illusion.

"There," Bill said, pointing toward a heavy oak door marked with brass numbers "201." According to Agent Reynolds's blueprints, the mansion's second floor contained the sleeping chambers where Julian Croix's transformed followers rested during daylight hours. "Guest bedrooms converted into vampire crypts."

I tested the door handle with holy water, watching the blessed liquid sizzle against metal that had been treated with supernatural influence. The room beyond was dark despite the morning sunlight that should have been streaming through windows. Heavy curtains blocked all natural light, creating the artificial night vampires required for daytime rest.

At the center of the room stood an ornate coffin that looked like it had been imported from European catacombs. The wood was dark with age, carved with symbols I recognized from Detective Miller's research into supernatural protection. But these weren't protective symbols---they were invitations, designed to channel and focus whatever psychic energy the amplification system generated.

"Holy water first," Irene said, opening one of Father Rodriguez's bottles. "According to the folklore, anointing the coffin should weaken any psychic defenses before we attempt the staking."

She poured blessed liquid across the coffin's surface, and the results exceeded our expectations. The carved symbols began to smoke and char, releasing clouds of sulfurous vapor that smelled like burning flesh. Whatever supernatural protections Julian Croix had placed around his sleeping followers, holy water was systematically destroying them.

But as the psychic defenses collapsed, something else took their place.

The air in the room grew thick and oppressive, filled with whispers that seemed to come from inside my own head. Not vampire voices this time, but something more personal, more painful. Someone I recognized but had hoped never to hear again.

You let me die, Ellie.

Detective Frank Miller stepped out of the shadows beside the coffin, looking exactly as he had during our last conversation six months ago. The same rumpled suit, the same tired eyes, the same expression of grim determination that had defined his approach to police work.

But there was something else in his face now---disappointment so profound it made my chest ache.

I trusted you to watch my back, and you let those werewolves tear me apart. All because you were too slow, too scared, too worried about your own survival to do what needed to be done.

I knew it was an illusion, a psychic projection designed to exploit my deepest guilt and regret. Detective Miller had died fighting werewolves because that's what good cops did---they put themselves between monsters and innocent people, even when it cost them everything. His death hadn't been my fault.

But the illusion spoke with Miller's voice, using words he might have said if he'd survived long enough to blame me for his sacrifice.

Look at what you've become, Ellie. A killer who justifies murder by calling it heroic. You drove a silver blade through Zelda's heart, and you tell yourself it was necessary. But we both know the truth---you enjoyed it. The power over life and death, the feeling of being judge and executioner.

"Don't listen to it," Bill whispered from somewhere behind me, but his voice sounded distant, muffled by the psychic interference filling the room. "It's not really Miller. It's just Julian Croix's psychic manipulation, designed to keep us from reaching the coffin."

The phantom Miller moved closer, and I could smell the familiar scents of cigarettes and aftershave that had defined our partnership during the months we'd worked together. Every detail was perfect, down to the way he held his shoulders when he was disappointed in someone's performance.

You could have saved me, Ellie. If you'd been faster, smarter, more willing to take risks for people you claimed to care about. Instead, you hesitated, and now I'm dead because you weren't good enough when it mattered most.

I pulled out one of the wooden stakes I'd prepared, noting how the holy water Father Rodriguez had blessed made the hardwood feel warm against my palm. If Miller's ghost was guarding this coffin, I'd have to get past him to reach whatever vampire was sleeping inside.

"You're right," I said, meeting the phantom's reproachful gaze. "I wasn't fast enough. I wasn't smart enough. And you died because I failed as a partner."

Miller's expression shifted to something that might have been surprise.

"But you know what, Frank? That's exactly why I'm here. Because I learned from watching you die that sometimes good people have to do terrible things to protect innocent lives. You taught me that being a hero isn't about feeling good about yourself---it's about stopping monsters, regardless of what it costs."

I stepped toward the coffin, and Miller's phantom moved to block my path.

You think killing makes you a hero? You think murder can be justified by good intentions?

"I think you'd rather see me kill vampires than let them kill more people like Margaret Walker and Zelda Kettleton," I replied, raising the blessed stake. "And I think the real Frank Miller would tell me to stop talking and get to work."

The phantom studied my face for a long moment, then stepped aside.

Do what needs to be done, Ellie. But remember---every life you take changes you. Don't let the this turn you into the monster you're fighting.

Miller's ghost faded, leaving me standing beside a coffin that contained one of Julian Croix's transformed followers. I pried open the heavy lid, revealing a young man who might have been handsome before vampire transformation had left his skin pale as marble and his features sharp enough to cut. He lay motionless in the artificial sleep vampires used to survive daylight hours, completely vulnerable to anyone who understood their weaknesses.

I positioned the stake over his heart, raised it with both hands, and drove it down with all the force I could manage.

The effect was immediate and horrifying. The vampire's eyes snapped open, filled with an awareness that would have been terrifying if he'd retained any capacity for movement. But the wooden stake had pierced his heart completely, paralyzing his supernatural abilities while his consciousness remained trapped in a body that would die slowly over the next three minutes.

He tried to speak, probably to beg or threaten or offer bargains that might save his existence. But wooden stakes through vampire hearts didn't permit final speeches. I watched his eyes until the light went out of them, then moved toward the door where Bill and Irene were waiting.

"One down," I said grimly. "How many more coffins are we looking at?"

"Agent Reynolds's blueprints show twelve guest bedrooms on this floor," Bill replied. "If Julian Croix has been using all of them for sleeping chambers, we could be facing a dozen vampires."

"Then we better get moving," Irene said, opening another bottle of holy water. "The sun won't stay up forever, and we need to finish this before they wake."

The second bedroom contained a female vampire who looked like she'd been a dancer before transformation. Her coffin was surrounded by mirrors that reflected nothing, creating an illusion of infinite empty space stretching in all directions. But when Irene poured holy water across the mirror surfaces, they cracked and shattered, revealing a room that was simply decorated with theatrical posters and dance shoes.

This time, the psychic guardian took the form of Irene's own doubts and fears.

The figure that materialized beside the coffin was Zelda Kettleton, but not as she'd appeared during our last conversation. This was Zelda as she might have become if Julian Croix's transformation had succeeded---radiant and otherworldly, possessing timeless beauty that vampire immortality promised to those willing to pay its price.

"You could have saved me," the phantom Zelda said, her voice carrying none of the desperation that had marked our final encounter. "You knew what Julian was offering. You could have helped me understand the choice I was making."

Irene stood frozen beside the dancer's coffin, staring at the supernatural projection of her friend with an expression of profound guilt.

"But you didn't trust me with the truth. You thought I was too weak, too desperate, too willing to make bad decisions. So you let me walk into Julian's trap without giving me the information I needed to make a real choice."

"That's not true," Irene said, but her voice lacked conviction. "We tried to warn you. We told you Julian Croix was dangerous."

"You told me he was dangerous to other people. You never explained that he was dangerous to me specifically, that his artistic philosophy was a recruitment tool designed to target people exactly like me. You let me think I could handle him because you were afraid of how I'd react to the truth."

I moved closer to Irene, noting how the psychic projection was affecting her ability to function. Unlike my encounter with Miller's ghost, this illusion was attacking Irene's confidence rather than her guilt, making her question decisions she'd made with the best information available.

"Irene," I said quietly, "you can't save someone who doesn't want to be saved. Zelda made her own choices."

The phantom Zelda turned to face me, and her expression shifted to something more forgiving than I'd expected.

"She's right, Irene. I chose to ignore your warnings because I wanted to believe Julian could give me what I'd been looking for. You tried to protect me, but I was more interested in the promise of artistic transcendence than I was in listening to friends who cared about my safety."

The projection moved closer to Irene, and for a moment the supernatural beauty faded, revealing the real Zelda underneath---frightened, desperate, but grateful for friends who'd tried to save her despite her own poor judgment.

"I forgive you for not being able to save me from myself. Now forgive yourself, and finish what you started when you agreed to help Ellie fight these monsters."

Irene wiped her eyes and picked up one of the prepared stakes, anointing it with holy water before approaching the dancer's coffin. The lid opened easily, revealing a young woman whose transformation had frozen her in the moment of perfect artistic expression, her face serene despite the supernatural predator she'd become.

The stake went through her heart cleanly, and she died with the same peaceful expression she'd worn in undead sleep.

"Two down," Irene said, though her voice shook slightly. "Ten to go."

We worked systematically through the mansion's upper floor, using holy water to break down psychic defenses before confronting whatever supernatural guardians Julian Croix had placed around each sleeping vampire. Every coffin was protected by illusions designed to exploit personal fears and regrets, but blessed materials proved effective against all of them.

A young male vampire who'd been a painter was guarded by visions of artistic failure and creative impotence. Bill faced projections of everyone he'd failed to save fighting the Crescent Club, supernatural voices blaming him for not being strong enough to protect innocent people from monster attacks.

An older female vampire who'd been a screenwriter was surrounded by phantom studio executives rejecting her work with increasingly personal and devastating criticism. I had to confront illusions of my father's disappointment, supernatural reproaches suggesting I'd dishonored his memory by becoming a killer rather than a proper detective.

Each psychic trial was designed to be personally devastating, tailored to exploit the specific fears and regrets that would paralyze that particular person. But holy water consistently disrupted the supernatural projections, and wooden stakes consistently killed the vampires once we could reach their coffins.

By noon, we'd eliminated eight of Julian Croix's sleeping followers.

The ninth coffin was different. Instead of being placed in a converted bedroom, it occupied a circular chamber at the top of the mansion's tower, surrounded by windows that had been painted black to block sunlight. This was clearly the resting place of someone more important than the artist recruits we'd been eliminating.

"This must be one of Julian Croix's lieutenants," Bill said, studying the elaborate coffin that dominated the tower room. "Someone he transformed years ago, with enough supernatural power to warrant special accommodations."

The coffin itself was a work of art, carved from what appeared to be a single piece of ebony and inlaid with precious metals that formed geometric patterns matching the amplification chambers we'd sabotaged in the basement. This wasn't just a sleeping place---it was part of Julian Croix's supernatural weapon system, designed to channel psychic energy through the mansion's most powerful vampire.

When Irene poured holy water across the coffin's surface, the reaction was violent enough to shake the entire tower. The blessed liquid didn't just sizzle---it exploded, creating clouds of vapor so thick we could barely see each other. The geometric inlays began to glow with supernatural heat, and the carved symbols writhed as if they were alive.

But the psychic guardian that materialized was more sophisticated than anything we'd encountered.

Instead of confronting us with personal guilt or fear, it attacked our fundamental understanding of reality.

The tower room began to shift and change around us, walls sliding into new configurations while the floor tilted at impossible angles. Up became down, left became right, and the painted windows showed scenes from different times and places---medieval battlefields, Renaissance palaces, modern city streets that wouldn't exist for decades.

"Julian's first convert," the thing in the coffin spoke without opening its eyes or moving its lips. "Made vampire in 1623, during the siege of La Rochelle. I have been sleeping for decades, gathering power, learning to manipulate human consciousness on levels your modern minds cannot comprehend."

The voice came from everywhere and nowhere, echoing inside our skulls with authority that bypassed normal hearing. This wasn't just a vampire---it was something ancient, predatory in ways that transcended physical violence.

"You think your blessed water and wooden stakes can destroy four centuries of accumulated supernatural power? You think the faith of one Catholic priest can overcome knowledge gathered from European masters who learned their craft when your country was still wilderness?"

The tower room continued its impossible transformations, creating geometric puzzles that hurt to look at directly. But I'd learned something important from our previous encounters---vampire illusions, no matter how sophisticated, depended on deception rather than genuine reality alteration.

I pulled out Detective Miller's rosary, holding the blessed silver against the ancient vampire's psychic assault.

The room's transformations slowed, then stopped entirely.

"Four centuries of supernatural power," I said, approaching the coffin despite the pressure that seemed to be crushing my chest, "but you're still vulnerable to the same weaknesses that killed vampires in medieval times."

I poured holy water directly onto the ancient vampire's face, watching blessed liquid burn through flesh that had survived since the 1600s. The creature screamed---not with its voice, but with psychic energy that felt like broken glass scraping against the inside of my skull.

But the scream faded as the holy water disrupted its supernatural abilities, leaving just another sleeping predator vulnerable to wooden stakes through the heart.

This death took longer than the others---nearly five minutes of conscious helplessness while the ancient vampire's accumulated power slowly drained away. But it died just like the younger vampires, proving that some vulnerabilities transcended age and experience.

"Nine down," I said, checking my watch. "Three to go, and then we find Julian Croix himself."

The remaining coffins were located in the mansion's basement levels, closer to the amplification chambers we'd sabotaged earlier. These were the newest converts, vampires who'd been transformed so recently they still retained most of their human appearance and limitations.

They died quickly and quietly, their psychic guardians too weak to mount effective resistance against blessed materials and prepared stakes. By two o'clock, we'd killed every vampire sleeping in the mansion except Croix. Twelve in total—the newest converts who needed close supervision during their early transformation period, plus a handful of lieutenants who served as his personal guard. The rest of his network had already been exported or were operating independently in other cities.

"Now comes the hard part," Bill said as we gathered in the mansion's main hall, checking our remaining supplies. "Julian Croix won't be sleeping in some converted bedroom. He'll be in the most protected chamber in the building, surrounded by every supernatural defense he can create."

I looked at the weapons we'd brought and wondered: these materials were effective against Julian Croix's followers, but he was something different. Four hundred years of supernatural experience, with access to amplification technology that could enhance his abilities beyond anything we'd faced.

"Then we find out if human determination can beat vampire arrogance," I said, shouldering my equipment bag. "We've come this far. We finish what we started."

The mansion felt different now that we'd eliminated Julian Croix's sleeping guardians. Lighter somehow, as if the supernatural oppression that had weighed on every room was finally lifting. But I knew that feeling was probably deceptive. The most dangerous part of our mission was still ahead.

Julian Croix was waiting for us somewhere in the depths of his supernatural stronghold, probably surrounded by defenses we hadn't anticipated. But we'd learned to fight vampire illusions, and we'd proven that traditional protective materials could overcome even ancient supernatural power.

Whatever happened next, we were as ready as three humans could be for a confrontation with a creature who'd been perfecting the art of predation since before America existed.

The question was whether being ready would be enough.

The Artist's Legacy

With the last of Julian Croix's sleeping followers dead, the mansion felt hollow, like a theater after the final curtain call. But the silence was deceptive. We'd eliminated his transformed army, but we still hadn't found the master himself or the heart of his operation. According to Agent Reynolds's blueprints, there were subterranean levels beneath the mansion that hadn't appeared on any public architectural documents.

"There," Bill said, pointing toward a section of the main hall where the marble floor showed subtle variations in color and pattern. "The blueprints show a concealed entrance to basement levels that go deeper than the amplification chambers."

I sprinkled holy water along the marble seams, watching the blessed liquid reveal hidden mechanisms that had been masked by supernatural illusion. What had appeared to be solid flooring was actually an elaborate trapdoor system, designed to blend invisibly into the mansion's architecture until activated by someone who knew its secrets.

The heavy stone slab slid aside with the grinding sound of machinery that hadn't been used in months, revealing a staircase that descended into absolute darkness. But it wasn't just darkness---it was an absence of light so complete it seemed to pull illumination out of our flashlights, creating shadows that moved independently of anything casting them.

"Stay close," I whispered as we began our descent. "Whatever Julian Croix has hidden down here, it's probably more dangerous than anything we've faced so far."

The staircase was carved from the same stone as the mansion's foundation, but the walls were decorated with murals that made my skin crawl. Not because they were grotesque or violent, but because they were beautiful in ways that felt fundamentally wrong. Painted figures that looked more real than life, captured in moments of artistic perfection that somehow conveyed the agony of their final transformation.

These weren't just paintings---they were portraits of Julian Croix's victims, preserved at the moment of their death.

The subterranean gallery opened into a vast chamber that must have extended far beyond the mansion's foundation. Cathedral ceilings arched overhead, supported by pillars carved with symbols that hurt to look at directly. But it was the contents of the gallery that made my blood turn to ice.

Julian Croix hadn't just killed his victims. He'd turned them into art.

Display cases lined the walls. What appeared to be incredibly lifelike statues posed in elaborate scenes. But as we moved closer, the horrible truth became clear. These weren't statues at all—they were actual bodies, preserved through some technique that maintained their appearance while trapping their consciousness inside paralyzed flesh.

Unlike the wine cellar portraits—which were just psychic echoes—these were the real people. Their consciousness hadn't been recorded; it had been trapped. They were still aware, still experiencing every moment, unable to move or speak or do anything except exist in whatever nightmare their minds created to cope with eternal paralysis.

"Jesus Christ," Bill whispered, approaching a display case that contained a young woman I recognized from newspaper photographs. "This is Sarah Lynch. She disappeared six months ago from a party in Beverly Hills." 'There's a difference between the portraits and these,' Irene said, her voice shaking. 'The portraits in the wine cellar were recordings—bad enough, but at least those people were already dead. These... these are still alive. Still conscious. Still suffering.'

Sarah stood frozen in a pose of artistic rapture, her arms raised toward an unseen canvas, her face expressing the joy of creative inspiration. A small brass plaque mounted beside the display read: "The Eternal Muse, preserved at the moment of perfect artistic transcendence."

But it was her eyes that revealed the truth. Behind the expression of artistic bliss, Sarah's eyes held an awareness showing some part of her consciousness remained trapped within her preserved body, forced to experience an eternity of motionless horror.

"They're still alive," Irene said, backing away from another display case. "God help us, they're still aware."

The gallery contained dozens of preserved victims, each one positioned in carefully constructed scenes that told the story of Julian Croix's artistic philosophy. Young painters stood before easels displaying masterpieces they'd never lived to complete. Musicians held instruments in performance poses that would never end. Writers sat at desks with fountain pens frozen inches above pages that would never be finished.

Each display was a monument to interrupted creativity, a statement about the relationship between art and mortality that Julian Croix had perverted into something monstrous.

"Look at this," Bill called from the center of the gallery, where a larger display commanded attention from every angle.

The centerpiece contained a familiar figure posed behind a typewriter, his hands positioned over keys he would never press again. Harrison Fitzgerald, the missing critic whose review had appeared in the Times, sat frozen in the act of writing. He'd been trapped like this for seven days, though the gallery's temporal distortion made it feel like months to him. The brass plaque read: 'The Perfect Critic, forever composing praise for artistic achievement that transcends human limitation.'

Harrison's face told a different story. While his body had been positioned to suggest enthusiasm for his task, his eyes held the desperate intelligence of someone trying to communicate a warning. This wasn't an echo or impression—this was the real Harrison Fitzgerald, fully conscious, fully aware, trapped in his own body for the past week.

The plaque beside his display read: "The Perfect Critic, forever composing praise for artistic achievement that transcends human limitation."

I moved closer to Harrison's typewriter, noting that the paper in the machine contained actual text. Line after line of praise for Julian Croix's genius, written in the same style as the fake review that had appeared in the newspaper. But hidden within the flowery prose were subtle distortions, word choices that created a pattern only someone looking carefully would notice.

"He's trying to warn people," I realized, pointing to the typewritten page. "Look at the first letter of each sentence."

R-U-N. H-E. C-O-M-E-S. A-T. N-I-G-H-T.

Harrison Fitzgerald had been turned into a living typewriter, forced to compose endless praise for his captor while desperately trying to embed warnings that might save future victims. The brass plaque indicated he'd been trapped in this condition for months, conscious and aware but unable to do anything except write the words Julian Croix wanted him to write.

"This is what he's been building," Irene said, studying the displays with growing horror. "Not just a vampire coven. A living museum dedicated to his artistic philosophy. He's preserving talented people at the moment of their greatest creative potential, turning them into permanent exhibitions of human artistic achievement."

The scope of Julian Croix's vision was staggering. This wasn't just serial killing---it was the systematic collection and preservation of human creativity, transformed into a monument to his own perceived superiority. Each preserved victim represented years of training, education, and natural talent frozen at the moment of its destruction.

But the gallery contained more than just preserved victims. Along the far wall, larger displays showed scenes that looked like frozen moments from theatrical productions. Groups of preserved figures arranged in elaborate tableaux that recreated dramatic scenes from literature and opera.

"These are from his films," Bill realized, studying a display that showed five figures arranged around a dinner table in what appeared to be a recreation of the Last Supper. "He's been using preserved victims as actors in his artistic projects, positioning them in scenes he can film without worrying about directing living performers."

Each tableau was perfectly composed, with lighting and positioning that would have taken hours to achieve with living actors. But Julian Croix had unlimited time to arrange his preserved cast in exactly the configurations his artistic vision required.

"That's how he's been funding his operation," I said, understanding the horrible economics of Julian Croix's enterprise. "He's not just making films with preserved actors. He's selling the tableaux themselves to collectors who think they're buying sophisticated art installations."

The brass plaques beside each display included price information and provenance details, indicating these weren't just personal projects but commercial ventures. Wealthy collectors who appreciated "unusual artistic statements" were apparently willing to pay enormous sums for what they believed were incredibly lifelike sculptures depicting classical themes.

Julian Croix had turned his victims into a luxury goods business, selling their preserved remains to people who had no idea they were purchasing actual human bodies.

But as we moved deeper into the gallery, studying the full scope of Julian Croix's collection, I became aware that we were no longer alone.

The feeling started as a subtle wrongness in the air, a sense that something was watching us from the shadows between the display cases. Not the trapped awareness of the preserved victims, but something active, predatory, intelligent enough to study our movements and plan its approach.

"We're being watched," I whispered, touching Pops under my jacket.

"I feel it too," Bill replied, scanning the gallery's shadows. "Something that's been waiting for us to get this far into Julian Croix's stronghold."

The attack came from above.

Something dropped from the cathedral ceiling with the fluid grace of a predator that had been planning its assault for several minutes. I caught a glimpse of pale flesh and expensive clothing before the thing landed directly on top of Bill, driving him to the floor with impact that echoed through the gallery like a gunshot.

This wasn't one of the converted artists we'd been fighting. This was something older, more powerful, more confident in its supernatural abilities. Julian Croix's first convert, the masterpiece he'd been perfecting for decades or possibly centuries.

The vampire looked like it might have been handsome once, before transformation had refined its features into something too perfect to be human. Its movements were economical and precise, indicating centuries of experience in supernatural combat. But it was the creature's eyes that were most disturbing---intelligent, artistic, completely lacking in human empathy or morality.

"Julian's greatest work," it said, speaking in a cultured accent that indicated European education. "Transformed in 1852, during his early experiments with artistic immortality. I have been his lieutenant, his student, his most successful demonstration of what vampire enhancement can achieve."

The thing that had been human lifted Bill off the ground with one hand, holding him at arm's length while studying us with the detached interest of a scientist examining laboratory specimens.

"You have eliminated our sleeping followers with admirable efficiency. But sleeping vampires are merely students, works in progress. I am a completed masterpiece, perfected through decades of supernatural refinement."

I drew Pops faster than I'd ever drawn before and put three silver bullets into the vampire's chest before it could react. The blessed silver burned through its clothing and flesh, creating wounds that smoked and sizzled. But instead of dropping Bill and retreating, the creature simply looked down at the bullet holes with mild annoyance.

"Silver causes discomfort, but I am no longer young enough to be seriously injured by conventional weapons." It threw Bill across the gallery with casual strength, sending him crashing into a display case that shattered around his body. "Decades of feeding on artistic talent have enhanced my supernatural abilities beyond what younger vampires can achieve."

Irene threw holy water at the vampire's face, and the blessed liquid burned through its skin like acid. The creature screamed---not with pain, but with artistic outrage, as if we'd just defaced a priceless painting.

"You dare damage Julian's masterpiece?" It moved toward Irene with speed that made tracking its motion almost impossible. "I am a work of art that took fifty years to complete. You have no appreciation for the careful refinement required to achieve this level of supernatural perfection."

I emptied the rest of my clip into the vampire's back, but the silver bullets only seemed to annoy it. This wasn't like the younger vampires we'd been fighting---this creature had accumulated enough supernatural power to shrug off weapons that had been effective against Julian Croix's other followers.

"Wooden stakes," Bill called from where he'd landed among the broken display case. "Traditional weapons. It's still a vampire, regardless of how old or powerful."

I pulled out one of the prepared stakes, anointing it with holy water while the vampire advanced on Irene. But the creature was faster than anything we'd faced, moving with predatory efficiency that came from decades of supernatural combat experience.

It caught Irene's wrist as she tried to throw more holy water, holding her immobilized while studying her face with artistic interest.

"You would make an excellent addition to Julian's collection," it said, tilting its head as if considering different poses for preservation. "The devoted friend, frozen at the moment of ultimate loyalty. Your preserved form could stand beside the detective, creating a tableau about human relationships transcending mortality."

The vampire's grip on Irene's wrist was strong enough to fracture bone, but it was applying just enough pressure to cause pain without permanent damage. This wasn't random violence---it was careful preparation for another preservation project.

I drove the blessed stake toward the vampire's back, hoping to pierce its heart before it could seriously injure Irene. But the creature sensed my approach and spun around, catching my wrist with its free hand and stopping the stake inches from its target.

"Predictable," it said, holding both of us immobilized with supernatural strength that exceeded anything human. "Julian warned me that you would attempt traditional vampire-killing methods. But I am no longer vulnerable to such crude approaches."

The stake felt warm against my palm where the holy water had soaked into the wood, but the vampire's grip prevented me from completing the attack. We were trapped, facing a supernatural predator that had evolved beyond the weaknesses we'd been exploiting against its younger companions.

"However," the creature continued, studying the blessed stake with genuine interest, "I must admit curiosity about your preparation methods. Holy water blessed by Catholic priests working with federal supernatural monitoring programs. Wooden stakes carved from furniture and treated with religious materials. You have been remarkably thorough in your research."

Bill appeared behind the vampire, moving quietly despite his injuries from being thrown across the gallery. In his hands was a broken piece of the display case he'd crashed into---jagged wood nearly two feet long, sharp enough to serve as an improvised weapon.

"Traditional methods," he said, driving the makeshift stake through the vampire's back with all the force his construction-worker strength could manage.

The effect was immediate and devastating. The vampire released both Irene and me, staggering forward as supernatural power began draining out of the wound in its chest. But this creature was too old and too powerful to die quickly---it would take several minutes for the wooden stake to complete its work.

"Impossible," it gasped, reaching behind itself to try to pull out the stake. "Fifty years of supernatural refinement. Julian's greatest artistic achievement. I cannot be destroyed by improvised weapons wielded by ordinary humans."

But the stake was buried too deeply for the vampire to remove, and its supernatural abilities were failing as the wood disrupted its immortal physiology. It collapsed to its knees, then fell forward onto the gallery floor, where it lay motionless except for the shallow breathing that would continue for another few minutes.

"How many more like that are we going to face?" Irene asked, rubbing her wrist where the vampire's grip had left marks.

"Hopefully none," I replied, checking our remaining supplies. The fight had cost us most of our holy water, half our prepared stakes, and all the silver bullets for Pops. We were running low on resources just when we needed them most. I could almost hear Pop's voice: Ellie, sweetie, a gun without ammunition is just a paperweight.

"Julian Croix is still somewhere in this complex," Bill said, studying the gallery layout. "And if that thing was guarding his collection, the master himself is probably in a chamber even deeper underground."

I looked around the gallery one final time, taking in the full scope of Julian Croix's artistic vision. Dozens of preserved victims, frozen in moments of creative transcendence, trapped in an eternity of conscious helplessness while serving as monuments to vampire superiority.

This was what we were fighting to stop. Not just random killings, but the systematic transformation of human creativity into decorative objects for supernatural predators who considered themselves artists.

"Then we finish this," I said, shouldering what remained of our equipment. "Whatever Julian Croix has waiting for us, we're going to end his operation permanently."

The vampire lieutenant's breathing stopped as we prepared to descend deeper into Julian Croix's underground complex. But I knew that death was just the beginning---somewhere below us, the master was waiting with defenses we probably couldn't imagine and power we might not be able to overcome.

The preserved victims watched us leave with eyes that held gratitude, hope, and desperate pleas for the freedom they would never experience again. We were their only chance for justice, their only hope that Julian Croix's artistic philosophy would die with him.

Whether we were strong enough to grant that hope remained to be seen.

Sanctum

The passage beyond the gallery descended through carved stone that felt older than the mansion above us, older than Los Angeles itself. Our flashlights revealed walls covered with symbols that predated any European influence in California---geometric patterns that seemed to shift and writhe when caught in peripheral vision. The air grew thicker with each step, heavy with an oppressive weight that made breathing difficult.

"The amplification system," Bill whispered, steadying himself against the stone wall. "We're getting close to whatever Julian Croix has been building down here."

I checked our remaining supplies as we moved deeper into the earth. Three wooden stakes, two small bottles of holy water, and my silver stiletto. Pops was empty, its magazine exhausted during our fight with the vampire lieutenant. We were walking into the heart of Julian Croix's operation with improvised weapons and prayers.

But I'd learned something important during our descent through the mansion's supernatural defenses. Traditional vampire lore wasn't just folklore---it was tested battlefield intelligence passed down by people who'd survived encounters with creatures like Julian Croix. Holy water burned vampire flesh like acid. Wooden stakes through the heart caused complete paralysis and eventual death. Garlic created barriers that disrupted vampire psychic abilities.

If Julian Croix could be killed, we had the tools to do it.

The passage opened into a circular chamber that felt wrong in ways I couldn't immediately identify. The proportions were subtly off, with a ceiling that seemed both too high and too low depending on where you looked. Carved alcoves lined the walls, each one containing candles that burned with steady flames despite the absence of any air circulation. But it was the far end of the chamber that made my blood turn cold.

A heavy wooden door stood partially open, revealing flickering light from whatever lay beyond. But the door itself was decorated with carvings that depicted scenes of transformation---human figures being changed into something else through processes that looked both surgical and artistic. Each panel told part of a story about the relationship between art and mortality, beauty and horror, creation and destruction.

"That's it," Irene said quietly. "Julian Croix's inner sanctum."

The door opened at my touch, revealing a private screening room that might have belonged to any Hollywood mogul if not for the details that marked it as something far more sinister. Red velvet seats faced a screen where images flickered in perfect clarity, accompanied by sound that seemed to come from the walls themselves. Crystal chandeliers provided ambient lighting that created an atmosphere of intimate theatrical presentation.

But it was the film playing on the screen that made my chest tighten with grief and rage.

Zelda Kettleton moved across the silver screen with ethereal beauty, her face glowing with artistic passion as she discussed her writing with someone beyond the camera's view. This wasn't the desperate, defeated woman I'd known---this was Zelda as she might have been if her talent had been recognized, if her dreams had been validated, if she'd never encountered Julian Croix's seductive promises.

The film showed her reading from manuscripts, laughing at private jokes, speaking about literature with the kind of intellectual excitement that had made her friendship with Irene so meaningful. She looked radiant, confident, alive in ways she'd never been during our brief acquaintance.

"Beautiful, isn't she?"

The voice came from the front row of seats, where a figure sat silhouetted against the screen's glow. Julian Croix turned to face us with the casual confidence of someone who'd been expecting our arrival for hours. He wore an expensive suit that looked like it had been tailored in Europe, and his features held the timeless quality of someone who'd stopped aging decades ago.

But it was his eyes that revealed the true nature of what we were facing. Julian Croix looked at us with the detached interest of an artist studying potential subjects for his next project. There was intelligence there, and aesthetic appreciation, but no trace of human empathy or moral restraint.

"I filmed this three days before her transformation," he continued, gesturing toward the screen where Zelda's image continued to move with lifelike grace. "She was discussing her novel, explaining how she wanted to capture the essence of human longing in prose that would outlast her mortal limitations. Poor child---she understood the goal but lacked the means to achieve it."

I kept my hand near the wooden stakes in my jacket, noting how Julian Croix remained seated despite our obvious hostility. Either he was supremely confident in his supernatural abilities, or the screening room contained defenses we hadn't identified yet.

"Until you offered to help her," I said, studying his face for reactions that might reveal tactical weaknesses.

"Until I offered to help her transcend those limitations entirely," Julian Croix corrected. "Zelda Kettleton possessed genuine artistic vision, but she was trapped within the temporal boundaries of human existence. Seventy years, perhaps eighty if she was fortunate, to develop her craft and create works worthy of immortal appreciation. I offered her unlimited time to perfect her abilities."

The film shifted to a different scene, showing Zelda in what appeared to be Julian Croix's mansion, discussing artistic philosophy with other young people who'd been drawn into his orbit. Her face held an expression of intellectual rapture, as if she'd finally found people who understood her creative ambitions.

"She came to my recruitment parties willingly," Julian Croix said, his voice carrying the careful modulation of someone accustomed to persuading reluctant audiences. "She listened to my explanations of what vampire transformation could offer serious artists. She asked intelligent questions about the relationship between immortality and creative development. She made an informed choice."

"You lied to her," Irene said from behind me. "You never explained what the transformation would actually cost."

Julian Croix's expression shifted to something that might have been mild annoyance, like a professor dealing with a student who'd missed an obvious point.

"I explained exactly what vampire transformation entailed---unlimited time to perfect her craft, freedom from human mortality and its petty concerns, elevation to a higher form of existence that would allow her to create truly eternal art. Miss Kettleton understood the implications completely."

"You never told her she'd become a predator who survived by killing innocent people," I said.

"I told her she'd become a superior being who transcended human moral limitations," Julian Croix replied. "The specific mechanics of vampire sustenance are merely technical details, no more relevant to artistic achievement than a painter's need for canvas and pigments."

The screen showed Zelda signing what appeared to be a contract, her expression serious but hopeful. Julian Croix had documented her consent, creating a record that would absolve him of responsibility for her subsequent transformation and death.

"But Zelda's transformation failed," I continued, watching his face for emotional responses. "She died because you couldn't deliver what you'd promised."

"Miss Kettleton's transformation failed because she retained too much attachment to human moral concepts," Julian Croix said with the clinical detachment of someone analyzing a failed experiment. "Despite our careful preparation, she couldn't release her commitment to conventional ethics. When the time came to embrace her new nature fully, she hesitated."

The film shifted again, showing scenes I recognized from the night Zelda had visited our apartment. But this version was different---instead of the desperate, manipulative creature I'd fought, the screen showed Zelda as she might have appeared to someone who saw her transformation as artistic triumph rather than moral catastrophe.

"She was magnificent during those final hours," Julian Croix said, his voice carrying genuine aesthetic appreciation. "Torn between her human limitations and vampire potential, suspended at the perfect moment of artistic tragedy. I recorded every moment of her struggle, preserving it as a masterpiece of psychological transformation."

I understood what he was telling us. Julian Croix hadn't just killed Zelda---he'd filmed her death, turning her final hours into entertainment for his own perverted artistic sensibilities.

"You son of a bitch," I said, reaching for one of the wooden stakes.

"Now, now, Miss Vance," Julian Croix said, raising one hand in a gesture that somehow froze my movement without any physical contact. "Before you resort to crude violence, perhaps you'd be interested in understanding why I've allowed you to penetrate so deeply into my sanctum."

The psychic pressure holding me in place was unlike anything I'd experienced during our earlier encounters with vampire abilities. This wasn't just supernatural strength or enhanced speed---Julian Croix was manipulating my nervous system directly, overriding my conscious control of my own body.

"You see, I've been studying your work for months," he continued, his voice taking on the tone of someone delivering a carefully prepared lecture. "Your elimination of the werewolf pack that threatened Los Angeles last October demonstrated remarkable artistic vision. The way you orchestrated their destruction---patient surveillance, strategic planning, decisive action when the moment presented itself---showed genuine aesthetic sophistication."

Bill and Irene remained motionless behind me, caught in the same psychic paralysis that prevented me from completing my attack. Julian Croix had disabled all three of us without apparent effort, proving that four centuries of supernatural experience provided advantages we'd underestimated.

"You're not just a detective, Miss Vance. You're an artist of destruction, someone who understands that meaningful change requires the complete elimination of corrupt systems. The werewolf pack represented a threat to human civilization, so you destroyed them. My vampire coterie represents a different kind of threat, so you've come here to destroy us as well."

The screening room began to change around us, walls shifting to reveal additional displays that hadn't been visible when we'd entered. Glass cases lined the walls, containing what appeared to be artifacts from Julian Croix's four centuries of existence. Weapons, documents, paintings, and photographs that told the story of his evolution from human artist to supernatural predator.

"I've spent four hundred years learning to create eternal art through the preservation of human beauty at moments of perfect transcendence," Julian Croix said, gesturing toward the displays with obvious pride. "But my work has always been limited by the passive nature of my subjects. Willing transformation produces superior results, but even the most enthusiastic convert lacks the dynamic tension that comes from genuine conflict."

One of the glass cases contained photographs of scenes I recognized from the subterranean gallery---preserved victims posed in elaborate tableaux demonstrating Julian Croix's aesthetic philosophy. But these weren't just random killings preserved as art. Each tableau told part of a larger story about the relationship between human creativity and vampire superiority.

"You represent something I've never encountered before, Miss Vance. An artist whose medium is destruction, someone who creates meaning through the elimination of corrupt influences. Your work demonstrates aesthetic principles that complement my own creative vision perfectly."

The film on the screen shifted again, showing scenes from our investigation---surveillance footage of our meetings, photographs of our preparations, recordings of conversations we'd thought were private. Julian Croix had been documenting our approach to his operation with the same artistic attention he'd devoted to Zelda's transformation.

"Consider the narrative structure of your campaign against my coterie," he said, his voice carrying growing excitement. "The initial investigation that revealed the scope of supernatural corruption. The personal loss that provided emotional motivation for your mission. The careful preparation and alliance building that preceded your assault. The systematic elimination of opposing forces leading to this final confrontation."

I tried to speak, to move, to break free from whatever psychic influence was holding me paralyzed, but Julian Croix's supernatural abilities exceeded anything we'd encountered from his followers.

He'd been feeding on artistic talent for centuries, accumulating power that made him nearly invulnerable to traditional vampire weaknesses.

"You've created a masterpiece of heroic narrative, Miss Vance. David facing Goliath, Saint George confronting the dragon, the lone gunfighter walking into the corrupt town's saloon for the final showdown. Your story contains all the classical elements of mythic confrontation between good and evil."

The screening room continued its transformation, revealing more displays that chronicled Julian Croix's artistic evolution. Paintings from the Renaissance showing his early work as a human artist, followed by increasingly sophisticated projects that demonstrated his supernatural development. Each piece showed technical advancement that would have been impossible within normal human lifespans.

"But every great narrative requires a proper conclusion," Julian Croix continued. "A resolution that provides emotional catharsis while demonstrating the artistic themes that motivated the entire work. Your story needs an ending that justifies the courage and sacrifice you've demonstrated during your campaign against supernatural corruption."

I began to understand what he was proposing. Julian Croix didn't want to simply kill us---he wanted to turn our mission into the climax of his own artistic project. We'd become characters in a narrative he was constructing about the relationship between human heroism and vampire superiority.

"I'm offering you immortality, Miss Vance. Not the crude transformation I attempted with lesser subjects like Miss Kettleton, but genuine artistic collaboration between equals. You would retain your identity, your memories, your moral convictions---everything that makes you effective as an artist of destruction. But you would gain unlimited time to perfect your methods and pursue targets worthy of your abilities."

The offer was seductive in ways I hadn't expected. Julian Croix wasn't promising wealth or power or conventional vampire abilities. He was offering the chance to continue fighting supernatural corruption forever, without the limitations of human mortality or the constant fear that age would eventually end my effectiveness.

"Think of what we could accomplish together," he said, his voice dropping to an intimate whisper that seemed to bypass my conscious mind and speak directly to deeper desires. "Four hundred years of experience in identifying and eliminating supernatural threats to human civilization. Your tactical abilities enhanced by vampire supernatural capabilities. No more rushed investigations or desperate improvisations---we would have centuries to plan perfect campaigns against every form of monster that preys on innocent people."

The psychic pressure holding me paralyzed began to ease, not because Julian Croix was losing control, but because he wanted me to be able to respond to his proposal. I could feel sensation returning to my arms and legs, though I suspected any sudden movement would result in immediate retaliation.

"What about them?" I asked, indicating Irene and Bill with a slight gesture.

"Your companions have served their purpose as supporting characters in your narrative," Julian Croix said with casual dismissal. "But supporting characters don't require preservation once the story reaches its climax. Their deaths will provide the emotional motivation you need to embrace your new nature fully."

I saw the trap he was constructing. Julian Croix would kill Irene and Bill in front of me, using their deaths to trigger the psychological transformation he believed would make me accept vampire immortality. My grief and rage would become the final ingredient in his artistic project, the moment of perfect beauty, ambition, and tragedy he'd been seeking to capture.

"You're insane," I said, testing his reaction to direct rejection.

"I'm an artist who's spent four centuries learning to recognize genuine creative talent," Julian Croix replied. "You possess abilities that would be wasted in a normal human lifespan. Seventy years, perhaps eighty, to develop your skills before age forces you into retirement or death. I'm offering you unlimited time to become everything you're capable of becoming."

The film on the screen shifted to show scenes from my investigation---surveillance footage of me interviewing witnesses, preparing weapons, planning our assault on his mansion. Julian Croix had been studying my methods with artistic appreciation, seeing patterns and techniques that even I hadn't recognized.

"Consider the aesthetic perfection of your approach to supernatural threats," he said, his voice carrying the enthusiasm of someone discussing a favorite work of art. "You don't simply react to monster attacks with crude violence. You investigate, you plan, you identify weaknesses, you prepare appropriate countermeasures. Your work demonstrates intellectual sophistication that elevates destruction beyond mere brutality into genuine artistic expression."

I looked around the screening room, noting details that might provide tactical advantages if the psychic paralysis lifted completely. The exits were clearly marked, but they probably led to passages Julian Croix controlled. The glass display cases contained weapons and artifacts that might be useful, but they were sealed and probably protected by supernatural defenses.

Our best chance lay in the traditional vampire weaknesses we'd already proven effective. Julian Croix might be more powerful than his followers, but he was still fundamentally a vampire---vulnerable to wooden stakes through the heart, holy water, and garlic barriers.

"I need time to consider your offer," I said, trying to buy us an opportunity to recover our tactical advantage.

"Of course," Julian Croix said, his expression showing satisfaction at what he interpreted as progress toward acceptance. "But time is a luxury we don't possess in unlimited quantities. European vampire authorities are en route to Los Angeles, sent to eliminate all evidence of supernatural activity that threatens species secrecy. They'll arrive tomorrow night, and they won't distinguish between my coterie and potential human witnesses."

The threat was real and immediate. Agent Reynolds had warned us about European vampire elimination teams, but we'd assumed they would focus on Julian Croix's operation rather than expanding their targets to include everyone who'd learned about supernatural activity in Los Angeles.

"If you accept my offer tonight, I can protect you from European intervention," Julian Croix continued. "Vampire authorities respect artistic achievement, even when it challenges traditional secrecy protocols. A collaboration between vampire artistic vision and human tactical expertise would be seen as innovative rather than threatening."

I studied his face, looking for signs of deception or uncertainty that might reveal flaws in his proposal. Julian Croix believed he was offering me something genuinely valuable---immortality, enhanced abilities, protection from vampire authorities, unlimited time to pursue supernatural threats. From his perspective, refusing such an offer would be irrational.

But I'd learned something important during my investigation of his operation. Julian Croix's artistic philosophy required the destruction of human moral boundaries. Accepting his offer would mean abandoning everything I'd fought to protect, becoming a predator who justified killing innocent people through aesthetic rationalization.

"What happens to Los Angeles if I refuse?" I asked.

"Los Angeles becomes a hunting ground for European vampire elimination teams," Julian Croix said matter-of-factly. "Agent Reynolds, the federal agents who provided you with intelligence, the police officers who've encountered supernatural evidence, the journalists who've investigated unexplained disappearances---everyone with knowledge of vampire activity will be eliminated to protect species secrecy."

The scope of destruction he was describing included hundreds of people whose only crime was learning the truth about supernatural threats to human civilization. European vampire authorities would kill federal agents, police officers, newspaper reporters, and random civilians to maintain the illusion that monsters didn't exist.

"And if I accept your offer?"

"If you accept my offer, we relocate to a more... accommodating jurisdiction where artistic collaboration between species is encouraged rather than forbidden," Julian Croix said. "Los Angeles continues its normal existence, ignorant and safe. Your friends live to pursue their own destinies. Everyone benefits from our mutual arrangement."

The projection screen shifted to show maps of Europe, focusing on regions where Julian Croix apparently had established relationships with vampire authorities. Castles and estates that looked like they'd been converted into artistic colonies where supernatural and human talent could collaborate on projects that would be impossible within normal moral constraints.

"Think of it as an artistic residency program," Julian Croix said, noting my attention to the geographical displays. "Unlimited resources, no bureaucratic interference, complete freedom to pursue targets that represent genuine threats to human civilization. We would work together to identify and eliminate supernatural corruption wherever we found it."

I began to understand the true scope of his vision. Julian Croix wasn't just offering individual immortality---he was proposing to create an organization dedicated to hunting monsters, staffed by vampires and enhanced humans who'd transcended conventional moral limitations.

It was seductive, terrifying, and completely insane.

"I need to discuss this with my companions," I said.

"Of course," Julian Croix said, though his tone suggested impatience with normal human decision-making processes. "But remember---time is limited, and the European teams won't delay their elimination schedule to accommodate your deliberations."

The psychic pressure holding Irene and Bill paralyzed began to ease, allowing them to move slightly without triggering immediate retaliation. Julian Croix was demonstrating good faith by giving us the ability to confer, though I suspected he was monitoring our thoughts and would intervene if we attempted anything he interpreted as hostile.

"You have ten minutes to reach a decision," he said, settling back into his director's chair. "After that, we proceed with or without your willing cooperation."

The film on the screen returned to scenes of Zelda, showing her transformation from hopeful artist to desperate predator to final death in our apartment. Julian Croix watched the images with obvious aesthetic appreciation, seeing beauty in moments that represented pure horror to anyone who retained human moral sensibilities.

Ten minutes to save Los Angeles from vampire elimination teams.

Ten minutes to decide whether accepting immortality from a monster was justified by the lives it would save.

Ten minutes to find a third option that didn't require abandoning everything I'd fought to protect.

The wooden stakes in my jacket felt warm against my ribs, blessed by Father Rodriguez and anointed with holy water that had proven effective against every supernatural defense we'd encountered.

Julian Croix might be four centuries old, but he was still just a vampire.

And I'd gotten very good at killing vampires.

The Beautiful Lie

"Ten minutes is generous," I said, reaching slowly for one of the wooden stakes in my jacket. "But I don't need that long to decide."

Julian Croix smiled with the patient confidence of someone who'd spent centuries learning to read human psychology. "Miss Vance, I appreciate directness in artistic temperament, but perhaps you should consider the full scope of what you're rejecting before---"

I lunged forward with the blessed stake, aiming for his heart with the speed and precision that had kept me alive six months ago. The holy water Father Rodriguez had used to anoint the hardwood burned against my palm, enhancing my grip as I drove the weapon toward Julian Croix's chest.

But four centuries of vampire experience provided reflexes beyond human capabilities by orders of magnitude. Julian Croix moved with fluid grace that made my attack seem clumsy and telegraphed, catching my wrist inches from his heart and holding the stake motionless despite all the force I could bring to bear.

"Admirable commitment," he said, studying the blessed weapon with professional interest. "But crude technique. You're approaching vampire elimination like a street fight rather than an artistic endeavor."

He twisted my wrist with casual strength, forcing me to drop the stake as pain shot up my arm. But instead of pressing his advantage with immediate violence, Julian Croix stepped back and gestured toward the screening room's displays with the manner of someone preparing to deliver a lecture.

"Violence will not resolve this situation to anyone's satisfaction," he said. "I could kill all three of you in seconds, but that would be wasteful destruction of irreplaceable artistic potential. You could continue your assault with traditional vampire defenses, but my accumulated power exceeds anything your preparations can overcome. We appear to have reached an impasse."

Bill and Irene moved to flank me, ready to coordinate whatever attack might give us tactical advantage against Julian Croix's supernatural abilities. But the screening room's architecture worked against us---too much open space for him to maneuver, too many glass display cases that could be turned into weapons, too few escape routes if our assault failed.

"Unless," Julian Croix continued, settling back into his director's chair with theatrical flourish, "I can demonstrate the true scope of what you're rejecting through more... comprehensive methods."

The air in the screening room began to change, taking on the thick, oppressive quality I'd learned to associate with vampire psychic manipulation. But this wasn't the crude mental pressure Julian Croix had used to paralyze us earlier. This felt different---deeper, more invasive, designed to reach memories and emotions I'd buried beneath months of professional focus.

"You know what I find most fascinating about your psychological profile, Miss Vance?" Julian Croix said as reality began to blur around the edges of my vision. "Not the guilt over tactical decisions during supernatural operations. Not the nightmares about people you failed to save. Those are merely symptoms of a much more fundamental trauma."

The screening room's walls started to dissolve, replaced by images that made my breath catch in my throat. A small apartment on Bunker Hill, decorated with furniture I'd helped select. Sunlight streaming through windows that looked out on a city where the most dangerous predators were human criminals rather than supernatural monsters.

"The real tragedy," Julian Croix continued, his voice becoming more intimate as the illusion strengthened around us, "is that none of it ever had to happen. The Crescent Club, Detective Miller's death, your transformation from Army medic to monster hunter---all of it was completely unnecessary."

The images solidified into a world I recognized but had never experienced. Los Angeles in the spring of 1949, exactly as it existed in reality, except for one crucial difference. In this version of events, supernatural creatures had never emerged from whatever shadows they'd hidden in for centuries. Werewolves, vampires, and other monsters remained myths and folklore rather than tactical problems requiring federal intervention.

"Consider what your life would have looked like," Julian Croix said as the illusion expanded to show scenes of domestic normalcy felt more real than memory, "if Agent Reynolds had never contacted you about unusual animal attacks in the Hollywood Hills."

I watched myself living a life that had been stolen from me by circumstances beyond my control. Working as a private investigator, yes, but handling normal cases---insurance fraud, missing persons who'd run off with lovers rather than been killed by monsters, corporate espionage that involved human greed rather than supernatural predation.

"No federal task forces," Julian Croix explained as the scenes played out around me with documentary precision. "No classified briefings about werewolf pack behavior. No tactical planning for assaults against creatures that could tear steel doors off their hinges. Just honest work helping ordinary people solve ordinary problems."

The illusion showed me coming home each evening to the Bunker Hill apartment, hanging up my jacket without checking for concealed weapons, sitting down to dinner without scanning the shadows for supernatural threats. It was the life I'd been living before October 1948, extended forward into a future where monsters remained fictional.

"And most importantly," Julian Croix said, his voice carrying growing warmth, "no reason to avoid personal relationships because of operational security concerns."

The apartment door opened, and my heart stopped.

Vivian Vanderbilt walked into the living room, wearing civilian clothes instead of a police uniform, her hair loose around her shoulders in a way I'd never seen during our brief partnership. But it was unmistakably her---the same intelligent brown eyes, the same confident bearing, the same smile that had made me look forward to our tactical planning sessions with anticipation beyond professional collaboration.

"Welcome home," she said, moving toward me with the easy familiarity of someone who belonged in this domestic scene. "How was the Kowalski surveillance case?"

The Kowalski surveillance case. Even in Julian Croix's illusion, Bill existed as a construction worker with normal problems rather than a federal ally fighting supernatural threats. The continuity was perfect, creating a world where all the same people existed but lived ordinary lives unmarked by monsters and violence.

"Wrapped it up this afternoon," I heard myself saying, though I had no memory of any surveillance case involving Bill. "Insurance fraud, just like we suspected. His work injury was legitimate, but he'd been taking construction jobs on the side while collecting disability payments."

Vivian nodded with the understanding of someone who'd heard similar stories before. In this timeline, she worked as a civilian investigator for the district attorney's office rather than serving as a police detective assigned to supernatural task forces. We'd met during a routine case involving municipal corruption, discovered professional compatibility that had developed into personal attraction, and begun building the relationship that werewolves and federal operations had prevented in reality.

"Good," she said, settling beside me on a couch I'd never owned. "That means we can focus on more important things."

She leaned against me with physical intimacy that felt completely natural despite never having actually occurred. This version of Vivian showed no awareness of werewolves or vampire investigations, no understanding that supernatural creatures posed threats requiring tactical responses. Her concerns were limited to normal human problems that could be solved through conventional law enforcement and legal procedures.

"Like what?" I asked, though part of me already knew what Julian Croix was offering.

"Like the fact that I love you," Vivian said, turning to face me with an expression of complete sincerity. "And the fact that you love me, even though we've both been too professional to say it directly."

The words hit me with emotional force that bypassed rational analysis. During our three weeks working together on the werewolf task force, I'd found myself developing feelings that mission requirements and operational security had prevented me from exploring. But in this timeline, those restrictions had never existed. We'd been free to pursue whatever personal connection developed between us.

"I've been thinking about our future," Vivian continued, her voice carrying the warmth of someone discussing plans rather than fantasies. "The district attorney's office has offered me a promotion to chief investigator. It would mean better hours, more regular schedule, time to focus on things that matter outside of work."

The illusion expanded to show glimpses of the life Julian Croix was offering---quiet domesticity unmarked by violence or loss, professional work that didn't require killing monsters, a relationship that could develop without interference from supernatural threats. Marriage, perhaps children, growing old together without fear that federal operations might separate us permanently.

"All you have to do," Julian Croix's voice said from somewhere beyond the apartment, "is accept that this is how things should have been. Acknowledge that your current existence is an aberration, a deviation from the natural path your life was meant to follow."

I found myself drawn deeper into the domestic scene, seduced by the possibility of normalcy I'd been denied by circumstances beyond my control. This version of Vivian represented everything I'd wanted during those three weeks in October, everything that had been destroyed when duty and personal attachment had pulled me in different directions.

"We could leave Los Angeles," Vivian suggested, her hand finding mine with touch that felt exactly as I'd imagined it might. "Move somewhere quiet, maybe up the coast. Open our own investigation agency, handle cases that matter to us. Build something together that belongs to us rather than the federal government or municipal authorities."

The apartment around us shifted to show a small coastal town where we could live without constant vigilance against supernatural threats. A place where the most dangerous predators were ordinary criminals who could be handled through conventional law enforcement techniques. No silver bullets, no wooden stakes, no holy water blessed by Catholic priests who understood the reality of vampire infiltration.

"This is what you really want," Julian Croix said, his voice becoming more persuasive as the illusion strengthened. "Not the guilt and trauma of fighting supernatural threats that most people refuse to believe exist. Not the constant fear that your next investigation might be your last. Just a normal life with someone you love, free from monsters and violence and federal operations that consume everything meaningful."

The temptation was overwhelming beyond anything I'd anticipated. Julian Croix wasn't just offering vampire immortality---he was offering the chance to undo every tragedy that had defined my existence since October 1948. No Crescent Club, no Detective Miller's death, no transformation from Army medic to monster hunter. Just the life I'd been living before supernatural creatures had forced me to choose between personal happiness and protecting innocent people.

"Ellie," Vivian said, using the informal version of my name she'd started employing during our final week working together. "What are you thinking about? You look like you're somewhere else."

"I'm thinking about how different things could have been," I said, understanding what Julian Croix was really offering. "How much simpler everything would be if monsters didn't exist."

"Monsters do exist," Vivian replied, but her tone suggested she was talking about human predators rather than supernatural threats. "Criminals who hurt innocent people, corrupt officials who abuse their authority, people who use power to exploit others. But we can fight those monsters together, through legal channels that produce lasting results rather than just temporary victories."

She was right, in the context of this alternative timeline. Human monsters were dangerous enough to require investigation and intervention, but they could be handled through conventional law enforcement rather than federal task forces equipped with silver bullets and wooden stakes. The work would be meaningful without being consistently life-threatening.

"But this isn't real," a voice said from somewhere outside the apartment, cutting through the domestic scene with sharp insistence. "Ellie, this is psychic manipulation. Vivian is dead, and no amount of vampire magic can bring her back."

I turned to see Irene standing in the apartment doorway, looking exactly as she had in the screening room rather than belonging to Julian Croix's alternative timeline. Her presence created a jarring discontinuity in the illusion, reminding me that I was experiencing artificial memories rather than genuine alternatives.

"Who is that?" Vivian asked, her expression showing confusion and concern. "Why is she talking about vampire magic? Ellie, what's going on?"

But the question revealed a fundamental flaw in Julian Croix's reconstruction. If monsters had never emerged from folklore into reality, Irene would have no knowledge of vampire magic or psychic manipulation. Her presence in the domestic scene proved that the illusion was incorporating elements from timelines that couldn't coexist logically.

"This is what Julian Croix wants you to see," Irene continued, moving closer despite Vivian's obvious distress. "A past where supernatural threats never forced you to make impossible choices. A world where you could have the normal life that monsters stole from you."

"But that's exactly what I want," Vivian said, her voice carrying desperation I'd never heard from the real person. "A normal life where we can be together without interference from federal operations or supernatural investigations. Why won't you let us have that?"

The reconstructed Vivian's emotional intensity felt wrong, unfamiliar. The real Vivian had been calm under pressure, intellectually curious about challenges rather than emotionally desperate for easy solutions. This version showed psychological patterns belonging to Julian Croix rather than the woman I'd known.

"Because accepting this illusion means abandoning everyone who's depending on you to fight supernatural threats," Irene said, pulling one of the holy water bottles from her jacket. "Margaret Walker, Zelda Kettleton, all the people Julian Croix will kill if his operation isn't stopped. Their lives matter as much as your personal happiness."

"What about my life?" Vivian demanded, her appearance beginning to flicker between the woman I'd loved and something artificial that wore her face without understanding her essential nature. "What about our relationship? Why should we sacrifice our future for people we've never met?"

The question struck at the heart of every moral dilemma I'd faced since becoming involved in supernatural investigation. Personal happiness versus professional responsibility, individual desires versus protecting innocent people from threats they didn't know existed. It was the same choice I'd made fighting the Crescent Club, when following protocols had cost Vivian's life but saved the mission.

"Because that's what the real Vivian would want," I said, finally understanding what was wrong with Julian Croix's temptation. "She died protecting people from monsters. She wouldn't want me to abandon that work for the sake of an illusion."

The apartment began to flicker and distort as I rejected its emotional premise, but Julian Croix made one final attempt to maintain psychological control. The reconstructed Vivian moved closer, her expression shifting between pleading and accusation.

"You're choosing strangers over the woman you love," she said, reaching toward me with hands that felt cold despite the apartment's warmth. "Just like you chose duty over saving my life last year. How many times will you make the same mistake?"

"I'm choosing to honor your memory by continuing the work that got you killed," I replied, stepping away from the false Vivian's touch. "Fighting monsters, protecting innocent people, making sure your sacrifice wasn't meaningless."

"My sacrifice was meaningless," the illusion snapped, its mask finally slipping completely. "I died for nothing, killed by creatures that shouldn't exist, forgotten by everyone except the woman who failed to save me. Accept Julian's offer, and you can fix that. Make it so I never died in the first place."

But the real Vivian had never been bitter about her work or resentful of the choices required by supernatural investigation. She'd understood the importance of protecting innocent people from threats they couldn't handle alone. Julian Croix's reconstruction revealed his fundamental inability to comprehend human moral motivation.

"The real Vivian is dead," I said, facing the illusion directly. "And I won't dishonor her memory by becoming a predator to ease my conscience."

Irene threw the holy water directly onto my face and hands, causing immediate burning pain that shattered what remained of Julian Croix's illusion. The blessed liquid felt like acid against my skin, but it also cleared my vision completely, revealing the screening room's actual layout and Julian Croix's position behind his director's chair.

The vampire's face showed rage beyond anything I'd seen from supernatural creatures, fury that transcended normal emotional responses. His carefully constructed psychic manipulation had failed to produce the result he'd been anticipating, and the rejection of his artistic vision seemed to affect him more profoundly than physical violence would have.

"Four hundred years of experience creating perfect psychological profiles," he snarled, abandoning the cultured academic tone he'd maintained throughout our confrontation. "Century after century of learning to offer subjects exactly what they need to accept transformation willingly. And you reject paradise for the sake of moral abstractions that provide no practical benefit."

Julian Croix rose from his director's chair with movements that blurred beyond human visual tracking, his supernatural nature finally emerging from behind the civilized facade he'd been maintaining. This was no longer an artistic genius offering collaboration between equals---this was a predator whose primary strategy had failed, leaving only violence as a means of achieving his objectives.

"If you won't serve as the willing climax of my artistic project," he said, his voice carrying four centuries of accumulated hatred for human moral limitations, "then you'll serve as an unwilling example of what happens to those who reject vampire superiority."

The screening room exploded into motion as Julian Croix attacked with the full power of his accumulated supernatural abilities, no longer constrained by aesthetic considerations or recruitment goals. This was vampire combat as it really existed---fast, brutal, and completely without mercy for anyone who stood between a predator and its intended victims.

Bill and Irene scattered to opposite sides of the room, trying to present multiple targets while I searched for weapons that might prove effective against Julian Croix's enhanced capabilities. The wooden stakes and holy water had worked against his younger followers, but four centuries of feeding on artistic talent had given him power that might exceed traditional vampire weaknesses.

The final battle had begun, and our survival would depend on finding ways to kill something that had been perfecting the art of predation since before America existed.

A Blade in the Dark

Julian Croix moved with speed that defied human perception, crossing the screening room in the time it took me to draw breath. His hand caught my throat before I could dodge, lifting me off the ground with supernatural strength that cut off my air supply completely.

"Four hundred years of artistic refinement," he snarled, his face inches from mine, showing teeth that had grown sharp as surgical instruments. "And you choose moral righteousness over immortal collaboration. Such a magnificent waste."

The screening room exploded into chaos as Bill hurled one of the heavy glass display cases at the projection equipment. The crash of breaking glass and sparking electrical circuits created enough distraction for me to drive my knee into Julian Croix's ribs with every ounce of strength I possessed.

The impact felt like striking a steel girder wrapped in expensive silk, but it loosened his grip enough for me to tear free and stumble toward the exit. Blood roared in my ears as oxygen returned to my lungs, but I could hear Irene shouting directions over the sound of electrical equipment dying in showers of sparks.

"The gallery," she called out, already moving toward the corridor that led to the subterranean chamber. "Bill, we need to reach the gallery where you can use the architecture against him."

Julian Croix turned toward Bill with predatory focus, abandoning his attempt to recapture me in favor of eliminating the human who'd dared to damage his carefully constructed screening room. But Bill was already in motion, using his intimate knowledge of the mansion's blueprint to lead us through passages that might provide tactical advantages.

"The support pillars," Bill shouted over his shoulder as we ran through corridors lined with Julian Croix's macabre artistic displays. "The gallery's cathedral ceiling is supported by carved stone pillars. If we can damage the right load-bearing structures, we might bring down sections of the roof."

It was a desperate plan that would likely kill us along with our target, but conventional weapons had proven insufficient against Julian Croix's accumulated supernatural power. Environmental destruction might be our only chance of creating damage severe enough to overcome four centuries of vampire enhancement.

The sound of Julian Croix's pursuit echoed behind us through the mansion's stone passages---footsteps that moved with inhuman rhythm, never seeming to tire or slow despite the supernatural speed he was maintaining. We had perhaps twenty seconds before he overtook us, and the gallery entrance was still thirty yards ahead through corridors that offered no defensive positions.

"There," Bill pointed toward the archway that led into the vast subterranean chamber where Julian Croix's preserved victims waited in their eternal tableaux. "Once we're inside, I can identify the structural weak points needed to collapse the ceiling."

But we never reached the gallery.

Julian Croix materialized in front of us with movement so fast it seemed like teleportation, blocking our path with supernatural reflexes perfected over centuries of predation. His expensive suit was torn from our brief struggle, revealing pale skin that showed no signs of exertion despite moving faster than physics should have allowed.

"Running through my own domain," he said, his voice carrying amusement rather than anger. "How delightfully theatrical. But this little performance has continued long enough."

He grabbed Bill by the shirt front and hurled him against the stone wall with force that would have pulverized every bone in a normal human body. Bill struck the carved stone with a sound like snapping timber, then collapsed in a heap where he lay motionless except for the shallow breathing that indicated life still flickered within his broken form.

"One obstacle removed," Julian Croix said, turning his attention to Irene and I with the casual confidence of someone accustomed to eliminating resistance. "Two remaining."

But while Julian Croix had been demonstrating his superior physical capabilities, Irene had been studying the corridor's architectural details with the focused attention of someone whose life depended on understanding structural vulnerabilities. The geometric patterns carved into the stone walls weren't merely decorative---they were functional components of Dr. Hayworth's amplification system, designed to channel supernatural energy throughout the entire mansion.

"Holy water," she said, producing the final bottle Father Rodriguez had blessed for our mission. "Ellie, the amplification system extends through every level of this building. If I can pour this onto the right geometric arrays, it might disrupt his power source at the fundamental level."

Julian Croix laughed with genuine amusement, as if a child had proposed to stop a locomotive with a toy sword. "Miss Stout, your folklore research has been thorough, but a few drops of blessed water cannot overcome centuries of accumulated supernatural enhancement. Observe."

He moved toward Irene with predatory grace, intending to eliminate her as efficiently as he'd disabled Bill. But Irene had spent weeks researching European vampire encounters, studying medieval accounts of supernatural combat that described holy water's effects on vampire physiology in precise detail.

Instead of throwing the blessed liquid at Julian Croix's face, she poured it directly onto the geometric arrays carved into the corridor's stone walls. The holy water struck the mathematical patterns with supernatural acid effects, creating clouds of sulfurous vapor that filled the narrow passage with smoke that burned our throats and lungs.

The results exceeded every optimistic projection we'd made.

The geometric carvings were integral components of the amplification system that had been channeling psychic energy throughout the mansion for decades. As the holy water corrupted their mathematical precision, Julian Croix's connection to his supernatural power source began to fluctuate wildly, then fail entirely.

"Impossible," he gasped, staggering as abilities that had sustained him since the reign of Louis XIV suddenly became unreliable. "The amplification matrix is designed to enhance vampire capabilities indefinitely. Blessed materials cannot disrupt electromagnetic resonance patterns that have been refined for centuries."

But they could, and they were doing exactly that.

Julian Croix's movements became visibly slower as the holy water ate through geometric patterns that had been focusing supernatural energy since the mansion's construction. His vampire strength and speed remained dangerous, but they were no longer beyond human ability to counter with proper timing and tactics.

"Now," I told Irene, pulling out one of our remaining wooden stakes while Julian Croix struggled to understand what was happening to his power. "While the amplification system is disrupted."

Julian Croix heard my words and spun toward me with speed that was still formidable but no longer impossible to track visually. His face showed rage mixed with genuine fear of mortality returning after centuries of assured immortality.

"You cannot kill me," he declared, advancing despite the obvious effects of Irene's sabotage. "I am Julian Beaumont, transformed in the court of the Sun King, survivor of European vampire wars that lasted decades, creator of artistic masterpieces that will outlast every human civilization. I am eternal."

"Maybe you were," I said, gripping the blessed stake with both hands. "But you're not anymore."

I drove the wooden weapon toward his heart with all the strength and precision I could muster in that moment. Julian Croix retained enough vampire ability to catch my wrist inches from his chest, stopping the stake's penetration through sheer muscular force.

"Crude implements," he snarled, twisting my arm with strength that sent lightning bolts of pain up to my shoulder. "Primitive methods. You believe traditional vampire-killing techniques can overcome four centuries of accumulated experience and refinement?"

But while Julian Croix focused on preventing the stake from reaching his heart, he'd forgotten about Irene and the architectural knowledge she'd gained from studying the mansion's supernatural construction alongside Bill's demolition expertise.

The gallery's entrance was flanked by massive carved stone supports that held up the corridor's vaulted ceiling. Irene had been examining their structural function during our chase, identifying pressure points where the right kind of impact could trigger catastrophic architectural failure.

She grabbed a chunk of broken stone from Bill's violent collision with the wall and hurled it at the nearest support column with accuracy that would have impressed a professional demolitions expert. The impact created fracture lines that spread up the carved pillar like spider webs, compromising the structural integrity that kept tons of stone ceiling from crashing down.

"Environmental traps," she called out, already moving toward the second support pillar. "Bill was right about using the mansion's architecture as a weapon."

Julian Croix released my wrist and whirled toward Irene, realizing she posed a more immediate threat than my wooden stake. But his movement was just slow enough for me to complete the attack he'd interrupted, driving the blessed weapon deep into his chest with a wet sound that echoed through the stone corridor.

The effect was immediate and devastating.

Julian Croix's eyes went wide with shock and agony as the wooden stake pierced his heart, disrupting the supernatural physiology that had sustained him since the seventeenth century. But this wasn't the quick death we'd witnessed with his younger followers---four centuries of accumulated power meant he would die slowly, remaining conscious and aware throughout the entire process.

"Impossible," he whispered, staring down at the stake protruding from his chest like an accusation. "I am a masterpiece of vampire evolution, a work of art that required decades to perfect. I cannot be destroyed by improvised weapons wielded by ordinary mortals."

But he could be paralyzed, which was exactly what the wooden stake was designed to accomplish. Julian Croix collapsed to his knees as supernatural strength drained from his limbs, then fell forward onto the stone floor where he lay unable to move despite complete awareness of his impending death.

"How does it feel?" I asked, drawing my silver stiletto while Julian Croix struggled to speak through vocal cords that barely functioned. "Lying there helpless while someone else decides your fate?"

His eyes tracked my movements as I knelt beside him, the blessed silver blade gleaming in the corridor's dim illumination. This was the moment every one of his victims had experienced---conscious awareness combined with complete inability to resist whatever was about to happen.

"Your artistic vision," he managed to say through lips that could barely form words. "You are indeed an artist of destruction, exactly as I claimed. This execution proves my point about the relationship between violence and aesthetic achievement. You're completing my masterpiece by becoming the final character in my narrative."

Even while dying, Julian Croix was attempting to transform his death into a philosophical statement about art and violence. He couldn't accept that sometimes monsters simply needed to be eliminated without deeper meaning or artistic significance.

"Maybe," I said, positioning the silver blade against his neck with surgical precision. "But you're still a predator who murdered innocent people to feed your artistic ego."

The silver stiletto had been designed for precise cutting rather than crude butchery, but decapitation required more force than the blade's elegant construction could provide efficiently. What followed was neither quick nor clean---Julian Croix's supernatural physiology meant his neck resisted the blessed silver despite the weapon's holy properties.

I had to saw through skin, muscle, and vertebrae with persistent cutting motions that required several minutes to complete. Julian Croix remained conscious throughout the entire process, his eyes holding expressions shifting between terror, fury, and artistic appreciation for the brutal intimacy of his own execution.

"Just in case, you bastard," I said as the silver blade finally severed his spinal column with a wet crack that reverberated through the stone corridor.

Julian Croix's head separated from his body with a sound like tearing leather, rolling several feet across the floor before coming to rest against the carved wall. His eyes continued to show awareness for nearly a full minute after decapitation, watching me with expressions I couldn't interpret before the light finally died out of them permanently.

I sat back on my heels, breathing hard from the physical exertion required to kill something that had survived since the age of absolute monarchy. The silver stiletto was coated with vampire blood that smoked against the blessed metal, creating vapors that smelled like sulfur mixed with burning copper.

"Is he dead?" Irene asked from where she'd been working to destabilize additional support pillars, preparing to bring down the corridor's ceiling if our attack had failed.

"He's dead," I confirmed, wiping the silver blade clean on Julian Croix's ruined suit. "Four hundred years of artistic immortality, ended by three humans with improvised weapons and holy water blessed by a Catholic priest."

Bill groaned from his position against the stone wall, slowly regaining consciousness despite injuries that would have killed most people. "Did we actually win?"

"We won," Irene said, moving to help him sit upright despite the obvious pain he was experiencing. "Julian Croix is permanently dead, his amplification system is destroyed, and his preserved victims are finally free from their eternal captivity."

But victory felt different than I'd anticipated. Looking at Julian Croix's severed head, I didn't experience triumph or satisfaction---just bone-deep exhaustion and grim awareness that this success had required moral compromises that would remain with me for the rest of my natural life.

"What about those European vampire elimination teams?" Bill asked, using the wall to help himself stand despite ribs that were probably cracked in multiple places.

"They'll arrive tomorrow night to discover Julian Croix already dead and his entire operation dismantled," I replied. "Perhaps that will satisfy their concerns about supernatural secrecy being compromised. Perhaps not."

Irene was examining the geometric arrays she'd corrupted with holy water, noting how the blessed liquid had permanently damaged mathematical patterns that had required decades to perfect. "The amplification system is beyond any possibility of repair. Even if other vampires wanted to continue Julian's artistic philosophy, they'd have to start completely from the beginning."

We made our way back through the mansion's corridors, past the screening room where Julian Croix had attempted to seduce me with illusions of normalcy, past the wine cellar where we'd destroyed his portrait collection, past the upper floors where we'd systematically eliminated his sleeping followers with wooden stakes and Father Rodriguez's holy water.

The mansion felt fundamentally different now its master was dead---lighter somehow, as if supernatural oppression weighing on every room was finally dissipating. But I knew that sensation was probably temporary. Los Angeles would always attract predators of various kinds, and some of them would inevitably be supernatural rather than merely human.

"What happens now?" Irene asked as we reached the service tunnel that would carry us back to the outside world and whatever future awaited.

"Now we return home," I said, shouldering my equipment bag for what I hoped would be the final time. "We clean our weapons, we submit our reports to Agent Reynolds, and we wait to see what other monsters emerge from the shadows to replace the ones we've eliminated."

The service tunnel led us back to the hillside overlooking Los Angeles, where the city's lights spread across the basin like stars that had fallen to earth. It was still Friday night---we'd infiltrated Julian Croix's supernatural fortress at dawn and emerged before midnight, though the combat had felt like it lasted for weeks.

"Fifteen hours," Bill said, checking his battered watch. "Fifteen hours to eliminate a vampire operation developing for eight months. Not bad for three ordinary people with improvised weapons and determination."

"Not bad at all," I agreed, though I was already contemplating the federal debriefing that would be required, the psychological evaluation that would determine whether I remained suitable for supernatural investigation, the questions about whether killing Julian

Croix had been absolutely necessary or whether alternative solutions might have been possible.

But those concerns could wait until tomorrow morning. Tonight, we'd prevented European vampire elimination teams from slaughtering hundreds of innocent civilians to protect supernatural secrecy. We'd stopped Julian Croix from expanding his artistic philosophy to other cities across America. We'd eliminated a threat that federal authorities couldn't address through conventional law enforcement methods.

"Come on," I said, beginning the descent toward the vehicles we'd concealed in the canyon below. "Let's evacuate this area before European vampires arrive to investigate the destruction we've caused."

The mansion continued to burn behind us---not with actual flames, but with supernatural energy being released as the amplification system collapsed completely. Whatever Dr. Cornelius Hayworth had constructed in the 1920s was destroying itself from within, taking Julian Croix's artistic vision along with it.

By tomorrow morning, there would be nothing remaining except ruins and unanswered questions that federal investigators would spend months attempting to resolve. But the crucial thing was that Julian Croix's operation had been permanently stopped, his victims had been avenged, and Los Angeles was safe from his particular variety of supernatural predation.

At least until the next monster decided to make Los Angeles their personal hunting ground.

Epilogue

Three weeks later

The afternoon sun slanted through the venetian blinds of my office, casting familiar patterns across the desk where I'd been cleaning my silver stiletto for the past twenty minutes. The blade gleamed like liquid mercury in the Hollywood light, showing no trace of the vampire blood that had coated it during our final confrontation with Julian Croix.

I'd been performing this ritual every evening since we'd returned from the mansion, checking the edge for damage, oiling the mechanism, ensuring the weapon remained ready for whatever supernatural threat might emerge from Los Angeles's shadows. Some habits, once formed in blood and necessity, became permanent fixtures in a life that had moved beyond normal concerns.

"Any word from Agent Reynolds about the European vampire teams?" Irene asked from the client chair where she'd been reading the afternoon edition of the Times. The newspaper had run a small item about "unexplained structural damage" discovered at an abandoned estate in the Hollywood Hills, but federal authorities had managed to keep most details out of public circulation.

"They arrived Saturday night as predicted," I said, testing the stiletto's balance before sliding it back into its shoulder holster. "Found nothing but rubble and unanswered questions. Reynolds thinks they spent about six hours searching the ruins before concluding that Julian Croix's operation had been permanently eliminated."

"And they were satisfied with that?"

"Apparently. No reports of European vampire elimination teams conducting operations against Los Angeles civilians. Whatever evidence they found at the mansion convinced them that the supernatural secrecy breach had been resolved through internal action rather than federal intervention."

I opened the bottom drawer of my desk and pulled out a bottle of rye whiskey that had been waiting for the right moment to be opened. This seemed like an appropriate occasion---three weeks after eliminating a four-hundred-year-old vampire, with no immediate supernatural threats requiring attention, and Irene sitting across from me looking like she'd finally gotten enough sleep to function normally.

"Drink?" I asked, producing two glasses from the same drawer.

"After the past month, I think I've earned one."

I poured two fingers of rye into each glass, noting how the amber liquid caught the afternoon light reminding me of California sunshine rather than the artificial illumination filling Julian Croix's screening room. Some associations would probably never fade completely, but they were becoming manageable rather than overwhelming.

"To Zelda," Irene said, raising her glass. "And Margaret Walker. And all the people Julian Croix preserved in that gallery."

"To the people we couldn't save," I agreed, touching my glass to hers. "And to making sure fewer people suffer similar fates in the future."

The rye burned pleasantly as it went down, carrying warmth having nothing to do with alcohol content and everything to do with sharing the moment with someone who'd seen the same horrors and made the same choices. There were perhaps a dozen people in Los Angeles who knew the truth about what had happened at 1864 Mulholland Drive, and only two of us had been there for the final confrontation.

"Bill's recovery is going well," Irene reported, settling back in her chair with the comfortable familiarity of someone who'd been spending considerable time in my office. "The doctors say he'll make a complete recovery from the internal injuries, though he'll probably have some interesting scars to explain."

"And the official story about his injuries?"

"Construction accident involving heavy machinery. Agent Reynolds arranged for appropriate paperwork to support that explanation, including workers' compensation benefits that should cover his medical expenses and lost wages."

Bill Kowalski had spent five days in the hospital after Julian Croix had thrown him against a stone wall with supernatural force. Three cracked ribs, internal bleeding, and a concussion that had left him unconscious for nearly twelve hours. But he'd survived, which was more than anyone had expected after watching him collide with carved stone at high velocity.

"Has he said anything about continuing supernatural investigation work?"

"He's expressed interest in serving as a consulting expert for federal task forces that might require demolitions knowledge in supernatural contexts," Irene said. "But he wants to avoid fieldwork that involves direct combat with creatures that can pick up grown men and throw them through walls."

"Smart man. There's a reason most supernatural investigation work is performed by people who don't have families depending on them."

I refilled both our glasses, noting how the simple domestic ritual of sharing whiskey felt almost surreal after weeks of planning vampire elimination missions and acquiring blessed weapons from Catholic priests. Normal human activities had taken on enhanced significance now that we knew how easily they could be interrupted by supernatural emergencies.

"Speaking of families," Irene said, "I received a letter from Dorothy Walker yesterday."

I paused with my glass halfway to my lips. Dorothy Walker was Margaret's mother, the woman who'd hired me to investigate her daughter's involvement with Julian Croix's artistic recruitment parties. The case that had started everything, leading us through vampire investigations and federal task forces to a final confrontation that had required killing a creature older than America itself.

"How is she handling everything?"

"Better than I expected. Agent Reynolds briefed her on the official conclusions of the federal investigation---supernatural predator eliminated, no additional threat to civilian populations, case closed with extreme prejudice. She knows Margaret was murdered by something that posed a genuine threat to other young people in Los Angeles."

"Does she know the details about what Julian Croix was actually doing?"

"Reynolds gave her the sanitized version. Dangerous individual with psychological obsessions who'd been targeting artists and creative people for exploitation purposes. No mention of vampires, preserved victims, or supernatural preservation techniques. Just enough truth to provide closure without compromising her mental stability."

It was probably for the best. Dorothy Walker had been through enough trauma without learning that her daughter had nearly been transformed into a supernatural predator before being killed and potentially preserved as an artistic display in Julian Croix's subterranean gallery.

"What about the other families? The people whose children disappeared over the past eight months?"

"Federal investigators are contacting them individually with similar explanations. Dangerous criminal operation targeting young artists, perpetrator eliminated, remains recovered and returned for proper burial where possible. Most families seem grateful to have closure rather than demanding detailed explanations about what actually happened."

I thought about the dozens of preserved victims we'd discovered in Julian Croix's gallery, young men and women turned into permanent artistic installations after being recruited through his philosophical discussions about immortality and transcendence. Their bodies had been released by federal authorities for burial, but their families would never know the full horror of what they'd experienced during their final months.

"Any indication that other vampires might attempt to continue Julian's work?"

"Reynolds says European vampire authorities have issued formal warnings against any similar operations in North American territories. Apparently Julian Croix's public exposure of vampire activity violated fundamental supernatural secrecy protocols that date back centuries. Any vampire who attempts similar operations will face elimination by their own species rather than federal intervention."

The rye was beginning to provide a pleasant warmth that made the afternoon sunlight seem brighter and the office furniture more comfortable. Three weeks of tension and hypervigilance were finally starting to ease as we confirmed that Julian Croix's death had genuinely ended the immediate supernatural threat to Los Angeles.

"What about us?" I asked. "Any official recognition for preventing European vampire elimination teams from slaughtering hundreds of innocent civilians?"

"The opposite of recognition. Agent Reynolds made it clear that our involvement in the Julian Croix operation never officially occurred. No federal records, no commendations, no public acknowledgment. As far as government documentation is concerned, we were never involved in supernatural investigation activities."

"Probably safer that way. Recognition from federal supernatural monitoring programs tends to make people targets for other creatures who want to eliminate potential threats."

I walked to the office window and adjusted the venetian blinds to block the direct sunlight that was creating glare across my desk. The view looked out on the same Hollywood street I'd been observing for two years, showing ordinary people pursuing ordinary activities---shopping, working, conducting business that had nothing to do with monsters or federal task forces or weapons blessed by Catholic priests.

"Do you miss it?" Irene asked from behind me. "The normal cases. Insurance fraud, missing persons who run off with lovers instead of being killed by vampires, corporate espionage that involves human greed rather than supernatural predation."

"Sometimes," I admitted, returning to my desk chair. "There was something to be said for investigations where the worst possible outcome was discovering that someone had been embezzling money or cheating on their spouse."

"But you wouldn't go back to that, would you? Even if you could somehow forget everything we've learned about supernatural activity in Los Angeles."

I considered the question while finishing my second glass of rye. Could I return to normal detective work, handling mundane cases that didn't require silver weapons or holy water or tactical planning for assaults against creatures that had been perfecting predation techniques for centuries?

"No," I said finally. "There's no going back once you know the truth about what's hiding in the shadows. Most people get to live their entire lives without learning that monsters are real. We don't have that luxury anymore."

"Do you regret it?"

"Learning the truth? Or killing Julian Croix?"

"Either. Both."

I thought about Zelda Kettleton's preserved form in Julian Croix's gallery, conscious and aware but unable to move or speak as she was transformed into a permanent artistic display. About Margaret Walker's body staged to look like suicide while her mother grieved for a daughter who'd been murdered by something that shouldn't have existed. About the dozens of other young artists who'd been recruited through philosophical discussions about immortality and transcendence.

"No regrets about learning the truth," I said. "Someone needs to know that supernatural threats exist and be prepared to deal with them when they emerge. As for killing Julian Croix..."

I paused, remembering the weight of the silver stiletto in my hand as I'd sawed through four centuries of accumulated supernatural enhancement. The brutal intimacy of decapitation, the way his eyes had remained conscious and aware for nearly a minute after his head separated from his body.

"No regrets about that either. He was a predator who'd been killing innocent people for his own artistic satisfaction. The world is demonstrably better with him dead."

"Even though it required becoming someone who could kill a helpless, paralyzed creature through extended cutting and sawing?"

"Especially because it required that. Julian Croix had power that exceeded normal human capabilities, resources that federal authorities couldn't match, and four centuries of experience in manipulating people who posed threats to his operations. Traditional law enforcement methods were insufficient to stop him."

I refilled our glasses, noting how the conversation had taken on the comfortable rhythm of two professionals discussing technical aspects of difficult work. Three weeks had been enough time to process the immediate trauma of supernatural combat, leaving us able to analyze what we'd done without being overwhelmed by emotional responses to violence we'd been forced to commit.

"Agent Reynolds offered me a position as a consulting investigator for future federal supernatural monitoring operations," Irene said, producing a business card from her jacket pocket. "Official liaison between civilian researchers and government task forces that require expertise in folklore and historical supernatural encounters."

"Are you considering it?"

"Are you?"

"He made me a similar offer. Consulting specialist in supernatural threat elimination, with federal resources and backup available for situations that exceed individual capabilities."

The business card Reynolds had given me was sitting in my desk drawer, along with emergency contact numbers for federal supernatural monitoring teams and authorization codes that would provide access to weapons and equipment that weren't available through normal civilian channels.

"It would mean more cases like Julian Croix," Irene pointed out. "Investigations that require killing creatures that most people refuse to believe exist. Violence that can't be reported or officially acknowledged. Psychological trauma that can't be discussed with anyone who wasn't directly involved."

"It would also mean preventing more situations like Julian Croix's preserved gallery. Stopping supernatural predators before they accumulate enough power to threaten hundreds of innocent people. Using what we've learned to protect people who don't know they need protection."

"Is that enough? Is the knowledge that we're doing necessary work sufficient compensation for everything we'd have to sacrifice?"

I considered the question while watching late afternoon traffic move past the office window. Normal people driving home from normal jobs, looking forward to normal evenings with families and friends who'd never know how close they'd come to becoming prey for a creature viewing human creativity as raw material for artistic projects.

"It has to be," I said. "Because the alternative is allowing things like Julian Croix to operate without opposition until federal authorities notice enough disappearances to warrant investigation. By then, dozens of people are already dead or worse."

"So we become monster hunters. Permanently."

"We become people who stand between predators and their intended victims. Whether that makes us heroes or just another variety of killer probably depends on perspective."

Irene finished her rye and set the empty glass on my desk with the decisive gesture of someone who'd reached an important conclusion. "When do we start?"

"Reynolds said he'd have our first assignment within two weeks. Unusual disappearances in San Francisco that might indicate supernatural activity. Missing persons who fit patterns similar to Julian Croix's recruitment methods."

"Artists and creative people?"

"Students at the San Francisco Art Institute. Three disappearances over the past month, all involving people who'd been attending lectures by a visiting professor from Eastern Europe. Local police assume they've run off to pursue bohemian lifestyles in other cities."

"But federal supernatural monitoring teams suspect something more serious."

"Reynolds thinks it might be another vampire recruitment operation, possibly connected to Julian Croix's European contacts. Someone who learned about his artistic philosophy and decided to continue his work in a different city."

The prospect of another supernatural investigation filled me with emotions I couldn't easily categorize. Dread at facing another creature with centuries of accumulated power. Determination to prevent more innocent people from suffering fates similar to Julian Croix's preserved victims. Grim satisfaction at having found work that utilized skills I'd never wanted to develop but couldn't ignore once circumstances had forced their acquisition.

"Two weeks should be enough time to acquire appropriate weapons and research San Francisco supernatural history," Irene said, already shifting into tactical planning mode. "I can contact the archival libraries at UC Berkeley and Stanford, see if they have historical records of unusual disappearances or unexplained phenomena in the Bay Area."

"I'll speak with Father Rodriguez about blessing additional holy water supplies, and look into acquiring silver bullets from the same source Reynolds used for our ammunition during the Julian Croix operation."

We sat in comfortable silence for several minutes, watching the afternoon light shift across the office walls as Los Angeles continued its normal operations around us. Somewhere in the city, people were falling in love, starting businesses, creating art, pursuing dreams that had nothing to do with monsters or supernatural threats or the constant vigilance we'd learned was necessary.

"Irene," I said as she prepared to leave, "do you think we'll ever be normal again?"

"Probably not," she replied, echoing the same conclusion I'd reached weeks earlier. "But normal was always overrated anyway."

"And are you okay with that? With knowing too much to look away if supernatural predators target innocent people again?"

"I'm okay with it because we're doing it together," she said, meeting my eyes with the steady gaze of someone who'd made peace with difficult decisions. "Whatever emerges from the shadows in Los Angeles, we'll face it as partners."

After she left, I remained in the office until the sun set completely, cleaning my weapons and organizing case files while the familiar sounds of evening traffic provided background noise. The silver stiletto had been sharpened to surgical precision, Pops was loaded with blessed ammunition, and the wooden stakes were treated with holy water that would remain effective for another week.

A stack of new cases sat on my desk---an insurance fraud investigation, a missing husband who'd probably run off with his secretary, and a corporate embezzlement case that would pay the rent for two months. Normal work for normal problems, the bread and butter of a private investigator's practice.

But underneath those files was Agent Reynolds's business card and emergency contact numbers that would provide access to federal resources if Los Angeles faced another supernatural threat. Because there would be other threats, eventually. Maybe not vampires, maybe not as sophisticated as Julian Croix's operation, but something would emerge from whatever shadows these creatures called home.

Los Angeles spread out below my window like a circuit board made of light, each illuminated building representing lives that would continue in ignorance of supernatural threats that lurked in the spaces between normal human understanding. Most people would never know how close they'd come to becoming prey for a creature that had spent four centuries perfecting techniques for turning human creativity into permanent artistic displays.

But some of us would carry that knowledge, use it to stand guard against the darkness, fight battles that could never be officially acknowledged or publicly celebrated. It wasn't heroic work in any conventional sense---just necessary labor performed by people who'd learned too much to maintain comfortable illusions about the nature of reality.

I locked the silver stiletto in the office safe along with the blessed ammunition and holy water supplies, but I kept one wooden stake in my jacket pocket as I walked to my car. Some precautions had become as automatic as carrying keys or checking locks, small rituals that provided psychological comfort in a world where predators might be lurking in any shadow.

The drive home took me through neighborhoods where ordinary families were settling in for ordinary evenings, watching television programs and discussing normal concerns that didn't involve federal task forces or creatures that had been perfecting predation techniques for centuries. I envied them their ignorance while simultaneously feeling grateful for the knowledge that allowed me to protect them from threats they couldn't imagine.

At a red light on Sunset Boulevard, I found myself thinking about Julian Croix's preserved victims, finally free after months of conscious captivity in his subterranean gallery. Their deaths had been avenged, their bodies returned to families for proper burial, their suffering ended through violent intervention that federal authorities couldn't provide through conventional methods.

Tomorrow there would be normal cases to investigate---insurance fraud, missing persons, corporate theft. The ordinary crimes that kept a detective agency profitable and provided a comfortable routine between supernatural emergencies.

But if something like Julian Croix emerged again in Los Angeles, Irene and I would be ready. Armed with knowledge gained through brutal experience, equipped with weapons that had proven effective against supernatural threats, prepared to stand between predators and their intended victims regardless of personal cost.

The light turned green, and I drove toward home through streets that looked exactly as they had three weeks ago, before Julian Croix's death had officially ended the supernatural threat to Los Angeles. But everything was different now---my perspective, my responsibilities, my understanding of what was hiding in the spaces between normal human knowledge.

Some changes, once made, became permanent fixtures in a life that had moved beyond conventional concerns. I was still a private investigator who handled normal cases involving normal crimes committed by normal people. But I was also someone who stood ready to fight supernatural predators when they emerged from the shadows, regardless of personal cost or psychological consequences.

And that was fine for now.

Ellie and Irene
will return
in

THE MUMMY ON THE MIRACLE MILE

www.ingramcontent.com/pod-product-compliance
Lightning Source LLC
LaVergne TN
LVHW091632070526
838199LV00044B/1027